WHATEVER HAPPENED TO PROFESSOR COYOTE?

~ a journey to the heart of the handgame ~

by

Bill Rathbun

Yerba Buena Press • Berkeley
www.yerbabuenapress.com

For Lida,
and to the continuing memory of
Gladys Mankins

Editor: Bob Rathbun
Book & cover design: Bill Rathbun
Cover graphics editor: Sandra Taylor, The Graphics Page

Some stories in this book have been previously published in different forms in *Sun Moon & Stars* and *The Destruction of the People*, by Coyote Man, © 1973 brother william press; in *Get the Buzz On* © 1972 brother william press, and in *Handgame* © 1993 Yerba Buena Press.

• ISBN 0-9631242-4-2 Trade paper
ISBN 0-9631242-5-0 Multimedia CD

Library of Congress Catalog Card Number: 99-91031

Yerba Buena Press • Berkeley
www.yerbabuenapress.com

WHATEVER HAPPENED TO PROFESSOR COYOTE?

~ a journey to the heart of the handgame ~

by

Bill Rathbun

Old Pancho talked about three ways of the path to power – the way of the healer, the way of the warrior, and the way of the handgame player.

This is the story of a curious professor who got close to some of the secrets of Indian power, and of his brother who went searching after him into the heart of the handgame.

1

The lake of eternal life

A long, long time ago there was no death. When people died, their relatives would haul the body up the mountain and throw it into a lake there. Next morning that person would come out young and whole again.

Coyote argued with the Worldmaker that this should not be! People should learn to weep and mourn, everyone should die forever, to make room for a new person.

Coyote argued and argued, but the Worldmaker never argued. He just got madder and madder the more Coyote argued. Finally they settled the issue. But trickster Coyote beat the Big Man that time.

The Big Man grew madder. He walked down toward a spring and pulled up a shoot of joint grass. He coiled it around into the shape of a rattlesnake and placed it down next to the water.

Old Man Coyote had a son who was a big Captain too. Young Coyote's wife sent her husband down to that spring to get some water. When he knelt down to dip the water, Rattlesnake struck out and bit him. Old Man Coyote found his son's body at the spring, and dragged his boy up to that lake in the mountains. He threw him into the water. The body just floated on the surface.

"I don't want it this way. I would rather have it the other way," old Coyote cried. He got together a big buckskin bag full of all his beads, and gave it to Worldmaker. He begged the Big Man to bring his boy back. The Big Man said nothing. He turned his back on Coyote that time and walked away.

Young Coyote's wife buried her husband on Pitch-off Mountain. She rubbed ashes on her face, and burned all his things there, all his clothes and baskets. She howled and mourned for her dead husband.

"We all have to die," Coyote said. "We have to make way for new people, or Earth will be too crowded."

2

The missing Professor

It had been a bad day at work, and when the phone rang again Chris knew it would be another problem.

"Next," he said half jokingly, "but prepare to take a number."

"Chris, this is Marv up in Ophir City. Your brother's disappeared. You seen him around?"

"Marvin!" Chris stammered. This wasn't the call he'd expected. "What do you mean he's disappeared. I just saw him the other day."

"You've heard from him since Saturday night?"

"No, I think it was Friday night down on my boat."

"Well, that was Friday and this is Monday, and he's missing. We were playing handgame over at the Pitch-off Mountain big-time Saturday night. I think he went out in the bushes or something between games. We'd collected the pot for the third game, and he never came back. He just disappeared. We started up the game without him and..."

"That was a mistake!" Chris interrupted. He didn't really believe anything serious had happened to his brother, the retired Professor Coyote.

"What do you mean by that?"

"No, never mind. What happened?"

"No. He wasn't around," Marv continued. "The bet was matched, and the other team was all ready to get on with the game."

"What happened?"

Chris started to worry. He knew a select few Indians in the foothills of the Sierras who didn't like white people messing around with Indian power, including him and especially his brother, the professor. But Chris wasn't playing with power – he was just a handgame player. He had learned the game years before while tagging along with his older brother Tom, the anthropologist.

"We started the game without him," Marv continued. "Must've been after midnight Saturday. Man, that game went back and forth all night long. They play the long game up there, you know. Sixteen counting sticks. Back and forth it went. We got 'em down to two sticks, then they came back and got us down to one stick, then we came back to even, then they got us down, then we got them down. It was after sunrise when we finally lost it. None of us remember Tom in that game, although I couldn't say for sure. I don't think he ever came back. I'm worried. He had his money in the game. He'd rolled over all his winnings from the first two games. And all his stuff is still in my truck. It doesn't look good. You know there's a few folks up here that don't much like you guys winning so many handgames."

It was a backhanded compliment, but it had truth to it. Chris and his brother Tom had been going to Indian big-times for most of their lives, and had many friends among the Maidu and other tribes of northern California and Nevada.

But at a big-time they were white people in an Indian world, and among their Indian friends there was often some friends' relative who bore a pent-up rage against the white man. Not without good historic cause – the century and more following the discovery of gold in California had been disastrous for all the native people, but for the tribes actually living in the gold country it was better described as genocidal. Soldiers rounded up most of the Maidu people a decade before Kit Carson's troops forced the Navajo on their long walk, and ten years later they were rounded up again and marched even farther when the fertile land they were originally driven to became coveted by white settlers. Those too old or too young or too weak to march were shot by the soldiers and left for dead.

Chris Livingstone's older brother Tom had spent most of his adult years collecting fragments of lost cultures, trying to piece together all he could from the memories of the oldest people he could find. He had published several scholarly papers and books on the old stories and songs from various tribes, and had once created a storm of controversy when he'd presented evidence indicating some groups of Indians may have originated in what is now America more than fifty-thousand years ago. Most anthropologists couldn't accept that idea, and the Professor was loudly lambasted by his colleagues. But Professor Thomas Livingstone was not one to be swayed or bothered by criticism, especially not since the University had granted him tenure some years before. And slowly, some skeptics were persuaded by his ideas and his evidence, which consisted of certain unusual rocks.

Tom's real specialty was the Maidu culture of northern California. When he was still looking for a thesis topic in his early days of graduate school, he could find the least amount of recorded music for these people of the northern Sierras. A few old moldy wax cylinder recordings of California Indian songs lay archived in the bowels of what was then called the Lowie Museum of Anthropology. Little was really known about them, even the speed at which many of the recordings were made and the true pitch and tempo of the music.

Some people felt Tom was messing around in Indian religion, while others felt he was playing a key role in preserving pieces of cultures on the verge of extinction. And recently, he and his brother Chris had been winning Indian money at the big-times.

"Yeah, you've got me a little worried, Marv."

"We're more than a little worried up here," Marv replied. "We spent all day Sunday looking around for him, asking around. Nobody seems to know much. Nobody saw him after the second handgame sometime around midnight. There was some trouble earlier with some drunks, but old Leonard says he took care of that. All the older people and friends up here are concerned, asking around.

"We looked all around up top on the dome of Pitch-off Mountain, where he headed off," Marv continued. "It's a beautiful place to walk around, but it's rugged. If you end up off the top of the dome, off the beaten trail, you could be in real trouble."

"Yeah, I remember that place well," Chris said. He thought about the landscape there. The top is flat terrain, but the dirt soon disappears and the ground becomes loose granite. Suddenly you find yourself way up on top of a huge half dome of slippery decomposing granite. A gentle crest yields to a gradual descent, then it gets steeper and steeper until the sheer rock face drops all the way down, some two thousand feet, to the Middle Fork of the Feather River. The people of the area call the dome the face of the Worldmaker. Stories tell of how old-time hunters used to drive deer over the ever-steepening rock dome, then hike down into the rugged canyon to carry back the meat.

"We think you ought to, you know, notify your family," Marv concluded.

Chris wondered. It wouldn't be the first time his brother Tom had disappeared only to show up again weeks or months later.

"But notify them of what?" he said. "Remember that time he ended up in Panama when we all thought he had drowned in Mexico? He's a coyote. You can't easily kill a coyote."

"He had his bucks on the game this time," Marv countered. "He left all his gear in my truck. He wouldn't leave his money and all his gear if he was going to take a hike, would he?"

Marv had Chris worried. It wasn't like Tom to leave all his stuff behind.

"You have got me worried, Marv. I don't know what I can do. Maybe you could call the police. Where are you now?"

"I'm in downtown Ophir City right now, but I'm not going to the cops! They might recognize me," Marv laughed. "Besides, the cops here won't go up there anyway. Once they get off the gravel road, its too rough. They'd beat up their new four-by-four. The last time they went up to the rancheria they got their new Suburban torn up so bad I think they're still using the old Bronco 'til the county has enough money to fix up the 'Burb'. They won't go back up there again if they don't have to. They'll let us Indians work things out among ourselves. But then, maybe if a professor was involved...."

At this point a mechanized operator's voice cut in. "Please deposit one dollar seventy-five cents for three minutes. Please deposit one dollar seventy-five cents."

Marvin fed several coins to the pay telephone.

"I don't know what I can do," Chris finally said, "but I feel like I've got to get up there."

"Right. I don't know either," Marv echoed. "But maybe you can at least pick up Tom's gear. It sort of gives me the creeps sitting in my truck."

- "What do you mean by that?"

"Well, it might be a dead man's stuff. In the old days we always burned someone's stuff when they died. But white peo-

7

ple like to keep all that stuff for themselves, fighting over who gets the cash and who dumps the trash!"

"Well, I'm not willing to say he's a goner yet," Chris continued. "He's always been like a coyote, you know. Coyote gets banged up or killed all the time in the old stories, but somebody always comes along and throws his bones or scraggly hide into the water, and next day there he is, a new coyote again. But you've got me worried, Marv, for sure. I've got to get up there."

"When?"

Chris made an instantaneous decision. "Tonight." Things had been going hard enough recently. He needed some time off. "I'll get out of here as soon as I can," Chris said. "But it might take some time. I've got a lot of stuff I've got to deal with right now, which is going to take a while. And it's a long drive up there, so it'll be late tonight, probably."

"Well, come up to the Pitch-off Mountain rancheria," Marv said. "I'll be back up there late today. I just came to town to give you a call."

"Right, I appreciate that, but don't wait up for me. I'm not sure when I'll be up there."

"Come up when you come. And bring your bedroll. Unless you want to use your brother's bag."

"Right," Chris responded, "I'll bring my own stuff. It's all in my truck anyway."

"I'll see you at the rancheria, then. We can go over to Leonard's in the morning. He'll have some coffee brewing. He knows more than me."

"What do you mean by that?"

"Well, you know, he's an old timer who's lived up here all his life. He knows everybody and everybody's family, he knows what's going on. Plus, I think he knows more than he's telling. We'll talk to Leonard in the morning. I've got to go now," said Marvin. "I'm out of coin. See you at the rancheria tonight, or in the morning. Call your family. Bye," and he hung up.

Chris sat pondering for a few moments. What did Marv really mean that Leonard knew more? It was like Marv knew more too.

Chris sat at his desk thinking about all his problems. The light on his phone blinked repeatedly, indicating more phone messages had come in while he'd been talking with Marvin, more problems, something that had to be dealt with immediately or sooner. But Chris had his own problems brewing now.

3

Monday still

In late afternoon Chris finally got on the freeway out of the city. The highway was packed with cars, packets of people jammed onto a huge river flowing in and out of the city, everybody going somewhere. 'What am I doing here? Why am I going up there?' he wondered. 'What can I do? Either he's okay or he's not okay. Either way there's nothing I can do.'

After he finally passed over the high bridge across the Carquinez Straights, where the Sacramento River joins San Francisco Bay, the traffic began to thin. Soon he was out of the Bay Area, and the rolling flaxen hills of the coastal mountains, golden red in the late afternoon sun, made him realize he was finally out of the city and going to the country again. The layers of stress brought on by life in the city began peeling away, and an old Indian traveling song popped into his mind. He began singing:

hedem yamani wi tu tu
wi tu tu wi tu tu wi tu tu
hodem yamani wi tu tu
wi tu tu wi tu tu wi tu tu

This song asks the local mountain spirits to protect people along their journey. Chris felt a little better.

mountain over here wi tu tu
wi tu tu wi tu tu wi tu tu
mountain over there wi tu tu
wi tu tu wi tu tu wi tu tu

He wondered for a moment how he'd ever gotten involved in all this. His brother Tom was the anthropologist. As more old Indian songs played through his head, Chris realized it was the music, the handgame songs, and the handgame itself, that had gotten him involved.

Many years ago the Professor had been invited by one of his best cultural informants, Pancho, for a weekend at the Bear Dance, an annual celebration of the coming of summer and the new year for the Indian tribes in the foothills and mountains of north-central California. This is the big event of the year for the Maidu. The Bear Dance is a time for all people and their relatives to get together, to have a big feast, to celebrate the spirits of the land with dances and handgames, and to learn to get along with each other. Over the years, Professor Livingstone realized that people from various tribes got together at these seasonal big-times not so much for trading, but for the gambling games. Items won in the handgames were later bartered and exchanged.

"It's time you learn some handgame, some real handgame," Pancho said one day when young Dr. Livingstone came to visit him at his cabin in the Sierra foothills. "Let's get up a team and go play some handgame at the Bear Dance next weekend. You bring your car, and we'll pick up some singers. You don't know what handgame's about until you play it."

Later, as an afterthought, the Professor invited his younger brother Chris. "Come on along. It might be an interesting experience for you."

4

The first Bear Dance

Back in the old days, even before there were human people, the animal people were always fighting one another. Worldmaker decided to put a stop to this. "You people, all my people, you have to learn to get along with one another. I'm going to put on a big-time, and you're all going to come. There'll be plenty of food and dances, and we'll all play handgame and have a good time."

But Pano, Grizzly Bear, was the biggest and meanest of all the animals. "I'm the strongest bear in the world. I don't have to come to your big-time," he said as he turned to run away. Worldmaker reached out and grabbed Pano by the tail. Pano got away, but the Worldmaker got that grizzly's tail. That's why Grizzly and all his relatives have a short tail today.

Sola, Rattlesnake, saw all this and said, "I don't have to come to your big-time either," and started to quickly slither away. Worldmaker picked up a piece of old acorn bread, hard as a rock, and threw it after Rattlesnake, hitting him in the back of the head. Rattlesnake got away too, but his head was flattened by the acorn bread.

Ever since, people have held a Bear Dance every year, trying to make peace with Bear and Rattlesnake, and with each other.

5

Through the valley to the foothills

Chris drove on and on, the endless freeway miles reflected by the monotonous repetition of Indian songs playing in his brain.

wai yo–
nameya wai yo-o nameya wai yo nameya wai yo
– wai-yo!
yoko wai o-o nameya wai o–

Near Davis he turned off the freeway and headed north on a state highway, straight and wide and at least as fast as the freeway. It was nearly dark now as he drove through the flood plain of the Sacramento River. A deep red twilight bathed the valley.

This once was the land of the fearsome grizzly bear and a mighty river. But the grizzly was long gone, and the river tamed by endless levees and dams.

He passed a dirt road that once led to Ben and Alvira's place....

Ben and Alvira – they're both gone now, but they were among the last of the Indians living in the Sacramento Valley. Ben was a tough old Indian doctor, and dirt poor. Alvira, an old woman then, with skin like the valley silt drying and cracking under the burning Sacramento sun, dug Indian potatoes from the same spots her grandmother had shown her years before. She knew all about the herbs that grew around her. Alvira sang and talked to the plants as she gathered them. When finished, she would silently thank the plant's spirit and leave some gift in the earth.

Ben was a singer too, and a kind of Indian doctor. If some person got sick they might come to Ben. "Kill or cure," Ben would say. "I've got to use strong medicine. If you have a problem, I might be able to help you." Or....

Professor Livingstone had met this old man and his companion many years before. He'd heard they were singers, and he wanted to collect their songs while he could, before their knowledge was lost forever.

One day Tom came bouncing along in his old beat-up Ford, up to the cabin where Ben and Alvira lived. Five or six rusting hulks of old wrecked cars lay scattered about the place – a sure sign Indians lived here. Tom had his old reel-to-reel tape recorder wired up to car batteries in the back seat of his car.

"I'm Ben Bane, and I'm a mean old man," said Ben, as he hobbled out. "What do you want?"

"I'm a friend of your cousin Jim," said Tom smoothly. "And I've come to hear you sing. I hear you're the best singer around these parts."

"You want to hear me sing. Eh? Well I might be able to come up with something for you."

The old man went into the cabin and soon came back with a cocoon shaman's rattle in one fist. He started to shake the rattle, singing. Strange sounds came from deep within his belly. The rattle he held seemed to shake his arm rather than the other way around. Ben sang for a long time.

"Hu yo, hu yo, ho!" Ben finally shouted out. He stopped. "How do you feel?"

"I feel good," said Tom. "I've never heard anything like that before."

"You bet you never heard that song, that's right. But you've got power, boy. I'll sing another song for you, more powerful even." Ben started singing another song.

After some time Ben stopped again and looked curiously at the kid.

"How you feel now?"

"Good. You're a good strong singer Ben. It makes me feel good just hearing you."

"Maybe I don't have the song adjusted quite right. You've got power, boy."

Old Doctor Ben sang and sang for young Doctor Tom this first meeting. These two became unlikely friends. Years later, when Professor Thomas Livingstone had learned more of Indian ways and was transcribing his old tapes, he realized Ben had been trying to poison him with medicine songs this first time they'd met. The professor thought Ben was great!

'Poison!' The thought burned in Chris's brain. Some of Tom's informants had been trying to poison him since he'd first met them, just because... he was a stranger.

The professor never let on that he knew what was up. He just wrote his papers and refined his interviewing techniques. With his good humor he'd always made his informants his friends – or at least he learned something from them.

It was night now, and the road had begun to climb out of the valley, winding upwards. Chris drove on, hypnotized by an old Maidu song playing incessantly through his brain. Suddenly he awoke from his trance.

'What's going on? This isn't right. I must've missed the turnoff to Ophir City,' he thought, now realizing he couldn't remember the last twenty miles of the highway, which was now climbing up Yankee Hill in the canyon of the North Fork of the Feather River.

He slowed, and after a short time he came to a turn off – a side road, part of the old highway, narrow but paved, and signed Yankee Hill Road – the way to Pancho's old place!

The synchronicity awakened Chris. He turned off the highway, and soon there was a wide spot on the side of the road where the trail wound down through live oak and manzanita scrub brush to the clearing above the Feather River where Pancho used to live.

Pancho is dead now, but he had been one of Tom's best informants and teachers. He was the original Professor Coyote.

Chris stopped and parked the truck. He'd been around Indians long enough to realize that this was where he was supposed to stay tonight. He picked up his sleeping bag from the truck, and headed down the short trail toward Pancho's old place.

The cabin was gone now – burned by the power company that Pancho had kept at bay during the long years of his tenancy. But a tall strong pole still stood in the ground where Pancho was going to build his ceremonial roundhouse. This was his spirit post, the center support for the lodge he never completed. "The sky is my kumi, my roundhouse, and this is my spirit pole," Pancho used to say, to justify the slow progress. He planned to build a traditional center-post roundhouse about thirty feet in diameter. But now, the post stood alone pointing up at the sky as seasons passed without further progress.

Chris spread out his sleeping bag next to the pole, and stared up at the incredible night sky. A loud chorus of crickets chirped continuously around him. The moon was not yet up, and the Milky Way looked like a hazy river swirling through the sea of stars.

At some point he fell asleep, and had a vision of Pancho, dressed like a logger, with red suspenders and cork boots. "You better get to know who your friends are," Pancho laughed, almost derisively, and disappeared. Then a strange bug, some kind of beetle, landed on the back of Chris's hand. Chris instinctively moved to brush it off with his other hand when he jolted awake.

"That was Pancho, I almost brushed off Pancho!" he thought in his dreamlike trance. He drifted back into sleep. The beetle came back.

"You've got to learn who your allies are," it said again, speaking more to his mind than out loud. "Your allies can help you if you know who they are."

6

Pancho

A black widow spider lived behind the old wood stove in Pancho's cabin. He let it stay there. He would talk to this pet, just like he would talk to a person, and regularly feed him a fly. He'd talk to plants, too – or, as he said, to the spirit behind the plant.

One time a strange plant grew next to his cabin, like a weed. Rather than dig it out, he'd talk to it each time he saw it. "Get out of here, you're no good! You don't belong here," he'd say. Next year that plant didn't grow back.

Some people thought he was poor, and would sometimes leave bags of vegetables for him on the roadside at the head of his trail. But he was a rich man, rich in power.

Pancho was probably in his sixties or seventies when young Professor Livingstone had first met him some thirty years ago. Age was hard to guess among the old people who still ate their traditional foods – they lived a long time, aged slowly, and usually died in some kind of accident.

Pancho was a handsome man, with a broad forehead and long gray hair swept back from a deeply furrowed face. High, prominent cheekbones and a narrow chin adorned with a thin, pointy salt-and-pepper beard gave his face a definite triangular shape.

He was strong and wiry – not big and barrel-like as many Maidu men today – and keenly intelligent. He spoke fluent English, occasionally interspersing his conversations with some Maiduan word or phrase to illustrate a point. And he knew many long stories and most of their songs.

Pancho told each story like a musical play, with many gestures and songs woven into it. In these stories every animal-person had its own special song. Its song, like its name, came from the calls these animals make in the forest.

Chris had met the Professor's friend several times. Tom considered Pancho one of his best cultural informants.

Pancho, on the other hand, considered Tom his best student. He felt he was getting old, and longed to pass on what he knew to younger people who would learn and appreciate and carry on the traditions. He couldn't find any of the young Maidu interested in the old ways. In those years modern Indians wanted the money and ways of the white man's world. Many were lost, part of neither world. But Tom had sought out Pancho, and Pancho interpreted that as a sign.

Pancho knew how to live off the land, the way his people used to live – eating larvae, berries and mushrooms; grinding acorns and leeching the bitterness from the flour with water; making cider from the manzanita berries. If he went on a long walk he often carried no food with him. He would just eat along the way, nibbling leaves, finding food under rocks or inside anthills – food that Chris could never bring himself to sample, but food that Tom, the curious professor, would always eat with seeming relish. "Yum – these yellow-jacket larvae taste like green corn!"

But Pancho lived in the white man's world too, working as a logger, 'sky-hooking for old man Crocket' as he used to tell it. He had several chickens, a rooster and a goat living in his front yard, and pet deer frequented his apple orchard. He also had a pet watchdog, a dog so well-behaved it would bark only once to alert Pancho when a stranger approached, and never once bothered the chickens or the playful deer.

Once, when middle-aged, Pancho and a partner hiked to a remote mountain lake, where a spirit lives. They talked to the spirit, then they both dove into the water and swam toward the center of the lake to seek their power. Pancho saw a big hole there, like a tube through the water. He swam down this hole, past giant frog-like beings who were trying to talk to him about Indian medicine. He went down and down. Strangely, he said, he found the water was warm and he didn't run out of air.

A light like moonlight glowed in the distance below him. He swam past white puffy clouds that seemed like giant mushrooms and puffballs. These were spirits, all trying to talk to him in the old language about medicine and power. He kept swimming down toward the light.

He finally popped out of the water and found himself next to some kind of spring in the world beneath this one. He got his power there. Then he dove back into the spring and swam until he found himself back on the surface of this world, in the middle of the lake.

His partner was there waiting for him, and dragged him out of the water.

"You see anything?"

"Ya, I saw something," Pancho answered.

There is a cave in a cliff about twenty or so feet above this lake. The Worldmaker made that cave to help the people get power. Pancho and his partner climbed to this cave, and smoked Indian tobacco to attract the spirits. They slept there, and that night a spirit came to Pancho and gave him a power song. After that, Pancho was on the path to being a doctor.

But those days were about over, and not many people came to him for doctoring any more. "It's not that I'm afraid of all these spirits and spooks," he would say, "I just don't like them hanging around when I can't use them!" Pancho knew all about the land he lived on and cared for. As he grew old, he could see much of his world disintegrating before his eyes. "They ought to give the land back to the Indians," he'd often say, "we'd take better care of it."

He knew the plants and animals that lived around him, big and small – their names and uses, and all the stories and songs about them his relatives had taught him. He wanted to pass all this knowledge down. Much of what Pancho spoke of over the years had gone onto Tom's tapes, or into his notebooks, and in later years published as source books on anthropology and ethnomusicology.

Pancho knew some things about the handgame, too! Almost every other thing he talked about at some point came back to the handgame.

"Why is the handgame so important?" Tom once asked.

"It is part of our religion," Pancho answered simply.

Tom had heard about Pancho many years ago, before the river was dammed, before the resulting lake flooded many special places. Tom knew he had to meet this old man – he must know some old stories and songs, and maybe some of the old language. So he stuck a bottle of Old Crow in a bag of groceries he bought – "it sometimes helps these old-timers become more loquacious and less confrontatious," he would say – and with his bags under one arm and a tape recorder under the other, he set off on the trail to Pancho's cabin.

"Who are you?" barked the old watchdog, once. Pancho came out from his rickety cabin with an ancient rifle under his arm.

"Hi, I'm Tom Livingstone," the professor hailed. "Your brother Fred said you're a good singer. I'm looking for some songs."

"Well you look like the devil to me, with all that stuff you're packing around. I thought you were one of those danged surveyors. You say you're looking for some song you lost?" he joked.

"No, I'm looking for the songs and stories that will be lost, once old-timers like you have passed along the big river in the sky – unless your knowledge can be saved," Tom retorted. "Know any Indian-chief songs?"

Pancho laughed. "Every story is a song," he said. On cue, a raucous blue jay squawked out his name and song from a nearby oak branch.

kasa kasa, ka sakasa

"Ka sakasa luan pi," Pancho sang in reply. "An Indian sings all the time, everything's a song." Then he added, "What do you have in that box?" pointing to the tape recorder under Tom's arm.

"That's a tape recorder. You teach it a song, and it can sing it back to you. Do you want me to show it to you?"

"Okay."

Tom put his heavy battery pack on the ground, lay the reel-to-reel tape recorder on a stump, and wired up the contraption. "There. Now just sing a song and this box will sing it back to you."

"No," Pancho said. "You sing a song. You white people always want to take something from the Indian. You sing. Give your song."

So Tom reached for some nonsense song from his childhood, and turned on the recorder.

froggy went a courting and he did ride
king kong kitchy kitchy kai - mi-o
with a sword and pistol by his side
king kong kitchy kitchy kai -mi-o
kim-o-kai-mo kai-mo-ki

way down yonder in a holler tree
the birds and the bees and the green green trees
king kong kitchy kitchy kai-mi -o

Tom stopped singing, rewound the tape and played it back.
"Froggy went a courting and he did ride...."
Pancho howled with laughter – maybe at Tom's funny
nasal singing, or maybe at the wonder of this recording box.
"... king kong kitchy kitchy kai - mi - o"
"What will the white man come up with next? How does
that thing work?" he asked.
"It's easy. There's a little man in there, and he remembers
everything we say on this tape here." Tom kidded him along.
"You press this here, and he goes back to sleep," he demonstrated. "When you want to wake him up, you press this here,
and then press this here."
Pancho started laughing. "I don't know about all that. You
do the pressing and I'll do the singing." So Tom got Pancho to
sing:

esto yamani, esto litl wito litl wito
esto yamani, esto litl wito litl wito
ya-man-ni, ya-man-ni
esto litl wito, litl wito

Pancho danced around, raised his leg once like a dog marking its place, and sang the song over and over, pounding a
walking stick on the ground to mark the rhythm.
"Litl wito! Ho!" he shouted out.
"Whoa! What's that song?" asked Tom.
"That's Coyote's dance. That's the devil, Old Man Coyote,
coming down this mountain, nosing around, talking to his stuff,
looking for something, just like you. Nosing around here, looking for something, anything. Do you think your man in the box
can learn that song?"
"Let's see," he said. Tom pushed a few buttons, and
rewound the tape back to the beginning of the vocables.

esto yamani, esto litl wito litl wito
esto yamani, esto litl wito litl wito
ya-man-ni, ya-man-ni
esto litl wito, litl wito

Pancho laughed. "That's right, just like you. Henom, Old Man Coyote. Coyote Tom!"

Pancho's eyes lit up. "That's some good singer you've got in that box, don't you think so?"

"Yeah, a very good singer. You think you can sing some more songs?" asked Tom as he pressed the fast-forward button to reposition the tape.

"I might be able to remember some songs. It looks like you've got something there that might help me remember even better," old Pancho said, eyeing the Old Crow whisky bottle Tom had brought

Liquor sometimes helped to break the ice with informants, but it also tended to slur their singing voices, or worse, degenerate the conversation into drunken disconnected memories. But Pancho had the look of an experienced drinker, one who could handle his liquor.

"Exactly what I was thinking," said Tom, taking the bottle from the bag. He opened it, poured a shot into the cap, took the first swig himself and passed the bottle and cap to Pancho.

"Exactly," repeated Pancho, sipping from the bottle. He took up two thick sticks from the ground and began pounding them together slowly.

honi no wan a honi no wan
honi no wan a honi no wan

"You gotta be warmed up for this one," he said, taking another sip.

honi no wan a honi no wan
honi no wan a honi no wan

He sang on in his soft baritone voice, keeping rhythm with this simple percussion instrument. Finally he ended the song with a loud clap of the sticks. "Ho!" he shouted.

"What does that song mean?" asked Tom.

"That song means you're gonna win at handgame!" said Pancho.

Then he added, "A lot of songs don't have words to them. Sometimes you'll hear a little critter singing in the forest, and you play with his song and make your own handgame song out of it."

"What's the handgame about?" asked Tom.

"It's part of our religion."

"But what's it about?" Tom persisted, pushing the little button on the tape recorder.

Pancho seemed to look at Tom a long time. Then he raised his eyebrows, opened his eyes wide and laughed.

"What's handgame about? It's about Indian power. Its about learning to see with your mind more than your eye. It's about hiding something from the other side. Its about something that's been with us, all of us, deep inside, all the time.

"But it's also about having fun," Pancho continued. "The animal-people all played handgame. Human people learned handgame from them. Our stories tell us that. It goes all the way back to the beginning of everything here."

"But how do you play it?"

"Well, let me get my bones and try to show you."

He went into his cabin and came right back out with a little deer-hide pouch. He pulled out two pair of little bones, each about the size of a man's little finger. Two of the bones were ivory white, and two were white with a black band marked around center.

"Here, take these, hide one in each hand, and let me guess which way you hold 'em." He handed Tom one white and one black-banded bone to hide.

Keeping the other set of bones, Pancho said "Roll 'em around, mix 'em up, hide 'em, one in each hand, and bring 'em out." He rolled his fists about each other, and demonstrated in exaggerated motion.

"Sing a good gambling song to try to call up the power. Hide the bones, one in each hand. If you have to, hide your fists behind your back. Maybe a little voice in your head will tell you which way to hide 'em. Bring 'em out when you feel good and ready, get your arms out from behind your back, but keep your fists closed and your hands apart. Hide 'em from me. Sing a good song to try to catch some gambling power."

Tom tried to sing Pancho's song:

honi no wan a honi no wan
honi no wan a honi no wan

He went on and on like Pancho had. Finally Pancho said, "Ok, I'm tired of hearing you sing that song. I'll call you now. Ho! *We!* Show me your bones. They're this way" he said, showing a white bone in his left hand and a black bone in his right. "You got the black bone over here, in your left hand."

Tom opened his fists to show the bones. Pancho was right. As they faced each other the bones matched.

"How'd you do that? Let's try that again."

"See, I win the chance to hide 'em now. Give me your bones," Pancho laughed.

"I thought you said that if I sang that song I was going to win," joked Tom.

"Well, that all depends on who's singing the song. And how well they sing it."

Tom gave the bones back to Pancho.

"So that's it? That's the game?"

"It's a little more than that. Each time the other guy guesses wrong, you win a counting stick. You've gotta win all the sticks to win the game. But that's just a start. When you play, each Captain has a partner. Or better, a whole team of partners, and you start out with two people hiding two sets of bones. But, this game's not over yet. Now its my turn to sing."

honi no wan a honi no wan
honi no wan a honi no wan

"You shouldn't sing your opponents' songs unless you can sing 'em better, can throw it back at 'em! See, I'm going to give it a try," laughed Pancho.

And he did sing it better. He expertly rolled the bones together in his hand, waving his arms around, then suddenly "Whup!" One hand was sticking out and the other was tucked away, hiding under the arm pit of the hand sticking out.

honi no wan a honi no wan
honi no wan a honi no wan

"Call 'em when you see where they are," said Pancho as he sang.

"How can I see them when they're hidden?"

"That's the point. Use your imagination. Try different clues 'til you find one that works. Follow your hunches. Learn to listen to your Luck. If you find your Luck you might win the game."

"Give me the other set of bones so I can use 'em to call," said Tom, starting to sound like Pancho.

"You gotta win 'em first to use 'em," countered Pancho. "We have both pairs of bones now. My partner Black Widow Spider Man here is hiding the other pair for me, down here," he said nodding his head toward the other pair of bones, now lying on the ground but partially covered with a dry leaf to hide them.

'How'd they get there?' wondered Tom.

"We've got both sets of bones now, so you gotta guess both sets. Me and my partner, we each have a marked bone and a white bone, one in each hand. Except my partner has his pair hidden on the ground down there, right in plain sight, because his hands are too small to hide 'em. Too small to see, even." Pancho laughed. "But you didn't see him hide the bones. You've got to keep your eyes on the bones." Pancho kept laughing as he sang along, swaying his body and waving his arms around.

"Call 'em as you see 'em, when you see 'em," Pancho said as he chanted.

"My people usually call for the black bone but sometimes the spirit might tell you to call for the white. You gotta agree on what you're callin' for before you can just point and say, 'They're over there'."

"You've got four choices:

"Both blacks on the left, over here," Pancho said, moving his left hand outward.

"Both blacks on the right, over there," he said, moving his right hand outward.

"Or both blacks on the outside, on opposite ends." He held out his right hand, with his little finger pointing off to the right and his thumb off to the left.

"Or both black bones on the inside, down the middle, between us," he said, with his right hand making a vertical chopping motion.

"You guess 'em both right, and your side gets their chance to hide 'em. You guess 'em both wrong, it costs you two counting sticks, one for each missed guess. If you split 'em, getting one right and one wrong, you win the set of bones you guessed right, but it costs you a stick for the set you got wrong. Once you've got both pairs of bones on your side, your team gets to sing and hide 'em. And so it goes until one team has won all the counting sticks."

Tom made a random guess, pointing to the right. "Over there," he said. Pancho showed the bones in his hands. Tom had missed. "Show yours too, Black Widow Man," Pancho said as he pushed the leaf off the bones on the ground. Tom had missed them too.

"I don't know about this game," complained Tom, half-jokingly.

"Oh, you'll like it plenty, once you find your Luck!"

Pancho and other old timers always used to talk about this thing called Luck, that they used in winning the handgame.

"Everyone must find their Luck. Keep trying different things, strange things, until you find something that works. Some people never find Luck. It runs away from them." Pancho said his brother found his Luck in a plant with leaves that look like a carrot. "That's one strong plant! If he doesn't want you to find him, he will hide when you look. His root's a long slender son-of-a-gun, like a skinny carrot. If he gets cut, white blood oozes out of him. When you want to use that plant, you talk to him real good, talk to him a long time, saying, 'The Old People did it this way and so do I. I want to talk with you. I want to use you in the handgame. I want you to show me which way to guess.'

"After talking to him, dig him up with a sharp stick. Don't touch him! Don't break the root! Don't make the root bleed either! If you break the root, put him back in the mountain, carefully tamp the soil around him, tell him you are sorry you hurt him, and leave.

"He's poison! When you've got him up, use sticks to put him in a pouch filled with leaves of Rattlesnake root. Keep the medicine wrapped around him to keep him warm. Carry that root only at certain times of day. Use him right or he will kill you. Keep him away from the house, under a rock, in a dry place, wrapped up in a warm bundle of Rattlesnake Medicine leaves. Every week or two, reach under the rock and get him out. Talk to him. Feed him... perhaps a deformed grasshopper or cricket. Talk to him as you feed him. If you don't talk to him once in a while, he will go away. He'll disappear. You look for him, but he left."

"How do you use that root?" asked Tom, always curious.

"All you need to do to use him is take him to a handgame and keep him nearby."

"But why keep a .poison fellow like him around?" Tom asked.

Pancho looked straight through Tom's eyes. "Because something tells you which way to guess during the handgame.

Maybe a little voice will talk to you. Or maybe you can look right through the other fellow's hand and see the marked bone. "But you're right," Pancho laughed. "My brother had one of those things. He called it his lucky root. He fed it deformed things, and wanted me to learn to use it. I said 'No, I don't want that thing!'"

7

Tuesday morning

Chris awoke as soon as the morning sun cleared the eastern ridge of the canyon. The chill of dawn dissipated almost instantly. He couldn't remain long in the sleeping bag. He looked around Pancho's old home-site. Nothing remained but the apple orchard and the old center-post, standing like an un-carved totem pole, a memory of some unfinished dream. He rolled up his bag and headed back up the trail to the old road where he had left his truck.

The day warmed rapidly. Summer was coming early, and the temperature would probably break the century mark before noon.

Chris skirted the downtown Ophir City area and drove out of town up the Olive Highway toward the Middle Fork of the Feather River. A few miles out of town he passed Julie's place.

Julie Steven! What a beautiful woman! Her voice was strong and powerful, and her spirit warm and friendly. She had liked Tom from the very first time they'd met.

When he'd first came to her place, Julie stood outside the trailer in her front yard.

"Hi," said Tom. "Your brother Jerry says you sing some great Indian songs."

> *a momoli momoli tai yandi tai yandi tai*
> *a momoli momoli tai yandi tai yandi tai*

she sang.

"I'm Julie and I love to sing," she said simply. "You've come to the right place."

Her voice was clear and booming, and she sang old work songs, acorn gathering songs – but most of all, handgame songs.

"I love the handgame! I've been playing handgame all my life," she said. "When we were kids we would sit around and listen while the old folks played. We'd find some sticks and beat the rhythm while they sang," she continued. "We learned all their songs, and sometimes made up some of our own. And then we would go up the hill and play among ourselves. Some older people didn't think young kids should play the game with them. They thought kids didn't know how to handle the bones with respect, or thought they'd bring them bad luck. But I don't think so. I think children should play, the sooner the better. Teach them the old ways."

Julie was another of Tom's best informants among the Maidu, and among the most knowledgeable. She knew much of the old language, even though it was forbidden to speak it when she was a young girl. "My grandmother was a doctor," she once said. "Women were often doctors in our culture. And why not?"

She knew the local herbs, where they grew, what they were used for, the old names for many of them.

She radiated warmth and friendliness. She was happy when she sang, and Tom liked to record her songs. But she was married, and her husband Marty was always jealous and suspicious, especially when he'd been drinking.

"What's that guy doing snooping around here?" Marty would ask. Julie would try to explain that Tom was a professor from the university, collecting all the pieces he could find of the old culture before they were lost forever.

"I don't care who he is. He don't belong here."

So Tom would only visit Julie when he knew Marty would be at work, and he always tried to leave well before Marty got home. But sometimes he'd get caught with his tape recorder on. That was never a pleasant scene.

a momoli momoli tai yandi tai yandi tai yandi
a momoli momoli tai yandi tai yandi tai

Marty Steven! Chris hadn't thought of Marty since Julie left him, several years ago. He wondered, whatever happened to them?

Chris continued onward toward Pitch-off Mountain, along the foothills rising east of the great valley, through vast oak parklands once tended by the Old People.

He was amazed at how much development had sprawled out from Ophir City since he had last been here. How long had it been? A long time!

He continued around the south part of the lake, near what used to be Bidwell's Bar, once a beautiful beach along the Feather River, now under 800 feet of water. He crossed the high suspension bridge spanning one finger of the huge lake, and continued up along the old Quincy highway, now a wide two-lane blacktop road.

After several miles he turned onto a smaller, slower blacktop road. Miles further, the pavement finally ended and the road turned into a wide dusty washboard, steadily climbing and turning with the contours of the land, up a long ridge between two branches of the Feather River.

Chris struggled to find the right speed to handle the shaking caused by the washboard road surface. He slowed down below ten, and the shimmies and dust clouds faded away. The old pickup bounced and rattled onward at this speed for another half hour or so, then the road leveled off. Chris realized he was on top of a high ridge, and a magnificent vista began revealing itself, flickering between the branches of the pine trees that obscured the view. He almost drove past a small unmarked turnoff that provided access to Pitch-off Mountain. He hit the brakes at the last second, and turned abruptly onto the little road, which immediately led to a circular drive viewing area and parking lot.

There were no signs anywhere – no DO NOT PARK signs, no NO OVERNIGHT PARKING, not even a SCENIC VIEW-POINT sign. Chris felt like a free man.

It had been years since he had been here, but he began to remember this special place. A good trail led off from the parking area, and Chris followed it a short ways up toward Pitch-off Mountain.

The dirt soon turned to rock, and the brushy terrain became a giant's stone sculpture garden. Huge white speckled rocks of various odd and fantastic shapes lay scattered about. Granite toadstools, anvil-shaped rocks, stone benches and faces lay scattered everywhere.

As Chris walked a little farther, the magnificent vista suddenly unfolded. He lingered for awhile to absorb the view, as the people must have done countless times before.

Down and to the west spread the huge Sacramento Valley, the flood plain of the Feather, of the Sacramento and the Yuba and many other rivers and streams. The great valley had long surrendered to agriculture. Gone were the elk and the antelope, the grizzly and the native settlements. A million people live there now.

To the southwest and in the center of the valley, the Sutter Buttes rose abruptly from the haze above the flat valley floor – the craggy weathered remnants of an ancient mountain range, rising high above the inland sea of people that formed the valley. The Old People thought these buttes were the giant round-house of the spirits. They believed the souls of the dead came here after leaving the body and revisiting all the places they had been during their time on earth. When the souls had finished visiting these places, they traveled along the Milky Way, the starry river in the night sky, to the great roundhouse inside these buttes, to sleep until the end of this world. Or, as some say, to spend the rest of time playing handgame with old friends.

Chris wondered, 'Is my brother's soul inside that mountain yet? No,' he thought, 'He is probably still traveling, because he has so many places to go to revisit.'

To the southeast he could see ridge beyond ridge into the Yuba River watershed.

Nearby, a patch of bald granite rose a head above the ridge-lines – the dome of Pitch-off Mountain.

Chris scrambled down the rocks, back down the trail to his truck, and continued on toward the dome – along the dusty washboard road, then off onto a smaller dirt road which soon got even smaller and rougher, then forked in three directions.

He had been here before, and instinctively knew which way to go. He took the fork that would eventually lead him to the rancheria, to the handgame players who had been gambling at the big-time on Pitch-off Mountain.

Soon the ground turned to barren, flat sheets of exfoliated granite – the dome of Pitch-off Mountain, the place where the Worldmaker sleeps until the end of this world. The face of the Worldmaker himself is frozen in the granite face of the dome – his eyes, his nose. The water stains on the dome wall mark the stains of his tears flowing into the the Feather River.

Chris stopped to hike out along the gently rising granite surface.

'What a spectacular place,' he thought. He heard a distant roar, like the wind rushing through the forest – but no wind blew, and he could see only a few stunted manzanita bushes.

The roar was the sound of the river rushing through the canyon, two-thousand feet below. Chris walked around trying to make it onto the highest part of the dome. But here he slipped on some loose gravel and started slowly sliding down the dome. He managed to grab hold of one branch of an old manzanita bush, thick as a strong man's arm, growing out of a crack in the granite. That stopped his slow slide. As he crawled back up the slope, Chris wondered how old that bush must be, to be so thick in this barren environment. What things had it witnessed in its long life? He was thankful it was there. He looked at his scraped elbow and gave up trying to get to find his way alone.

'I'll look around this place more thoroughly later, after I've met my friends down the road,' he thought as he made his way off the dome and back to his truck. He got in, and continued the last few miles to the Pitch-off Mountain rancheria.

A huge gnarly old oak tree marked the outer boundary of the rancheria. A branch, well over a foot thick, had been formed into a huge hoop when the tree was still young and its branches supple. Other old oaks in the area had fallen to the loggers' saws, or had been sprayed by the Forest Service. This tree had been spared only because it had been part of an active settlement.

Chris took the right dirt fork here that led to the run-down rancheria.

The rancheria system in California is unlike the reservation system of most recognized tribes. The Maidu never fought a war with the American soldiers, and thus were never 'rewarded' with a big reservation. The soldiers merely rounded-up all the Indians, killed whomever could not make the long trip, and marched the rest at gunpoint to Round Valley in the distant Coast Ranges. The Round Valley Reservation was originally more like a prison camp for the several disparate tribes of California Indians driven to it than it was a tribal reservation

Indians who worked for a white man or who managed to run away from the soldiers and hide in the canyons eventually resettled the foothills and ended up living on rancherias, which are tiny enclaves of land, more or less ceded to whichever Indians happened to be living there.

Big Bob sat half-in his huge old Cadillac Sedan de Ville listening to a tape of handgame songs when Chris drove into the rancheria. The '70's vintage Caddy was about the only car big enough for Big Bob to fit into. Even then, he'd had to remove the rear seat and move the front seat all the way back just to fit more-or-less comfortably behind the steering wheel.

Big Bob had huge hairy hands with stubby fingers and thick curved fingernails, which now tapped time to a handgame chant playing on the tape. Big Bob was the man who broke up whatever fights might occur at an Indian big-time. Nobody wanted to tangle with him.

Chris hadn't seen Big Bob in nearly six months. He was a casual friend, whom Chris and Tom had faced many times over the past twenty-five years in friendly handgame competitions.

Big Bob greeted Chris as he stopped his truck by the big old Caddy.

"Hey guy, what'd ya do, stop for lunch on the way up to breakfast here? We thought we might see ya last night."

"It's a long way up here. I started dozing on the way up, and pulled over for awhile last night. Guess I got going a little late this morning." Chris didn't feel like mentioning he'd rested at Pancho's old place. "How's it going, BB?"

"Real good, all considered. Ya come up here to get your brother's stuff?"

"Yeah, and to figure out what happened."

Chris rolled his old truck over to the outdoor kitchen and parked.

Summers in the foothills bring days that frequently top 100° F. After the last spring rains, many Maidu people move their cooking and sleeping activities outdoors. In this country it's not unusual to see an old refrigerator outside serving as a cupboard, and gas stoves functioning under the shade of a big oak tree, with overstuffed chairs and couches scattered comfortably about. Chris had always thought this was a perfect and practical synthesis of the old and new ways of life – living outside, under the dome of the sky, but able to light a stove with the turning of a knob.

Old Leonard rose from the worn couch sitting beneath the shade of the white oak that shaded the kitchen area. He was a silver-haired gentleman, built like a barrel, but not fat. He owned a small well-kept farm that adjoined the rancheria.

"Hi Chris. Leonard Johnson." He nodded toward Chris. "I know your brother well. I sure hope nothing's happened to him."

"I remember you, Leonard. I met you years ago."

Leonard looked Chris up and down with a friendly smile. He could see the family resemblance, but couldn't recall meeting the Professor's brother before. "When was that?" he finally asked.

"Years ago. Too many to count anymore. It was that year Tom had his summer students up to try to help build a roundhouse here. You brought us all that fresh meat from the deer you shot in your garden. I probably looked just like all the other student helpers back then."

"I remember that now," Leonard said. "Too bad that kumi never got built here, over where the old camp used to be."

"Yeah," Chris continued, "after we had gotten all the cedar shakes cut, the family here decided they didn't want a roundhouse built unless an Indian doctor blessed it, and they couldn't figure out who that was going to be."

"That's like our people," Leonard said, "one half don't like what the other half does. You get three of us together and you get four different opinions. Our people don't get together and agree on anything."

"Yeah," Chris said, "they more-or-less ran us out of here that time. The cedar rotted, and my brother learned another lesson. I haven't been back here since, but I still make it to some big-times and other get-togethers a few times a year – to see old friends and play handgame."

"Well, that was all a long time ago," Leonard said as he eyed Chris again. "It looks like you've put some meat on your bones since those days."

"Well, what do you expect, after twenty years of good eating?"

"Well, we grow out as we get older. Then we start shrinking again. Looks like you're still growing though. Come on, let's sit down in the kitchen. I'll put some coffee on."

A young thin man came over to Chris.

"Hey man, how's it going?"

"Hey Vinnie!" Chris reached out to hug the young man.

Vinnie, a traditional dancer and the youngest son of one of the Maidu dance leaders, was now in his sophomore year studying anthropology at Chico State University.

Chris had met Vinnie a dozen or more years ago at a big-time, when Vinnie had been only about eight years old. Vinnie and his young playmates had put their nickels and dimes together to make a pot of less than a dollar. The kids had challenged Tom and Chris and their team to a handgame – which, to the amazement of all, the children quickly won. Chris never forgot that game.

A large, muscular sullen looking man of about thirty approached.

"What's he doing here? I thought he was dead," he asked anyone who would answer, nodding toward Chris.

"This is Professor Livingstone's brother," Leonard tried to introduce Chris.

"Yeah, so what's he doing here?" The man asked again, looking at Leonard and avoiding Chris's eyes. Chris felt annoyed at being referred to in the third person. He answered for himself.

"I'm here to find out what happened to my brother. He was up at the dome for the handgames the other night, and he disappeared."

The man continued to address Leonard, avoiding Chris's look. "He don't belong here either. Tell him his people don't belong up here."

Chris felt decidedly uncomfortable, and moved to say something for himself, but Leonard jumped in first.

"Now, this is a family place, Frank. You don't speak for our family, or for me or for anyone but yourself as far as I can see. I invited Chris over here for coffee."

That seemed to shut up Frank. Chris felt that after Marvin had called him, he didn't need any invitation. Frank glowered briefly at Chris and then walked away.

"Don't mind Frank," Leonard said, "he's still fighting the white and Injun wars. Come on, let's sit down in the kitchen here."

Marvin walked over from the shed behind the kitchen area in a nimble and eager stride. Marv was one of Chris's favorite people among the Maidu. He had played often with Tom and Chris in the handgames, and was usually full of humor and good spirits. Today he looked more serious, and the typical broad grin was absent from his handsome face.

Marv was ageless – he looked the same age now as the day Chris met him some twenty years previously, but he had seemed ageless and handsome even then. He had been a traditional dancer, but his joints and back were no longer what they had been, even though he always looked trim and fit. Now he worked as a mechanic at a car dealership in town, and spent his summer weekends either fishing or helping out at some of the big-times and other get-togethers.

Marv shrugged his shoulders. "Well, I talked with a couple other people, but I still don't know what happened to him."

"That's what I came up here to find out from you folks – what happened," Chris said.

"Let's have some coffee and a talk," said Marv.

"Here, I brought up some of the good stuff," volunteered Chris as he went back to his truck and returned with a brown bag containing a pound of yesterday's roast ground premium coffee. "Put some of this city stuff in your pot and brew it up. It'll stand up the hair on your chest!"

Marv took the bag and opened it up to smell. "Ah, all right!" he said, passing the bag to Leonard.

"I got some brewed already," Leonard said. "We can use this stuff for the next pot."

He brought out five large cups and a big jar of white sugar, and filled each cup from the pot. Chris eagerly awaited the coffee, whatever kind it was. It had been since yesterday that he'd had any, and it was already almost halfway through today. He sipped the black brew. It was... pretty good for camp-coffee. Strong, but bitter.

"Any sugar?" asked Leonard.

"No." Chris usually liked his coffee with a dab of cream to smooth out the bitterness, but no sugar, and no milk. Cream, or straight black. He knew they didn't have cream here, maybe evaporated milk at best, so he continued to sip it black.

"Cream?" asked Leonard.

"Sure, if you have it, a bit of cream would be perfect."

"If we have it!" Leonard opened a can of evaporated milk. 'Oh well,' Chris thought, as he splashed a bit of evaporated milk into his coffee. "Perfect," he said. He took a couple more sips from the big mug, then brushed a few leaves off the couch cushion as he settled onto the old sofa.

"So what happened."

Marv sat down on a worn over-stuffed chair beneath the big oak tree as he began.

"I don't know what all happened, really. It seemed like a nice get-together, everybody having a good time and nobody causing any real trouble that I know of, except that earlier thing with the punks. We watched a couple handgames while the Feather Falls bunch cleaned up on a group of Nevada Paiutes from Wadsworth. I manned the barbecue for a while and couldn't get in on the first game. But after the Feather Falls boys had all that good Nevada money in their pockets, we challenged 'em, and got some of that Nevada money for ourselves. Tom was really hot! He guessed 'em right most every time he called 'em. But they were pretty hot too, and the game took a while, 'til we finally found our song and won it. Then we had some barbecued venison and acorn soup, then played 'em another game. That one took even longer, but we won that too. Sometime in the middle of the night we started another game. It was getting late, but the Feather Falls folks wanted one more chance to get some of that Paiute money back. Tom went off to the bushes. I don't remember seeing him again after that."

"Who all was on your team?" Chris asked.

"Me and Tom, and Vinnie here, and Big Bob for a while, and Leonard. There were lots more people sitting around, but I don't remember who all bet on our team."

"I faded out before the last game ended," added Leonard. "I guess I didn't want to win that bad, to play all night. I went off to stretch my legs too, then just ended up resting in the back of my truck instead of going back to the game. But I don't remember Tom in that last game. I don't think he ever come back."

"Did you hear any cars leave in the middle of the night?" Chris asked. "Do you think Tom could have gotten a ride out with someone?"

"No, not after that last game started, not that I can remember, and we asked other folks about that. Nobody heard cars coming or going during that last game. Of course, during the game you wouldn't hear a car over the drums and the singing. Not unless it was a loud one, or some drunk spinning his tires on the rock."

"What about earlier. Marv said some young punks hassled Tom earlier in the afternoon. What was that about?" Chris persisted.

"Oh, that was just some drunk kids trying to hit him up for money to buy more booze. They wanted him to pay 'em 'royalties', to pay something for the stories and songs he'd published."

Leonard paused. "One of them was my grandnephew Kevin. I took him aside later and taught him some lessons he had apparently never learned yet. I told the rest of 'em all to get out of here and sleep it off. They left, and I didn't see 'em come back."

"Who were they?"

"At least a couple of 'em come from up around Greenville," Leonard said. "Two of 'em I didn't recognize, and Kevin said he didn't know where they come from either, except the one who was a brother of the dancer from Indian Valley, Mike Jackson. Nobody from around here, except Kevin."

"You don't think they came back?"

"No, someone would've seen 'em or heard about 'em," Leonard said.

"Even in the heat of a hot handgame? Over all the singing and drumming?"

"Well, if we were guessing and the other team was singing, I would've heard 'em. I don't like listening too long to the other team's songs." Old Leonard laughed. "It's bad luck if you listen to their songs too long! I think I would've heard 'em or seen 'em, if the other side was singing. But if we were singing, maybe not. I was still awake for quite a while after I lay down in my truck, listening to the gambling songs, and I didn't hear any cars, comin' or goin'."

"What do you think, BB?"

Big Bob paused, then smiled. "Maybe Professor Coyote ran off with an Indian woman. Maybe he wanted to disappear. We looked around Sunday and didn't find no trace of him. Maybe a bear got him," he grunted.

As Big Bob spoke,.Chris suddenly wondered why BB had been playing on Tom and Marvin's team. Big Bob had always captained his own team, as far back as Chris could remember. Chris couldn't recall a time when BB played on their team. He always ran things himself, he wasn't the type of man to let someone else do the guessing for him. But then, Chris only saw Big Bob a couple times a year, there were probably lots of things he didn't know about him.

"Well, I know you guys have all done this before, but I'd like to walk around up on the dome myself, just to feel out the spot," said Chris.

"I kinda figured you would," said Leonard, "I would want to do the same thing myself. Let's get some water, and then pile into my truck."

8

On Pitch-off Mountain

Pitch-off Mountain was less than two miles from the rancheria – probably less than one mile as the crow flies. Over the rough and rutted road it took over a quarter hour to drive to it. They probably could have walked to it in the same time.

Leonard pulled his truck off and parked where the road crossed an outcropping of the granite surface. Chris, Vinnie and Big Bob climbed out from the back of the pickup, and Leonard and Marv came out of the cab.

"This place up here is sacred to our people," Leonard said, apparently to Chris. Leonard headed up toward the crest and Chris followed, with Marv and Big Bob bringing up the rear.

'I was just here,' thought Chris. 'How could I have gotten lost?'

Two huge granite rocks stood upright on the flaking granite surface atop Pitch-off Mountain. One looked like a giant coyote head, and the other nearby monument looked exactly like a stooping, naked, pregnant woman, her head bowed and draped with a blanket of stone. Chris could see her eyes in the rock, her smile, her hair, and the crack of her buttocks half-covered by a large bush.

"This is Worldmaker's Woman, frozen in shame after Coyote had his way with her," Leonard said. "We call her Ino O. This is a special place. People with trouble having kids come to this rock from far away. If you rub against her in a certain way she will help you. But if you don't know how to use her, or use her wrong, she will hurt you, make you sterile, or worse. So they say, anyway. These rocks reflect things that happened in ancient times."

They slowly walked around the barren surface toward Pitch-off Mountain dome.

"What's the story about this place?" Chris had heard it before but wanted to hear it again, wanted to remember it.

"Well," Leonard began, "a long long time ago, the world was full of killers and dangerous places. Worldmaker come through here after he made the land, getting it ready for the people he was making. A stump told him about this mean old woman who lived here on Pitch-off Mountain. Whenever some young man would come along here, up to the crest of the dome to look out over this world, the old woman would sneak up behind him, give him a hard push, send him sliding and falling down into the river canyon below.

"Worldmaker had to put a stop to this, he had to make it safe for the people that would live here. He come up the crest here, right to that spot over there, and looked way out across the canyon. He knew that old woman would try to push him off the dome, but Worldmaker had a magic walking stick. When the old woman moved to push him, he stretched his stick way out across the canyon to balance himself, and stepped aside. As the old woman fell down into the canyon, Worldmaker saw that she was his grandmother. Now he cries for the old woman, for his grandmother, because he had to kill her here to make the world safe for us."

Chris had heard that story before. He wanted to hear another story, the story behind the big fertility rock there, where the punks had been messing with his brother.

"What about those big rocks – Ino O you called it?"

Leonard was happy to find someone interested in the old stories of the land.

"Still a long long time ago, the people held a big-time up here on Pitch-off Mountain, just like we did the other night. Old man Coyote lived here then, with the Worldmaker and his wife. The Worldmaker's wife was a beautiful woman, and Coyote wanted her. She was Worldmaker's wife, but old Coyote broke all the rules. While everyone there made acorn bread, Coyote decided that he would create a diversion, so he could sneak the woman away for a little love making. Coyote prowled away from camp, and shot a man with his bow and arrow.

"'We're being attacked, we're being attacked,' Coyote hollered, as he ran back into camp, throwing around pieces of acorn bread. In the ensuing panic Coyote grabbed Worldmaker's woman and sneaked her away, saying 'Quick, let's hide here in the bushes.'

"Worldmaker come upon 'em while Coyote was having his way with her, and he turned 'em both into stone, right here, where you can still see them frozen in shame. All these other blocks of rocks around are the pieces of acorn bread that Coyote threw. It's a fertility rock now."

Beyond the big rocks they came to the handgame area. Two logs still lay opposite each other, where just a few nights ago players pounded out the rhythms of their handgame songs. Remnants of a fire smudged an area between the logs.

Vinnie looked around, as if he were looking for tracks or footprints in the rock.

Chris wondered, 'What am I looking for, what am I doing here?' but he walked back and forth like Vinnie, looking at the ground, gazing around the rockscape. After some while they continued up toward the crest of the dome. Just a hundred feet or so beyond the crest Chris was drawn to a large flat area in the granite landscape. Another smudge mark in the center of the area marked the spot where someone had recently made a campfire.

Vinnie walked around the area as he looked intently down at the ground. He got on all fours, and brushed his hands along the ground in a broad sweeping motion.

"This is a dance ground!" he eventually proclaimed. "See, this area has all been recently swept clean. If you look around the rest of this mountain you'll see lots of little rocks and pebbles. But look here – it's all clean. We dancers always make sure our dance ground is clean and clear of all little pebbles and sticks before we dance. We dance barefoot, and when we pound our rhythm into the earth it can be real painful pounding your heel into a pebble! But there are no pebbles anywhere around here... Hmmm... recently used."

Vinnie called out to the others. "Hey Marv! Leonard! BB! Come over here and check this out."

When they came over Vinnie said "Look at this! This is a dance ground. Was somebody doing the deer dance up here Saturday? I didn't know there were dances here last weekend."

"There wasn't, not that I know of," said Leonard. "This was a handgame get-together. Many handgame players are also dancers, like you, Vinnie, and if they're dancing, its hard for them to play handgame too. The dancers have to dance when their leader says, but sometimes the handgames just go on and on. No telling when they'll end. So we keep our handgame get-togethers separate from the seasonal dances here. But at big-time get-togethers like the Bear Dance, you got lots of people and lots of handgame players, so they'll gamble with or without the dancers."

"There wasn't no deer dance up here Saturday," Big Bob grunted. "This must be left over from sometime before."

"But not much before," Vinnie protested. "I don't know, I bet within a week this place would need sweeping again. And those coals aren't very old, it looks about the same here as down by the handgame area, and we know when those were made."

"There wasn't no deer dance here," Big Bob stated emphatically. "You wasn't dancing. Do you know anyone who was dancing?" He was almost challenging Vinnie.

"No, I wasn't dancing, and I didn't see anyone dancing. Still doesn't mean somebody wasn't. It's a nice place to have a dance here." Vinnie started prancing around like a coyote.

"Well, there wasn't no deer dance here. That's just some old campfire someone had up here. But it don't matter, there's probably been lots of dances up here before."

'No,' Chris thought, 'it doesn't matter if some outfit danced up here Saturday night. A lot of people aren't into the handgame, but why would they hold a dance away from the rest of the crowd, where nobody would see it. And why was Big Bob so adamant that it never happened? And if it never happened, where did this dance ground in front of us come from?'

Chris walked farther out along the top of the huge dome. The late morning sun burned mercilessly overhead. The rock became more barren as it steepened. Just a few twisting manzanita bushes pushed up through the cracks in the decomposing granite.

From here Chris could hear the roar of the Feather River rushing nearly half a mile below him through Pitch-off Mountain Canyon.

Beyond, in the distant haze, he could see the rising hills of the Coast Range. If he stretched his mind he could almost see the land where he had come from the day before, the western edge of the Maidu world. But try as he might, he couldn't see the river that he could hear rushing nearby, but far below, at the base of the rock dome.

"Watch your footing. You can't go much farther than this. It just gets steeper and steeper," cautioned Leonard.

Chris knew that already. "It's awesome," he said. "You feel like you can see half the world from here, but you can't even see the river just below us."

"This is where the old-timers used to come to hunt sumi, long ago," Leonard said. "They'd get a hunting party together, hide one man back there, hide another over by that edge of the clear area, maybe another over there," he said, gesturing toward the brushy edges of the flat rocky area. "Some hunters might wear a deer hide, dress up like a deer to hide their human smell, some might wear antlers on their head. They'd partly surround a bunch of deer. But they wouldn't go after the leader or the strongest ones, they'd go for the stragglers, the old ones having trouble keeping up with the rest of the herd. That's the ones they'd go for. They'd hide downwind, then start moving in to cut the deer off from escape. Hunters move in, deer moves back a little ways, away from the hunters."

Leonard gestured with his hands and arms, describing the hunt in his motions. "Whenever deer might get through the line of hunters here, maybe somewhere around there a bunch of feathers dangling from a bush spooks her back. Hunters get closer, deer moves away, farther down the dome. Then someone opens up with a whoop, another man comes hollering down from over there, the deer takes off running down the rock. The ground gets steeper and steeper. The deer begins to cry, because she knows what's happening. The deer slides and crashes down the cliff, then you hike down into the canyon and pick up your good sumi," said Leonard with a chuckle as he patted his barrel-like belly. "Of course nowadays we just pop 'em up on top here with a rifle."

"Wouldn't the river just wash the deer carcass downstream?" asked Chris

"Naw, there's lots of big rocks down there. And there's a flat area, more or less, right below Salmon Falls, when the river's low. If the river's running real high it might be another matter. But it's a tough place to get to. Coyote made it that way. "Worldmaker wanted to make it easy for people to get food," Leonard continued. "He wanted to put Salmon Falls in a nice easy spot where people could just walk right up and grab a good salmon to eat. But old Coyote wanted none of that! He argued that the salmon should come way up the river, to the most dangerous and treacherous place in the canyon, so that the young men could show the girls and women how brave and strong they were.

"Worldmaker never argued. Coyote won that time, so the people had to go way down to the falls to get their salmon.... I speared fish there when I was a boy. I haven't been down there for, oh, thirty, forty years or more. There's an old trail about a mile from here, on the way back toward the rancheria. Fishermen go down there sometimes, but it's a good tough hike. The government come in and tried to make it safe back when I was a boy. It was a tough trail before then, but they just messed it up, trying to put safety rails into the crumbling rock. Made it more dangerous than ever! They put holes in the rock for their support poles as they carved a trail across the face of God! But that just made the face crumble away more. Safety rails on an Injun trail! Dang government morons! Just inviting people who shouldn't to go down there and get themselves killed."

"Can you show me the trail?" Chris asked.

"You don't want to go down there," interjected Big Bob. "What do ya want to go down for? The river's raging, nothing but whitewater and big boulders down there. It'd take ya the rest of the day just to get down and back. Wouldn't give ya any time to look around. And there's probably nothing to find there anyway."

Chris wondered how Big Bob knew so much about conditions in the bottom of the canyon. He was such a huge man Chris had trouble visualizing him scrambling down into a river canyon, but apparently he had been there before. Either he had been much younger and lighter then, or Big Bob must have enormous strength and balance.

"Well, somehow I've got to go down there," Chris said. "I mean, my brother was up here a few days ago, and he just vanished. That just seems like one of the few places he might be... down there."

A momentary horror came over Chris as he imagined his brother slipping or being driven off the cliff like a deer in the old hunt. How long would it take a person to tumble two thousand feet?

Chris felt he had to somehow justify to Big Bob his urge to go down into the canyon, even if it would be a futile trip. "Besides, its so blazing hot up here I've just got to get near some water."

"Well, you can do what ya want," said Big Bob, "but I'm not going down there. I've gotta take care of some business back at the Goose Farm."

"That's all right, I can go down alone if you show me the trail head." Chris was intent on getting down to the base of the dome. If anything were to be found it would be found there.

"I'll go down with you," Vinnie volunteered, "I've never been down there, and it's probably safer to go down with a partner."

"Well I have been down there, years ago," said Marv, "I remember some mighty big trout that'd stare back at you from those deep pools along the rocks. I might just get my fishing gear and head on down there with you two."

"Well, I'm a little too old to be going down in a young man's place like that," Leonard said. "And I've got some farm work I've got to tend to. But you boys go on down there. If you haven't been there, it'll be a place you'll never forget."

"I've got to get some supplies from my truck back at the rancheria," said Chris.

"Yeah, I've gotta get some gear too," added Marv.

"Well, hop back in the truck and we'll head back to the rancheria. I'll show you the way to the trail head up here."

9

Robin Woman

Why didn't the Professor call? She was more hurt than angry, but now she really needed his help. He had finally agreed to come to dinner at her place, and she had spent all Monday afternoon preparing everything, making it just right. But he never showed up, never even called. She'd ended up letting the lasagna cool in the oven all night, while she stewed her emotions in wine and waited for the phone which never rang. Half-glass by half-glass she'd polished off the liter of six-year old Merlot bought just for the occasion, then slipped into the two-year old Zinfandel before she was out for the night.

Tuesday was a rough day. She took a couple aspirin in the morning trying to fend off the headache-that-wouldn't-go-away. Aspirin dulled the pain, but didn't mask it. It wasn't the sharp killer-pain of a migraine or cluster headache, it was more a low dull pain in the back of her brain that had been with her for over a year now and never really went away. No one had been able to cure it, and the last doctor she went to speculated it might be more psychological than physical. She didn't go back to him.

Robin Ann Marquez, still a student at age thirty-three, needed, hopefully, one more semester to get her PhD, if she could just get her thesis pulled together in time. That's where Professor Thomas Livingstone was supposed to help. She was stuck on a few key points, and Tom had agreed to hash them out with her. She was stuck on him also. In fact, Tom was the reason she was studying anthropology in the first place.

She had started her university career late, after too-many years of a bad early marriage, and had no idea what she wanted to do with her life until she enrolled in Tom's Petrymythology of the Sierra Indians class. There he had made the ancient past come so alive to her that she knew she wanted to get into the field and learn more.

More than that, he had shown an interest that started to germinate in her a new self-confidence. Before her enrollment in the university, she'd thought of herself as an underprivileged mixed blood minority struggling to make it in a white man's world. Tom made her aware that her relatives included Maidu and Yacqui Indians, and that she was mostly Maidu herself. It gave her a cultural heritage that had been missing all her life, and an intuitive connection with native people everywhere. It had also given a direction to her future life.

She was fascinated by the Professor. He was outgoing and fun-loving, and by far the smartest person she had ever met. She flirted with him frequently, but felt he'd always been a bit too hung-up on the professor-student relationship taboo. But now the Professor had taken an early retirement after getting into a departmental feud, and none of that teacher-student taboo stuff should matter anymore. But where was he now?

He was a wise friend and mentor – and old enough to be her father. But he was also... interesting and fun to be with. He knew a lot of what little has survived of the ways of the original Californians and the medicines they practiced. That was where she most needed his help. He also knew a lot about the so-called Martis Complex people, and that was also where she needed him now.

She was confused about some seeming discrepancies in the basic timelines of the Maidu and Martis people, and needed to bat around some ideas with the Professor to get the last two chapters of her thesis finished.

All morning she struggled to pretend to be alert during her seminar, but her mind roamed everywhere but here. Why hadn't he at least called her? Why had he stood her up? Was he okay?

By the time eleven o'clock came, she was glad to get off campus for some strong coffee. Something had to wake her up and get her going, to get her through the day, so she could get through one more week, so she could just get through one more semester.

She cut across Sproul Plaza, where a street preacher raving about the coming end of the world competed vainly for ear-space with a pick-up percussion band improvising a lively Caribbean beat.

Robin headed down Telegraph Avenue a few blocks, threading her way through waves of students years younger than herself, past colorful street vendors and scruffy panhandlers, to what had become her off-campus office – the Caffe Med.

She ordered a double cappucino and a scone, and found a small table by the wall.

'Did something happen to him?' she wondered, 'or was he just trying to run away from me?'

She sipped her coffee, and watched the menagerie of people around her. Eventually, she turned her thoughts to the things she had to understand in order to finish her thesis.

The stories of the Maidu, passed down through centuries of oral tradition, point to their being among the original people of the northern Sierras – true American aborigines. There is no migration story in their mythology, and several surviving stories reflect times of one or more great floods that covered the world. Each time, a new world eventually emerged around This Place, where the Maidu people still live today. Oral stories going back to mythological times describe many rocks and landforms of the region. But other evidence indicates the Maidu were relative late-comers to the region – perhaps as late as 1200 CE. How could they be both original people and late-comers? She was confused. She thought about some of the old stories that are part of the oral mythological record.

But there were also other hard facts: linguistic studies indicated the Maiduan languages diversified from neighboring languages some four thousand years ago; the climatological record locked in tree rings showed there were two periods of extended droughts in the last two thousand years, lasting at least a century each. Could the People have survived in their area during those droughts, or did they migrate? Where did they go?

Then there was the archaeological record concerning the so-called Martis Complex, named after the Martis Valley in the high Sierras where their artifacts were first recognized in the 1950's.

The Martis stayed mostly around the Yuba and American rivers and the Tahoe area. They probably migrated with the seasons like most of the hunter-gathering people, following the food, moving up into their higher cooler mountain camps in summer and back to their homes in the lower foothills and valley in winter. They used simple basalt tools, not chert or obsidian or flint, and they didn't use a bow and arrow. That's how to identify them. What little is known of them comes from their artifacts. Nothing is known of the culture.

The Martis people disappeared around 600 CE, and the later Maidu culture appeared in the area by about 1200. Of course, in dating ancient sites it's much easier to determine when a site was last used than when it was first used. Were the Martis people earlier ancestors of the Maidu? Were they even a

Penutian language people? Did the Martis migrate during the long periods of drought, intermingle there with different tribes, where they learned different tools, and then migrate back? Or were they a totally separate people from the Maidu, brought to extinction by something – centuries of drought? Would a people, forced to migrate from their ancestral lands by climatological change, return twenty or thirty generations later? Or was it more likely that a different people came into the Sierras when it could again support a human population?

And then there was the Maidu star map that Tom had created after years of interviewing dozens of old timers. This consisted of a hand-drawn picture of the June night sky with the names of stars and constellations the various old-timers recognized from their stories. What bothered Robin was the polar star. The map showed the north star Polaris as 'the Anchor'. This was the point around which the night sky circled, and the name made sense. But there was also the star Vega, called on the map 'the Big Man'. Thirteen thousand years ago, more or less, Vega was itself the polar star. Why would people call this star the Big Man unless the name went back to those times when the Big Man was the polar star? It seemed plausible, almost likely, but impossible by the currently accepted doctrine. Did this name go back to Martis times? Or earlier?

She finished off her doppio as she mulled over these and other things, then went to the pay phone to call Tom's house again. When the machine answered, she hung up. She'd already left enough messages, and didn't want to seem like a desperate pest. Then she remembered Tom's brother Chris. She found his work number and rang his office. She got another recorded greeting that said he'd be out of the office for a few days, but this time she left her name and number with a message to call her as soon as he returned.

10

Worldmaker and Sunflower Girl

Worldmaker passed out and had a crazy dream. "I had a dream about grizzly bears. On this kind of day, water comes. I see water everywhere, covering This World."

And Worldmaker began to sing:

hainu hainu hainu hainu

When he finished, water started coming. It flooded the whole country.

Worldmaker put up a big pole, like the center pole of a roundhouse. That pole stretched from below the ground to above the sky, however far that might be.

All the animals were drowning, but as the water came up, Worldmaker climbed onto the big pole. As the water came higher, Worldmaker climbed higher. Sunflower Girl followed right behind him. She was a beautiful woman in those days. Water came up. Worldmaker moved up. Sunflower Girl moved up right behind him. Pretty soon Sunflower Girl looked around. Water covered everything. No mountains, nothing but water. She sang about water, singing that the water should drop so they could get back down to the land. But the water kept getting higher, so she had to keep moving higher up the pole.

Finally, the water stopped rising. By then the country was nothing but water, far as the eye could see. Worldmaker started singing, singing to the Big Deer in the sky, asking Big Deer to stick his hind leg down through the hole in the sky.

Big Deer lives in the world above the sky. He stuck his big leg down to Worldmaker, who drew the main cord from Big Deer's ankle and set him free again. He split the cord into thin strands, then split them again, and again. Then he sang for birds to come, and pretty soon birds were fluttering around the big pole, Mudhen Woman and Blackbird Woman. Worldmaker tied one end of each strip of cord to the pole. Blackbird Woman flew off with the cords to find some place to anchor them. To the north she tied one to a big pile of rocks. At two or three places to the east and south she tied the ends to mountains sticking out of the water. To the west, the cord was short and wouldn't stretch over the water. 'I've got to find something to tie this to,' she thought, and found another big rock.

Then Mudhen Woman dove down in the water to look for mud. Blackbird brought a few sticks and weeds, and pretty soon they had a good pile built up around the pole.

Then Worldmaker sang for Robin Woman, and soon she came – Cheezpahpah – down from the world above, with a pile of mud to build her nest around the pole.

Worldmaker watched all this, singing all the time. When Robin Woman finished her nest, Worldmaker stuck his big right foot into it and began shaking it, kept shaking, shaking, and the pile of muck grew bigger and bigger. Then he put his left foot into it, started shaking it. No telling where all that muck came from, but pretty soon it covered the world, and there was land over the water.

Worldmaker crawled down his pole and looked around. Pretty soon Sunflower Girl came down too, and started to grow in the mud. To this day she hangs on a little pole in the ground, singing away.

Sometime later Worldmaker went on an inspection tour of this new world, getting it ready for the People he was about to make.

11

Pitch-off Mountain Canyon

The trail down into the canyon began as an easy hike. Easy – except for the heavy pack that Chris carried on his back. It had been at least a few years since he had done any serious hiking, and he was starting to feel the lack of conditioning as he puffed down the trail. He wondered if he really needed all the stuff he was carrying.

Big Bob had warned him it was a long hike, so they had planned to spend the night at the bottom. Chris carried everything he might need: sleeping bag, food, cups, utensils, pots and pans – and the Peet's coffee, coffee pot, bag of Melitta filters, and a couple gallons of fresh water. More than enough for the three of them to eat comfortably while camping overnight down in the canyon. Vinnie carried just a small day-pack, and Marv carried only his fishing gear.

As the weight of the pack bore on his shoulders with every step, Chris kept wondering if he really needed all this stuff. Not thinking of anything he really wanted to do without, he tightened up the waist belt of the backpack to put more of the weight on his hips, and grunted on.

After some distance the trail passed into the shade of a large buckeye tree, and crossed a small spring-fed creek. They all paused here to refresh in the shade next to the clear cold water. Then, after a brief respite, they trudged onward down the trail, which now moved out of the shade and back into the heat of the overhead sun. There were no trees here, just patches of poison oak and the shining dark green leaves of yerba santa occasionally growing out of cracks in the granite.

At one point the trail crossed remnants of an old road, probably marking some old mining operation from the previous century. Chris stopped to survey the terrain. The trail continued on through switchbacks, up and down across more ravines as it twisted its way downward, whereas the old mining road continued steadily downward toward the river for a few hundred yards, then disappeared.

Marvin and Vinnie talked about the Eagle Dance. Marv thought the dance had changed in the last sixty years from a dance that celebrated Eagle's spirit and the majesty of his hunt, to a newer dance, as Vinnie and his group of Maidu dancers now performed it, climaxed with the Eagle being shot at the height of his flight by a white man's rifle.

Chris stopped by the old mining road. "You guys go on ahead, I'll catch up with you down the trail" he said, as Marv and Vinnie passed. "I'd like to check out this old road."

"Well, don't wander too far off the trail," Marv cautioned. "What seems like a trail around here turns into washes, and water can go a lot of places a man can't."

"I'll catch up."

Marv and Vinnie continued along the main trail. Chris walked a short way down the old road. A distant roar from the yet unseen river in the canyon below permeated all sounds, like a strong wind blowing through trees. Chris paused, then continued down the old mining road to see if he could get a view of the river, and where his brother might have fallen.

A rusty old cable, thick as a man's arm, protruded out of the road and ran a few dozen yards, ending next to a huge rusted pulley contraption – remains of some long abandoned enterprise. Beyond these ruins the road seemed to continue. The old tracks deepened into ruts and gullies. As the track steepened it became clear that this was no longer a road but a steep wash, dry now but obviously awash with large amounts of water at some times of year.

Chris remembered Marv's warnings about getting too far off the trail, about the same time he realized this trail went nowhere. As he turned to head back up, he slipped. The decomposing granite flaked off beneath his feet, and he fell on his back, sliding feet first and slow motion down the steepening gulch. As he picked up speed he grabbed a manzanita branch growing out of the rock. It slowed him for a moment before breaking off. He kept sliding, picking up a speed as he tried desperately to slow down. He grabbed at an outgrowth of yerba santa plants as he went by, but his hands just stripped the leaves off the stalks.

Heart pounding, he tried to use his heels and fingers to slow himself. The steepening of his descent offset whatever braking he could effect He could see one last clump of bushes ahead of him, before the wash ended in a long drop to the river. He reached out and grabbed the branches as he slid by. Leaves stripped off the woody stalks until they finally... stopped him.

Chris lay there on the steep rock incline, shaking in panic, his heart racing. Still clinging to the bush, he finally recovered enough to evaluate his predicament.

Death waited for him a thousand feet below. Somehow he had to roll over and crawl back up to the trail. He tried several times to change his position, but every time he moved at all, he started to slip.

After a while he realized his problem – his center of balance was thrown off by his back pack. If he could just take off the pack he might have a chance of getting out of here. He could always figure out how to retrieve the pack later. With his heels dug in and one hand always clinging to the bush, he managed to wriggle out of the pack's harness. The pack itself, once free, slid quickly away, over the edge and gone.

It happened so fast it was astonishing. Everything he had needed, everything that he had carried on his back for the past hour was now gone. He had nothing. But now he needed nothing, nothing except a chance to get out alive. And if he couldn't do that, he'd need nothing anyway.

Without the pack, he found he could now turn over and move more easily. Only then did he fully notice the bush that had saved his life – poison oak. It didn't matter. He thanked the bush profusely, speaking to it out loud, like to a regular person. He reached into his pocket and left a cigarette as a gift to the spirit behind the bush that saved him. Then, using his fingers and toes, he managed to slowly crawl back up the wash.

He crawled out of the erosion through masses of poison oak. What could it hurt now? He was already thoroughly exposed, but it would be a day or two until any rashes would break out. Besides, poison oak was now his friend, his ally. It had saved his life. He reached a point where he could stand up again and claw his way up through scrub oak and manzanita. Finally, he pulled himself over a small hill and ended up on the main trail again.

Directly in front of him, painted into the cliff face at a bend in the cliff-side trail, a pictograph, a painted spirit-face, stared at him. The synchronicity caught Chris off guard.

He moved toward the pictograph, and instinctively froze. Immediately above and to the right, a large diamond-backed snake peered at him from its ledge on the rock. 'Rattlesnake!' he thought. He felt he was looking at the Spirit of the canyon. What was it trying to tell him?

His mind answered. 'You have come to this place without asking, without preparation, without permission. That is why you nearly died. Wake up!'

He spoke with his mind to the spirit of the canyon. 'I come here as a visitor to this place. I come here to look for my brother, or my brother's spirit. I am your friend. Please help me, and show me the way."

He had a sudden urge to leave a gift of tobacco for the spirit. He reached into his pocket to see if he still had the pack of cigarettes. In modern times a single cigarette might be considered an appropriate gift to leave for a spirit. Chris didn't want to be cheap here. He had just come back from Death's reach. He tucked the entire pack of cigarettes into a crack in the cliff face beneath the pictograph.

He felt safe now, happy to still be alive. As he hustled down the trail, trying to catch up with his friends, he sang the song that always made him feel safe.

hedem yamani wi-tu-tu, wi-tu-tu, wi-tu tu wi tu tu
hodem yamani wi-tu-tu, wi-tu-tu, wi-tu tu wi tu tu

The final leg of the trail was carved into the side of the cliff face, a descending ledge of switchbacks zig-zagging down the crumbling, nearly vertical wall of decomposing granite. In some places handrails made of galvanized steel pipes, supported by more pipes stuck into weathered holes drilled into the crumbling granite, provided more psychological comfort than physical safety.

The river was visible now, maybe five hundred feet below, and the roar of the raging water grew louder with every step he took.

Near the end of the switchbacks a thin curtain of water trickled down the face of the cliff and across the trail, which was now just a thin ledge cutting across the slippery rock a few hundred feet above the river. Beyond the seepage Marv and Vinnie waited for Chris.

Chris gingerly eased himself across the slippery wet spot and joined his friends. They made no mention of his absence. How long had it been?

"Wonomi, the One Who Never Dies, sleeps in this rock mountain," Marv greeted, raising his voice above the roar of the river and waterfalls below. "These are his tears, Wonomi's Tears." He gestured up the wet cliff face toward a point where a dark manganese-stained crack in the rock showed where a spring originated. "Wonomi cries here. That's his eye way up there, and this is his face, this whole rock wall. He cries for his grandmother. That's the story anyway. I think he cries for all his people now."

Marv turned to look down the canyon below. "The river's pretty high now from all the spring runoff, you can see that. Not sure how much were gonna be able to get around down there. There's a fisherman camp at the bottom of this trail, it should be up high enough to be out of the water. We'll make camp down there and then see what we can see. But it will be loud down there. This is Thunder's place. We won't be able to talk above the sound of the river, so we should do our talking here." He looked at Chris and then added "What happened to your back pack?"

"Oh, I got off the trail back there, and came to a spot where either the pack had to go or we both would go." Chris tried to be nonchalant about his near-death encounter. "Didn't need all that stuff anyway. Sorry about the food. We'll have to make do."

"That's okay, we can find our own food, if you're willing to eat like an Indian. There's food right there," Vinnie said, pointing to a mound of pine needles just below the trail in a sunny spot between some rocks, where a small pine had found its niche in a crack.

"That's a wood ants' nest. There'll be plenty of ants' eggs inside the ant pile. I was eyeing them while we waited here for you. We can eat them raw or fry them up on a hot rock. Scrambled ants eggs is actually real tasty."

Vinnie was getting on a roll. "And there're lots of manzanita berries around, dry and from last year, but still real good for you. And this water here comes from Worldmaker's Tears, we can see the spring way up there, so we know the water's good."

"Yeah, and I saw a rattlesnake back there, maybe you can go get some rattlesnake meat too," Chris jockeyed back.

"That wasn't a rattler, that was a gopher snake," Vinnie responded. "We saw it back there too."

Marv patted the fish creel hanging from his shoulder. "Don't worry, I've got us all covered." He sized up Chris from head to toe with the bemused smile of an experienced woodsman looking at a city-person in the wilderness.

"I told you about getting off the trail, didn't I?" Marv said. "You gotta watch your step around here. There's only one way down unless you can fly or turn yourself into water, and this is it. But we're almost there now. We'll make camp down below here, and then check around. I'll go to the natural foods store for some trout, since you lost our dinner," he said with his trademark smile. "Vinnie can fix up his ant eggs for an appetizer."

"Why do you call this Thunder's place?" Chris asked.

"In the beginning, all the people spoke the same language," Marv said. "And they all played handgame. Thunder used to live down here, and he was a big gambler. You can still see the place where his roundhouse used to be. He played handgame against the different animals, and he beat every one of 'em. That's why they're all the way the are today. When Thunder roared, Mouse cowered, and became the little animal he is today. But one day Thunder gambled against two magic twins who had more power. He couldn't beat them, they had more power, and Thunder had to go live in the sky."

12

The songs of the canyon

The switchback trail ended, and the path, what there was of it, became a scramble down and around a ravine piled with truck-sized boulders, which finally emptied onto a flat sandy area tucked against the rocks above the river. Here the sound of the river overpowered everything, except the visual landscape – rushing blurry white water sweeping around and through enormous smooth sun-bleached boulders; curvaceous sculpted granite masses, speckled white, carved and polished by the power of water.

Against the cliff, away from the center of the river, white water swirled into a long, deep, blue-green pool. Upstream, a huge waterfall spanned the canyon as the tumbling river dropped through a boulder field. Farther upstream, just beyond these rapids, the Fall River fell down Feather Falls, adding more power to the water rushing by.

The sound of all this rushing river was overwhelming, oppressive at first. Chris tried to shout out to Marv that he would go look downstream, but the effort was futile. He could feel his own shouting voice in his chest but the sound never reached his own ears. Now was obviously a time for work without talk, for mental processing and basic tasks, and not for words.

Marv signaled that he was heading up the river with his fishing gear. Chris set out downstream, looking around and organizing some wood for the evening campfire.

Firewood was not hard to find. Dry driftwood was lodged everywhere throughout the boulders in the highest parts of the riverbed, carried down some time ago by waters running even higher than today.

Chris scrambled around the camp area, gathering wood and looking for... a sign, his brother's hat, maybe his sunglasses, maybe his own backpack – something.

He peered over a boulder into a deep clear pool. Below, a huge trout hung motionless in the water. Chris made a slight movement, and the fish disappeared into the deep blue-green, hiding somewhere beneath the rocks. Chris thought of all the stuff that had been in his pack, and was now gone. He hoped Marv would have some good luck.

In the old days the salmon used to come all the way up here from the ocean. Old-timers said sometimes it was so thick with salmon that a man could just stand on a rock in the river and spear as many as he needed. This was the end of the long river road for them, the falls were a formidable barrier. The end of their road, but the beginning of their road also – the place of their birth, the place where their ancestors spawned, the place where they spawned after their long journey down the Feather River to the Sacramento, to the Delta and San Francisco Bay, to the wide expanse of the open ocean world, and then some-day back to the Bay and up the Delta, back up the same rivers to this very spot where they were born.

But the dam at Ophir City ended all that in the 1960's. The state built a fishery below the dam, and the salmon never got up this far anymore.

The huge old trout in the pool beneath Chris now seemed symbolic of that end of the run, like it evolved from some steel-head salmon trapped long ago in fresh water, barred from its ancestral journey to the sea by the white man's dams, surviving just as native cultures have survived the past century by living on in tiny isolated enclaves, evolving and surviving, barred from their ancestral dream voyage by encroaching civilization.

The first thing Chris would do whenever he set up a new camp was gather firewood. Collecting wood now gave him something to do as he scrambled among the hot boulders look-ing for his brother's body. It was hard for him to admit to him-self that this was what he was doing – looking for a body. What would it be like if he found it? Would it look like a body? Would it be all in one piece? What happens to a body when it bounces two thousand feet into a pile of giant boulders?

He left another armful of wood at the campsite. Then he surveyed the canyon, trying to determine where something falling from the top of the dome might land. Above him he could see only a few hundred feet of the rocky canyon wall. The top of the granite dome, rising some two thousand feet above him, lay hidden. He remembered roughly where Marv had pointed out Worldmaker's eye and the seepage that was his tears. Chris figured a hundred yards or so downstream from where he now stood would probably be just about below that spot.

Vinnie came into camp with something wrapped up in his shirt. 'I'm not eating any ant eggs,' Chris thought. He indicat-ed to Vinnie that he would go downstream again. Vinnie stayed in the camp, apparently singing while he emptied the contents of his shirt onto a rock, but no song could be heard above the roar of the river.

Chris spent the afternoon searching the canyon beneath the dome, scrambling over and around huge water-polished boulders. He found an agility he hadn't felt in years, and within a short time he hopped from rock to rock with a natural balance and fearlessness, as if he had spent all his life in river canyons.

He searched for some sign of his brother's body, but found nothing. Like Big Bob had said, the canyon had been swept clean by the raging spring runoff, except for a line of driftwood debris high above the water line. Along the debris line Chris found nothing but firewood, which he gathered and left in small piles to cart back to camp later.

Chris saw a deep green pool that seemed like an oasis of calm in the wild white water of the river. Collecting more firewood in the intense heat of the afternoon seemed senseless, so he pulled off his clothes and dove into the icy pool. The cold water washed away all the heat, the dirt and grime, and, he hoped, the poison oak resins from his body. Shimmering light played upon the bottom of the riverbed. On the far side of the river a small bird, a water ousel, nervously dipped its legs as it made its way along a white rock above the river. Suddenly it flew and dove into the water and disappeared.

He hauled himself out onto a house-sized boulder. The hot rock beneath him warmed his cold wet body, and the smooth indentation he rested upon seemed like a hard but comfortable couch carved in polished granite especially for him to enjoy.

The light of day slowly faded into dusk, and the noise of the rushing water pressed all his thoughts deep within his brain. His mind was almost empty now, his thoughts squeezed below the threshold of consciousness by the relentless force of the deafening sound of the canyon. As he dozed he could hear the river singing.

When the light faded, he picked himself off his resting spot and made his way back toward camp. He saw Marv hiding on the rock above the deep hole with the big trout in it, dangling his line into the water. When Marv saw Chris, he shrugged his shoulders as if to say "No fish tonight, this old sucker's too smart."

Chris gathered another of the piles of wood he'd collected, and with both arms full he hopped from rock to rock back upstream to the fisherman's camp where they were spending the night.

Marv returned to the camp soon also. Vinnie already had a good fire going. Chris dropped another armful of wood next to the fire circle and sat down on a stone next to them. Marv and Vinnie snacked on some fried ants eggs seasoned with caddis flies that Vinnie had cooked up on a hot flat rock in the hearth.

"Mmm, try these, they taste like dried shrimp," Marv seemed to say, although Chris couldn't hear a word.

Even though hunger pangs pulled on his stomach, Chris couldn't bring himself to join them. With tightly closed lips he shook his head and smiled. He had an aversion to eating bugs and larvae and slimy creatures, even if they were now crisp and crunchy. 'There's plenty to find to eat if you're willing,' he thought. 'I'm just not hungry enough yet.'

Marv enjoyed watching Chris's plight, but soon the appetizers were gone, and Marv reached over to his fishing creel and pulled out his trophy, a whitefish about fourteen inches long.

"All right!" Chris cheered, but the words never got further than his stomach. Marv put the cleaned fish on the hot rock that Vinnie had used to cook the ants eggs, then skewered it with a thin stick, and positioned it over the coals. The fish baked, and soon he, Chris and Vinnie were licking their fingers around the fire. Nothing could be heard above the roar of the canyon.

The water's roar, and somewhere beneath the roar the subtle sound of rocks rattling in the riverbed, washed away any words they might try to utter. The embers of the fire beneath the slot of sky above the canyon walls mesmerized the three campers. They sat around the fire throughout the night, each taking turns poking the embers and feeding pieces of wood to the coals, all lost in their own thoughts.

In the embers Chris saw a woeful face staring back at him. He remembered Pancho talking about this old man in the fire. Old Man Fire. If you see him staring back at you from the embers with glowing woeful eyes... feed him, give him a piece of food – the fish head. Chris watched the woeful eyes of the man in the fire as he fed him all that was now left of Marv's trophy fish.

He stared into the coals, and thought about fire. How useful it was, how powerful. He wondered how long had people known how to use fire? He tried to remember pieces of the story, as Pancho had told it....

Chris threw some more wood on the fire. Vinnie and Marv were in some kind of trance, mumbling soundless songs as one or the other occasionally poked at the coals

Chris listened to the sounds of the canyon. Beyond the circle of the campfire, almost felt rather than heard, rocks and boulders rattled against the bedrock as the river rushed through the canyon – music hidden in the roar of the water. Chris wondered, 'Is this the song of the spirit whose face I saw painted on the canyon wall?'

Behind the roar of the water, perhaps within it, a continuous droning chant could be heard:

o momoli momoli momoli mom
o wonomi momi momoli mom

Listening closely, through the sounds of water rolling through his head he could almost hear a handgame song:

o wonomi momi momoli mom
o momoli momi o wonomi mom

This was Wonomi's place, and all around was the sound of his water, momi. Somewhere above them, Wonomi's tears trickled down the rock face of the dome. Chris picked up a stick and began pounding a rhythm on the rock to accompany the tune rolling through his brain.

wonomi momi wonomi momi

wonomi momi wonomi mom

The song took form as endless varations played through his brain. He wondered if Marv and Vinnie heard the same song as they beat their sticks upon a rock. Though he could not hear them above the roar of the canyon, their bodies seemed to be swaying in unison to the same rhythm and chant that now circled through his mind.

wonomi momi wonomi mom
wonomi momi wonomi mom

The song looped through his head in endless variations throughout the night, as the three campers fed driftwood to the woeful old man in the embers.

13

The theft of fire

A long long time ago, all the animals were people, and
they all spoke the same language. The animal-people here did-
n't have fire then. They ate raw food because they didn't have
coals to cook it. Once in a while they could get a red-eyed bird
to stare at a piece of meat for a long time. It would turn a little
white around the edges – that's all. They wanted to cook their
food, and knew what fire was, but they didn't have any. Only
the bird-people, who lived in the Coast Range far to the west
across the Great Valley, had fire.

One day this tribe of animal-people all went swimming at
a place in the Feather River called Long Hole. While they
swam there, all the other animals mocked little blue-belly
lizard. Lizard left the pool crying. He climbed up the side of the
canyon to a rock where he could look across the Great Valley
to the Coast Range, where the bird-people lived.

As he cried, his eyes shrank and he could see very clearly. Smoke. Smoke in the Coast Range. Lizard ran back to the swimming hole.

'Smoke, I saw smoke in the Coast Range.'

Lizard took the other animals up to the lookout. 'See it there, see the smoke!' He pointed with his little finger.

The other animals looked but they saw nothing. In those days Deer had eyes as big as saucers. The animals sewed Deer's eyes closed until they were the size they are today. Then Deer could see the smoke too.

'If the bird-people have smoke, they must have fire,' one of them said.

After some convincing they all agreed it must be fire. 'Wouldn't it be nice if we could have our own fire to warm ourselves on a cold night, and to cook our food?' they thought. They all agreed they needed fire and should go get some of it.

They got together a little war party to go over to the Coast Range and steal the bird-people's fire.

Coyote, as always, elected himself leader of the expedition. 'Well, cousins, you all know I'm smarter than you, so you'll need me.' And off they went to steal fire.

No telling how long they traveled, but sometime at night when they sneaked closer they discovered the smoke came from inside the bird-people's roundhouse. Mockingbird perched on the roof and was the lookout, because he could stay awake all night.

'If any one of us can steal that fire, I can,' said Coyote. 'Besides, I have a good place to carry it.'

He sneaked off to the roundhouse, but the big guardian bird on the roundhouse roof cried out 'Enemies coming!' Coyote felt that he was lucky to escape alive, and ran back to the others.

'If I can't get it, none of you can,' Coyote said.

But the other animals all had to have their try.

Finally, after each of the other animals tried to sneak up on the bird-peoples' roundhouse and got spotted by Mockingbird, little Mouse said 'Let me try. I can steal the fire from the bird-people.'

All the other animals laughed at him.

'You can never succeed. We have all tried. You'll just be picked up and eaten by the bird-people.'

But Mouse scurried off with his little flute, intent to get some fire.

When he came to the roundhouse, Mouse saw that Mockingbird seemed to be asleep. Every so often Mockingbird jerked his head up and sang

Enemies coming
I see them! I see them!

Then his head fell down and he went back to sleep.

Mouse scooted up the cedar wall, onto the bark roof, past Mockingbird, up to the smoke-hole, and down the center post of the roundhouse

Birds everywhere! It was a tough outfit. Three big, mean-looking birds – Eagle, Red-tailed Hawk, and Owl – perched in a circle with their wings outspread, guarding something. But all the birds were asleep.

Little Mouse chewed up all their baskets. Then he sneaked under the big birds' wings and found a pit filled with ashes. The fire was stoked down for the night, but Mouse burrowed through the ashes and found some hot coals. He scooped some coals into his elderberry flute, and hurried out of the round-house.

Mouse rushed back to the war party. 'I got the fire, I got the fire,' he squeaked.

'Well done, cousin, good job,' said Coyote as took the flute from Mouse. 'I've got a better place to hide this.' He took the coals from the flute and stuffed them up between his hind legs.

'YELP, YELP, YELP,' Coyote hollered as he flew through the air with hot coals shooting out of his behind.

The bird-people woke up when they heard Coyote's hollering.

'Our fire is gone! Stolen!' They all flew out of the round-house with a vengeance.

The animals took off toward the Sierras, taking turns carrying the fire. First the bird-people swooped down on Turtle, since he was the slowest runner. Turtle ducked into his shell. The birds tried to spear him – the marks can still be seen on Turtle's shell.

'If we can't spear Turtle, what are we going to do with him?' the birds said.

'Please don't drown me,' Turtle cried.

'That's it, we'll drown him!' They picked him up and dropped him into the Sacramento River. This couldn't have made Turtle happier, and he swam to the bottom of the river.

Next was Skunk. Skunk was a slow runner too, but the birds backed off quickly when Skunk gave them a whiff of his medicine.

Meanwhile Fox and the other animals passed the stolen coals from one to another as they fled across the valley.

The bird-people got a big rain storm to come up. Rain, spears and lightning struck everywhere. The animals all got under this huge animal, bigger than an elephant, called a *kohunoya*. The kohunoya could only come out at night, for light would change them into stone.

They hid underneath the kohunoya until Deer said, 'I'm a fast runner, let me give it a try.' He put the coals between his hind legs and bounded to the Sacramento River. There, Deer hid the hot coals inside a hollow part of a buckeye tree and swam across the river before running off to hide. The dark hocks on a deer today mark the spot where Deer carried the burning coals. After that, the people used buckeye wood for their fire-makers.

When the bird-people got back to their roundhouse, they were so mad at Mockingbird for falling asleep that they whipped him to death.

At night, Mockingbird still calls out in his sleep. And in early Fall, dead mockingbirds lie all over the forest floor.

14

Coffee at Leonard's

Chris, Marv and Vinnie hiked out of the canyon early next morning, before the sun cracked the canyon rim. A few hundred feet above the river, the canyon's roar lifted and they could talk again.

"That was something!" Chris exclaimed. "We didn't find out anything, I guess, but I've never been to a place that just takes you over like that. I feel like I've been dreaming for the past day."

"Yeah, I was hearing spirits down there too," said Vinnie, "singing in the canyon all night long. Did you hear them – like a chant or song coming from the river, rocks pounding on rocks in an endless song, *wonomi momi wonomi mom, wonomi momi wonomi mom.*"

"Wow, I heard that too, all night long," Chris exclaimed. "Maybe we heard each other singing the same song. I don't know what to call it, except the howl of the river."

"No, I heard the same song," added Marvin, "and I couldn't even hear myself singing it. We couldn't possibly hear one another. The spirit of the canyon gave us all that song. You know what that means, don't you?"

"Yeah, it mean's Worldmaker's water," answered Vinnie.

"Yeah, right, Wonomi momi. But it really means we should be handgame partners," Marv raised his eyebrows while nodding his head. "That's our *hilom soli* now – our gambling song. The spirit of the canyon gave us this song, and it should bring us luck. We didn't find your brother's body or anything of his for that matter. That's a good sign, really. And we were given a handgame song here. That's a good sign too, good luck on both counts."

They trudged up the trail, singing their song.

wonomi momi wonomi mom
wonomi momi wonomi mom

This time they stayed together, in a column. Chris didn't stray from the trail for side trips or sight-seeing, they were a team. They had spent the night in the roaring canyon together, and the spirits gave them a song together. Now they trudged up the trail together.

It was a long hike, zig-zagging up across the rock face, barren but for the sparse plants struggling to survive in occasional cracks in the face of the Worldmaker.

They got off the dome and wound their way around the first creek crossing when Chris realized he had walked right past the pictograph on the cliff face. He had meant to stop there, to see if the spirit face was really there – or if all those cigarettes were still there too.

As they moved away from the heart of the canyon and onto a regular earthen trail, the flora changed to tangles of manzanita, sugar pines, buckeye trees, and poison oak. As they ascended, Chris began to itch between his fingers, and remembered his brush with poison oak. Last year's berries were still on the manzanita bushes. Marv had once told him manzanita was an antidote for poison oak, so Chris pulled off some dry berries to chew. The berries were like small rose hips, tasty but dry and tough, and small hard pieces stuck between his teeth and in his throat. Then Chris remembered you were supposed to make a tea of the berries.

They made good time, and by midmorning they arrived back at Marv's new pickup parked under the shade of a big buckeye tree. They threw the fishing gear into the back of the truck, and took the short drive back to Leonard's.

"How was the expedition?" Leonard greeted them as the three drove up.

"Slim pickings, but great scenery," Marv replied. "We didn't find any sign of Tom. Our esteemed expedition leader here lost all that city coffee down there," he nodded, grinning toward Chris, "and I only caught one small whitefish. The granddaddy trout down there are just too smart."

"Well, I got a fresh pot of Folger's on. I take it you boys could use some coffee."

"Well, some water first, and then the coffee," Chris panted, the manzanita dust still clinging to his throat. "That was a long hike up. By the way, did I leave any cigarettes around here somewhere?"

"Here you go – I know you don't smoke your own stuff anyway, you just leave cigarettes all over the countryside and smoke OP's – Other Peoples brand," Marv grinned, holding out his pack of Pall Malls.

Chris took one of Marv's cigarettes, and sat down in one of the overstuffed chairs. Leonard brought a pitcher of water and a pot of coffee.

"So," he asked Chris, smiling, "you know how that whitefish got so many bones, don't you?"

"Why?"

"Down there in the canyon, at Thunder's place, Whitefish and Eel wanted to play some handgame. 'We don't have anything to bet, how are we going to gamble?' they wondered. 'Let's play for our bones' one of 'em said. Whitefish won that game. That's why he has all those bones, and Eel has none. He lost 'em all to Whitefish."

"So is that why they sometimes call it the bone game?" Chris laughed.

"No, Whitefish won all Eel's bones, see" Leonard laughed.

Chris eventually directed the conversation back to his missing brother.

"I keep thinking about those punks that were giving Tom a hard time last Saturday," he ventured, as he examined the poison oak rash on his hands. "Can you tell me more about that?"

"Well," Leonard said, "I took the Professor over to visit my Aunt Eleanor earlier in the morning, then dropped him off along Bean Creek on the way back home. Later in the day I was driving down Pitch-off Mountain Road, and for some reason decided to stop by Ino O. That rock's a special place," he added, "I like to go there."

After a moment Leonard continued. "When I got out of my truck and started walking up, I saw that group hassling Tom. I think some of 'em come from over around Indian Valley. Two or three of these guys held him against the rock. It looked like something that needed breaking up right then! Those boys wanted to mess him up, but they backed of when the saw me comin'. But the Professor shook it off with a laugh, saying it was all something for his next book."

"Why were they after him?" Chris asked.

Leonard went on. "I asked 'em what's going on. One of 'em said the professor stole his great-grandfather's gambling song, put it on a record and made a lot of money on it. They thought he owed 'em."

"That's not true!" objected Chris. "He gets a little money from his pension, but that's about it!"

"Well," countered Leonard, "turns out some the professor's tapes ended up in the university museum, and the university published a collection of recordings a while back. I think the whole collection of tapes is about a hundred and twenty five bucks. More money than anybody up here can afford! But the professor said he had nothing to do with it, he was retired now, and just as upset as these boys, because the tapes got published without his knowledge or advice, done by some other professor's student, with some missing notes, and so forth. But Tom was credited with some of the recordings, and these guys figured he owed 'em money for it since they're their great-grandfather's songs. But they were drunk, I broke it up pretty easily, told 'em they never would've even known about their great-grandfather's songs if it hadn't been for Professor Coyote and people like him. They've got some respect for their elders left, even when they're drunk. I cooled 'em off and told 'em to go sleep it off before they hit the road and beat it. I don't think they come back, I didn't see 'em around after that."

"How can you steal a song?" Chris protested. "The old people wanted to sing for him, wanted to share what pieces they could remember of the old ways. They knew their culture was almost dead. They wanted to save what was left, so that maybe it could survive, be revived."

"We know that. We know what the professor did. I learned some songs from his recordings, and I learned this place right here used to be like the capitol of our little country. I can show you where the house pits are. I wasn't interested when I was young. We were ashamed to be Indian. We wanted to learn to be like the white man. Your brother wanted to learn to be an Indian. It's strange."

"Who told them that Tom had stolen their great-grandfather's song?"

Leonard waited a moment to answer. "I asked them that. They said Big Bob told 'em."

Leonard looked a bit concerned for a moment, then continued. "He probably told 'em that Professor Coyote's tapes were being sold by the University, and that they cost a hundred twenty-five bucks a set, something like that."

Chris felt a flush of anger at how things could be misconstrued.

"Well, the only money he's made from you guys is from playing handgame with you," Chris laughed. "Using your own songs against you. Some of them are Coyote Tom's songs now – he saved them with his tape recorder."

"Well the way you and him sing some of 'em, they might as well be yours," chided Marvin, with laughter beaming through his eyes and voice. "We sing 'em a little different up here, a little slower."

"It's all this modern world stuff, Marv," Chris laughed. "Things just tend to move faster nowadays, just look at the highways. You gotta keep up, or the rhythm will run you down!"

Chris joked, but Marv had a point. Sometimes their handgame team would get so excited as a winning song went on and on that they would subconsciously or otherwise develop a faster and faster rhythm until the older people would mock them, to let them know they were butchering the song by singing it so fast.

"I wonder how Big Bob heard about that tape, and why he told those kids," Chris said.

"He was looking for stuff about his own people," Leonard replied, "over in Berkeley at the University. There was supposed to be some old wax cylinders with his grandfather telling stories about the grizzly doctors, with some parts in the old language. But he couldn't find 'em. Then he saw this other collection of tapes. He felt the Indian people should at least be entitled to copies of their own music and stories. He got mad when they wouldn't give him a copy of the whole set. He's got a point there."

"There was something else," Leonard continued. "Between Big Bob and Tom, about something they found together down at the Goose Farm rancheria. When they dug out a new barbecue pit a couple weeks back, they found a soapstone bowl and an Indian pipe, way down deep, about four or five feet. Tom thought this was the ancient peoples' stuff, several thousand years older than the newer stuff. Big Bob was worried some of Tom's friends at the University might get wind of the find, and want to do a big dig at the site. Tom said there hadn't been much ancient stuff found in this area, and it looked like the ground there was undisturbed by modern activities. He said he wasn't interested in digging up any old sites, but Big Bob was real worried someone might find out about it."

"I heard about another big dig south of here," Vinnie jumped in, "down in the Yuba River area around North San Juan. A rich site, but on land that had been used for cattle feeding for years. Livestock wallowing around in the mud years ago had jumbled all the artifacts around and they couldn't get any meaningful layers and dates. But it was almost all Martis stuff, with a little bit of Southern Maidu stuff mixed in."

"What kind of stuff are they teaching you at the University?, Vinnie?" Leonard interjected.

"Mostly cultural anthro, but I'm taking a physical –"

"No, I mean what kind of stuff are they teaching you there? You talk about Maidu and Martis and all those names, but they're just white-man's names that don't mean anything," old Leonard lectured. "Vinnie, you know we are *Tai* here, but I'll bet your books don't even have that word in them. They call us all Maidu or Concow. Your people from up the river are *Notu'koyo*, but your books call you Mountain Maidu or Northern Maidu or what-not. And the tribes south of here, that the books call Southern Maidu or Nisenan, they call themselves *Tanku*. That's what we call 'em, too. But the white man calls us all Maidu today. We all got stuck together under the same name. You know why. they call us all Maidu don't you?" Leonard asked.

Chris eagerly answered, to show he too knew a thing or two about anthropology.

"Well, like with most tribes, the name the whites give them usually means 'people' in their language."

"Yeah, more like 'person'," Leonard continued. "Some white men come upon some of our people once a long time ago, and asked 'who are you?' And someone said 'I'm a person, *maidum*'. And so all the people with a similar language were called Maidu."

"It's just like with our Paiute friends over in Nevada," Marv pitched in. "A long time ago, Fremont I think it was, came upon some people north of Pyramid Lake, and started talking to them, or trying to. The Indians didn't understand a word. They wondered what this white man was trying to say, and they talked among themselves. 'What could they want?' The only thing strangers would want to know in this desert was 'where is the water?' So they pointed and answered *paiute* – the water is over there.

"'Oh, some kind of Ute,' the whites thought, so the Pyramid-Lake Indians came to be known to the whites as the Paiutes – the 'water-is-over-there' people."

"We are *Tai*, here," Leonard said. "That's what we've always called ourselves, and that's what the neighboring tribes called us. But that's okay." Leonard looked at Chris with a big grin. "We call you white men *wo'le*. No matter if you're English or German or Portuguese, you're all wo'le to us."

"Maybe more like woolly," Marv jested, rubbing his face to mimic the beard on Chris's face.

"Right, the woolly white men, like the wooly mammoth. But you're just jealous 'cause you can't grow this much wool on your face," Chris jested back, rubbing his beard.

"But what do you call the ancient people, the old Martis people or whatever?" Chris asked anyone who could answer.

"Spirits," Leonard said. "We call them spirits, *kukini*, when we find their old stuff, their stone bowls and what-not. It's dangerous to even touch that old stuff."

Leonard sipped his coffee as he thought, then his voice changed a little as it always did when he began another story.

"Years ago," he continued, "a bunch of Tai went to a big-time in the Tanku's country. These Tai people played the handgame there, and filled their bellies for several days. After these Tai left, the Tanku began to get sick. They called for a doctor. The doctor heard something moaning. He traced the sound to a rise overlooking the camp. Hidden on the rise he found one of those old pounding bowls lying on its side with its hole pointed right toward their camp. Feathers dangled from the top of the hole. When it moaned, it squeezed closed a little and blood trickled out of its mouth."

Leonard shook his head. "Wasn't it terrible, to fill your belly at someone's place, and then try to poison them? Some of the old-timers were mean! No wonder the Tanku hated us. But we're not that way anymore."

Leonard took another sip of coffee then continued. "Big Bob was adamant that they re-bury the ancient stuff where they found it. He said it was bad luck, bad medicine. If some kid got hold of it, it could cause some serious sicknesses. He was right. We don't want more of our ancestors' stuff ending up in base-ment storage shelves of some museum!"

Leonard stood up to pour a little more coffee into his cup. "White people say others lived here before us," he continued, "because they never had a bow and arrow, and therefore must be different people. But how do they know? Our stories tell us we are the original people here, from This-Place. So these so-called Martis people must be our ancestors, the same people as us, Tai people. Anyway, it's better not to dig around old camp-sites. Let the dead stay dead," old Leonard said solemnly.

"Ye wenai," a couple of voices asserted, like an 'Amen'.

"Well, we need to do more digging around to find out whatever happened to Tom," Chris said. "But I don't think that involves digging up the grounds. We need to spread our efforts around, fan out in different directions, to find out what hap-pened."

"Well, I'll poke around," Leonard volunteered, "I'll talk with the kids too, to see if they know something. The young people see or hear about things that we old folks never know.

"And Vinnie–" Leonard turned toward Vinnie who was sitting on the arm of one of the old couches.

"What do you want me to do?"

Leonard continued. "One of those punks has a brother who's a dancer with that outfit up in Greenville. That's a natural for you."

"Yeah, we dance up at Indian Valley in a couple weeks," Vinnie replied. "The Greenville dancers will be there for sure. The Big Head dancers should be coming down, and I think there'll even be the Miwok dance group. It'll be awesome. You should all come up. There'll probably be some pick-up handgames too."

"Vinnie, you hang around some of those guys, see if any of them had it in for the professor," Leonard suggested. "And talk to that dancer, see if you can get to know him and anything about his brother, the one who was with the group hassling Tom. Find out all you can about them. And see if they performed any kind of dance up on Pitch-off Mountain last weekend. Dances that might have been kept secret. Ask around who knows what, without trying to be too nosy. Somebody knows something. I'd like to learn more about that dance ground."

"And I'll call the sheriff's office, report the professor missing, maybe they can mount a search," volunteered Chris, trying to keep things on track.

"Yeah right, good luck," pitched in Marv. "You can fill out a form, but the cops won't help you. They never help us out here, and they'll never help you! But, you probably should make some kind of notification... other people gotta be notified too. Your family. Do what you have to do, and so will we."

Marv continued after a moment. "Tom was kind of a big man, and he was a white man, not just another drunk Injun like Marty, so maybe the cops will take more interest."

"Marty? What about Marty?"

"Oh, he disappeared last year, seems like. Nobody knows what happened to him. Nobody cares, really. We saw him last fall at the Feather Falls big-time, but nobody's seen him since. He was drinking up there pretty heavily, already pretty drunk when he got there. You know they don't like drinking in their roundhouse there. They told him he couldn't come into the roundhouse with his beer. He got pretty mean, saying he was gonna kick everybody's butt. But he's all bark, you know. He's been pretty much on a constant drunk since Julie left him. I hear his boss finally fired him for not showing up for work, figuring he was just off on another drunk. Nobody's seen him around since, and nobody's really going lookin' for him either. His boss finally filed a missing persons on him when he learned that nobody had seen him for a month. He had more enemies than friends, if he even had any friends left. We figured he must've driven off the road somewhere. The bottle killed him, however it happened."

Vinnie piped up: "You know, maybe the bottle didn't kill him. Maybe we have a *hudessi* here."

Nobody said a thing. Hudessi? "What do you mean hudessi?" Chris asked. "I thought a hudessi was the warrior guy who moved so fast he dodged all the arrows shot at him."

"That too, but you know – hudessi," Vinnie said, "a man-killer. They used to live around here. They wouldn't just kill one person, they were serial killers. They'd kill to get power – the more people they killed the more power they got, and the faster they became. When the mood came to them they'd kill again and again. They were like the psychopathic killers of the old culture. And we know there's a killer around here – remember that body they found last summer down by Bean Creek? All torn apart?"

"Yeah," Marv said, "they said a bear probably killed him and ate part of him. I don't think they ever did figure out who it was."

"That's what they thought at first, but they figured out he was stabbed with a sharp wooden stick before he was mauled.

And now we have two more people gone," Vinnie argued, "Tom and Marty, and who knows who else over the past years. If nobody's looking for Marty, how many others have there been that nobody's looking for?"

Vinnie continued. "Some hudessi dressed up in a grizzly bear hide to go kill their prey. Maybe somebody who had offended him somehow, or maybe a stranger. He'd wait for him to go out in the woods, then stalk him and kill him. Grizzly-men, they called those hudessi. They'd hide behind the hide to conceal their identity. They'd maul their victim to make it look like a real bear kill.

"Nobody knew who the hudessi was, because if he knew you knew, he'd kill you too. But usually people would figure it out. Then they would get together and figure some way to get rid of him. That was the old way."

There was a long silence. Leonard looked intently at Vinnie. The fact that he brought up the hudessi indicated Vinnie was sure nobody present was this man-killer.

Vinnie continued. "I saw a huge bear here the other night. Or at least I thought I did then. I told my friends at the time I thought I saw a grizzly, but they all laughed, saying the grizzly was extinct here for ages. But it was the biggest bear I ever saw, and it had a big hump. But just now I realized, maybe I saw a hudessi."

"Well, I don't know," Leonard sighed, "we called 'em *maidum pano*, grizzly-persons. They used to live around here. People hunters. They wouldn't always use a grizzly hide. Some of 'em would just roll their victim off Pitch-off Mountain, after they'd killed 'em, to make it look like someone had slipped and fallen off the dome.

"Some of the old grizzly-bear hunters used to turn into maidum pano," Leonard continued, "if they wore that hide too much. They'd wear a grizzly hide when they went out to hunt the grizzly. But you wear that hide too much, you turn into a grizzly. That's the only way people can turn into a grizzly."

Leonard paused. "There might be a maidum pano around. There have been some funny things going on around here. But this is Indian country," he said, getting out of his chair, ending the discussion. "How about another cup of coffee?"

"That sounds good to me," Chris replied. "I've gotta hit the road pretty soon anyway, and get on with life in the other world."

"Well, why don't you plan to come up for the Indian Valley big-time? We can meet together again up there in a couple weeks, weekend after next. You'll probably need to get away from the city by then anyway," Marv grinned.

"Besides, I hear there's a bunch of Injun's that'd like to win some money back from you guys. They might have a chance if old Professor Coyote's not driving your team anymore," Leonard added.

"Oh I don't know about that. I've picked up a little luck of my own over the years. But I need to have some Injuns to play on my side, to help me remember some songs and hang on to my money. Know any volunteers?" Chris jousted back.

"Oh I suppose we could find a few to salt your team with, before we pick your pockets," Marv teased.

The good natured jostling continued a while, then Chris started to pack up the truck for the trip back home.

Leonard said. "Come back up here anytime."

Marvin added "And bring up some handgame players with you. We'll play handgame anytime. We need some of that city money up here. You know some of the same songs we do – even if you do sing 'em faster!"

"See you in a few weeks at Indian Valley," Vinnie hailed.

15

Coyote's trip to the world above

A long time ago, a big bird from the world above this world would sometimes come down to this country to hunt. He'd swoop down and carry off people through a hole in the sky, back to his home in the world above. He would catch all kinds of people, but usually he carried off human children – they were the easiest to catch. He killed off most of the humans in this world that way.

One day he carried off two more human children, two young girls. This was back when all the animals were people, and they all spoke the same language.

Coyote decided to put together a rescue mission, to go save those girls. He appointed himself the leader of the group, as usual, and they headed off with the girls' parents to find the world above this one.

They couldn't fly there like the Big Bird did, through the hole in the sky, but Coyote knew of another way to get there. Old Man Mole had a roundhouse at the eastern end of the world. Mole could use his big hands to push up the edge of the sky, to let people slip into the world above.

Coyote and his friends traveled eastward toward Mole's place. No telling how long it took them to get there, clear to the edge of this world. But that was the only way Coyote knew to get to the world above.

When they finally got to the roundhouse at the east end of this world, Mole agreed to shove up the edge of the sky so the group could jump through.

But Mole knew Coyote, he knew Coyote would pull something foolish. Mole held him back until last. When it was his turn to jump through, Coyote waited and waited until just the last moment before the sky came crashing back down. But he waited too long. The sky smashed him in two, leaving the head-half on one side and the tail-half on the other. Coyote got killed that time.

The rest of Coyote's party waited for him on the other side of the sky. 'What's wrong, what happened to Coyote?' they wondered. Pretty soon Mole pushed up the sky again and tossed through the other half of Coyote. One fellow picked up one half and another fellow picked up the other half and they dragged the parts up to a big spring on the other side, and tossed them in.

They made camp nearby, and next morning here comes Coyote, a new man again. 'What happened? Where have I been? I must have been dreaming again.'

16

A stop in Ophir City

Chris decided to stop by Ophir City on the way back. He pulled into a gas station to get directions, but it took a phone book and the local map on the window of the station to get proper directions to the Butte County sheriff's office.

A blast of cold air greeted him as he walked into the office.

"I need to report a missing person," Chris announced to the heavyset woman behind the counter.

"A deputy will have to help you. Why don't you take a seat?"

At that moment a boyish-looking man in a uniform walked through the door and headed for the coffee maker behind the counter.

"Oh Mickey, this man needs to fill out a missing persons," the heavy woman addressed the man.

"Okay, no problem." The young man filled his coffee cup and picked up a notebook and a few papers. "Step back here, let me ask you a few questions." The young man held out his hand. "Mickey Whittaker."

Chris reached out to shake his hand. "Chris Livingstone."

The young deputy sat down at a clear desk and leaned back in his chair. "So Mr. Livingstone, what can I do for you?"

"I need to report my brother missing. He disappeared up at Pitch-off Mountain last weekend." Chris sat down on a hard wood chair next to the desk.

"What was he doing up at Pitch-off Mountain?"

"He was up at an Indian handgame. The people up there put on a big-time a couple times a year."

"Uh huh." Mickey jotted some notes on a pad. "What's a handgame?"

"Oh, it's an old Indian gambling game." Chris regretted the words as soon as they came out. "But it's not so much a gambling game, it's really a game of power," he tried to correct, but the retraction just seemed to get him in deeper.

"So your brother was up there gambling? With the Indians?"

"Yeah. He's an anthropologist."

"Were you gambling up there too?" The gambling issue seemed to be taking a direction Chris didn't like. He was glad to redirect it.

"No, I was down in the city. In the Bay Area." Chris avoided saying 'Berkeley'. He had learned through the years that people form an immediate impression if you tell them you're from Berkeley. It was like telling a person in Montana that you were from California.

"I got a call Monday that my brother was missing. Actually, the handgame isn't so much about gambling as we white people know it. It's more like a game of dowsing, like learning to see things that aren't obvious to the eyes."

"Uh huh, right. When did your brother go up to Pitch-off Mountain?"

"Last Saturday. He rode up with one of his friends from Chico."

"And you say you got a call Monday?"

"Right."

"And this is Wednesday. Why did you wait to report him missing?"

"Well, I drove up from the Bay Area Monday night. I talked with some of the people who were there, and looked around myself. A few of us even hiked down into the canyon yesterday, to see if we could find anything."

"And I gather you didn't?"

"No, the river was really high. We didn't find anything."

"Well, I don't expect you would. Anything that comes down that canyon most likely ends up in the lake. We get two or three cases a year of fishermen who disappear up there. Fish and Game usually finds pieces of them in the upper lake region, following year. If anything happened to your brother up there it'll probably be next year 'til his remains show up, if they ever do. You've been down there, you say. You know what that country's like then."

"It's a wild river all right."

"Yeah, wild, and it's a difficult country to patrol. Full of washed-out back roads and some people who have no respect for authority. We tried to shut down some after-hours drinking outside a place near Berry Creek last month. It turned into an instant riot. They virtually destroyed our new patrol vehicle, smashed all the windows out, and more. Officers won't go up there without backup now, and we don't have that many officers to spread around. The county's nearly broke as it is. That Suburban's still not back in service yet. We'll probably have to wait 'til next fiscal year to get it fixed. Anyway, I need you to fill out this form. I'll file it with my report here. We'll notify Fish and Game over at the lake, to be on the lookout for another floater, or his bones."

A floater: that's what they would be looking for. Chris filled out the missing persons report, but he now realized what

Marv was talking about. There would be no search party, they weren't interested in trying to find a lost living person. They would just file this form in some data base, and whenever some body parts were found they would try to match the body part with the information in the data base. Then the case would be closed, another successful conclusion. A fishing accident, they would probably call it.

Chris completed the form as best he could, and talked a little more with Deputy Whittaker. Then he left the frigid sheriff's office and walked into the stifling heat of a summer's afternoon in Ophir City. But it wasn't summer, it was still only May. This was shaping up to be a blistering summer in the Sierra foothills.

He felt his stop had been a waste of time. 'Marv was right. These people won't be much help.'

Getting back into his truck was like entering a solar oven. With all the windows down he began the long drive back. "Let your people know," Marvin had told him. But let them know what? He still didn't know what, if anything, had happened to his brother.

The hot air blasted through the open windows as he got onto the fast two-lane highway and headed south down the Sacramento Valley. Orchards of olives flashed by, then peaches and walnuts, more olives, then an orange grove. Food was abundant everywhere.

Past Marysville, he knew he should stop in Sacramento to tell his aging mother something. He didn't know what he'd say. She was an old woman, living alone, still physically healthy, more-or-less alert but perhaps bored or tired of a long life. Her children had long since left the roost, hardly ever wrote or called, and except for major holidays, rarely visited. She spent her time between tending her flower gardens, waiting for the mail, re-reading old books, and writing to her family and friends, hoping to obligate them to write her in return so something would come to her mailbox.

He continued on the highway toward Sacramento rather than taking the cutoff that would have brought him back to the Bay area. He drove past more huge orchards – peaches, nectarines, plums, walnuts, almonds. Then came the miles of rice fields, then tomatoes, onions, potatoes, corn, beans, more rice, more tomatoes – tomatoes bio-engineered to be so tough they could be picked by an automated harvester with no danger of bruising or bleeding. Tens, hundreds of thousands of acres of produce flashed by his windows as he blasted down the valley highway.

In the old days this land was the marshy flood plain of the Sacramento and all the northern Sierran rivers, home of wild native grasses taller than a man could reach. Indian foods and medicines, some never known to modern botany, were once abundant.

This valley was also once home to the ferocious grizzly bear, *pano*, now officially extinct in California – the last one sighted was back in the 1920's, and he got shot dead for letting himself be seen! Now and again some woodsman will tell you he saw one a few years back up at such-and-such a place. Just like Vinnie said he saw a grizzly at the big-time.

The grizzly was the main beast the Old People had to worry about – at least before the white man came. Sometimes weighing over a ton, a grizzly could tear apart a large man with the ease of a modern man tearing a shirt.

But it was not just grizzly – the animal – that was a danger to the Old People. There was also the grizzly-man, maidum pano. Chris had heard of these psychopaths before Vinnie mentioned them. Pancho had talked about these man-killers, who were still common in the Sacramento Valley and Sierra foothills when he was a boy. He said they were more feared than respected in his community – a bad kind of man who would sometimes put on the skin of a grizzly and go out at night to hunt his enemies. The grizzly-man was somebody nobody wanted to cross. Chris wondered if any grizzly-men might really still be operating in inaccessible areas of the Sierras, out of reach from the law.

Chris remembered what Vinnie had said about the grizzly man. He would stalk and kill his victims, then maul them with his grizzly claws to make it look like a real bear attack. Or he would drive them over a cliff, alive or dead....

The traffic became intense on the road Chris drove now. The only grizzlies here were in the hearts of the truckers as they roared their huge rigs down the two lane state highway – fearless, the biggest beasts of all, capable of mangling anything that got in their way.

Chris pulled off onto a county road when he could, and followed the grid line eastward at a quieter pace, cutting over to the old river road that followed the levees down the valley. It was cooler by the river, the groves of trees along the water seemed to clean and cool the air, even though they provided Chris little shade as he drove southward along the bank of the Sacramento River.

Here the river was wide – flat, swift, smooth, the water of many rivers: of the Feather, the Yuba, the Bear, the Pit, the McCloud, all the drainage of the northern Sierra and the southern Shasta and Lassen regions. Were it not for the dam at Ophir City, some of this water may have been in Pitch-off Mountain Canyon yesterday.

He drove down the levee road along the river into old West Sacramento, past gas stations and taco houses, then up and over the old bridge across the river into the downtown of Sacramento proper. His mother lived alone east of the capitol area, in an old middle class residential area of brick houses and tree-lined streets. She was out in her front rose garden when Chris drove up.

"Oh Tom, I'm so glad you stopped by. You boys never come to see me anymore."

"I'm Chris, mom."

"Oh I know you're Chris, I don't know why I do that. I must be getting old."

"That's not it, you've always done that," Chris laughed.

"Come on in and I'll fix up some dinner. I have a steak I've been saving for you boys in the freezer. I'll thaw it out in the microwave and we'll fry it up."

This was a family ritual. Their mother always wanted to feed her boys, especially with steak, whenever they visited – and they didn't visit her often enough. They had their own lives now, they had for years, she realized that.

She relished the times they'd all get together for the big holidays – Thanksgiving and Christmas – but beyond that they didn't see one another much, even though they lived only ninety miles apart. She wrote letters regularly, and her sons would call her back occasionally.

Until recently she had lived with her two older sisters, but one had died last year and the other had a stroke shortly afterwards and had to move to a care facility. Now she was alone, the youngest of her generation at eighty-seven years, but still able-bodied and strong willed. Chris knew she couldn't live alone for long, but neither Chris nor his brother the Professor could live with her either.

She was a gardener, and loved to spend time in her rose beds. Chris knew the time would come someday when his mother's health faded too, but she was still pretty alert and healthy, even if she did hold some odd opinions.

But Chris's mind was on his brother now. Their mother had always said it was unnatural for a child to die before its parent. Now Chris was wondering how to bring up the matter.

"Come on in and sit on the couch, Tom, make yourself comfortable. I'll just get this steak out to thaw."

"Chris."

"Oh, there I go again. See, I am getting old."

He didn't know how he was going to break the news. He didn't want to upset her, especially since he really didn't know anything for sure. He decided to just say it.

"I was just up in Ophir City. I heard that Tom was missing after an Indian big-time, so I went up there, looking for him."

She was in the kitchen now and didn't respond. He decided to be more blunt.

"I think something might have happened to him up there, mother."

"Oh he'll be all right. He's been going to those things for years. Chris will be all right."

"Tom."

"I know that, Tom."

"Chris."

"I know that. You're Chris. He's Tom. I'm not that bad. I just say the wrong word sometimes. But Tom will be all right. I'm sure he's all right. Why would anyone want to hurt Tom?"

"Well, for one, because he's a white man. There's some Indians that don't like white people messing around in their world. For two, some people think he stole some of their songs."

"That's silly. He's an anthropologist, he's spent his life helping those people from what I gather. Why would they want to hurt him?"

"Because he's white, mother. Because he's not an Indian. Because he was trying to find out about the Power the old people talked about. Because he was especially interested in the plants they used, little known herbs and roots. Some people think he's messing around in Indian power. Especially some of the younger Indians. If he had any Indian blood in him it'd be different. Then they'd see him as one of their own. Maybe even a shaman. It gets pretty racist sometimes.

"Still, almost all the people I've met up there are real friendly," Chris continued, "real nice people, full of humor and personal honesty. I can't see any of them wanting to hurt Tom, except maybe a few punks. The people really like Tom. But they have good reason to hate the white man generically."

"But not to hurt Chris. He never hurt them."

"Tom."

"Chris, Tom, it's just a name, you know what I mean. He never hurt them. Besides, he does have Indian blood in him. You both do. I suspect most people do by now."

"What do you mean by that?"

"Your father's grandfather was a Pawnee Indian from Kansas."

She went to a closet and came back with a box of photographs.

"Harold never wanted you boys to know. His grandfather was adopted by George Livingstone, a wealthy Englishman living in Kansas, when he was five years old, after his family had been killed by some settlers for rustling their livestock."

She brought out an old sepia-tone photograph of a group of people of all ages, dressed in their best clothes, posing stiffly for the camera. She pointed to a middle-aged man with high cheekbones and long black hair, wearing a dark double-breasted suit.

"This is him here. White Cloud. And this is your grandfather Clinton here," she said, pointing to a young well-dressed dark-haired man in the old photo. He also looked a lot like an Indian.

"Your father was ashamed of it, he wanted his ancestors to be from England or Scotland or Germany like the other white people. He was ashamed of the Indian part, and never mentioned it because he didn't want anyone to think he was an Indian."

"But why didn't you say anything about this before, after dad died?"

"It just never came up. But I probably should have, especially since you boys seemed to be so interested in the Indians and all that. I just never thought much about it, until now."

Chris thought a long moment about this development.

"Well, it's not what you are but what you think you are," he said at last. "Or maybe what *they* think you are. The Indians knew Tom as a white man, even though he knew more of Maidu culture than a lot of them. But it's crazy, it's all mixed up, people are all mixed up now. Nobody's pure-blood any-more. Some Indians are half-white and a quarter Chinese and still all Indian. They're Indian because they identify with that Indian part of their culture, with its values. But still, they most-ly live like white people – many follow white man's religions and go to white man's churches, live in square rooms with arti-ficial light, watch the latest soaps and sitcoms on TV. We don't call them the wannabe-white people. But if we so-called white people – half Chinese and quarter Portuguese or smidgeon Injun' that we might be – if we start following the old people's teachings about caring for the earth and living simply, we're scorned as wannabes, the Want-to-be Indian tribe. Or worse."

'It's silly."

"I think it doesn't matter, in the long run. I think the land shapes the genes of all the people that live on it." Chris scratched his rashes. The poison oak was starting to spread all over his body.

"You mean like a dog and his master grow to look like each other?" she said.

"Yeah, right, kinda like that. Especially if you're both eat-ing the same food." Chris laughed. "We'll all be looking like cows pretty soon."

Then he continued. "Anyway, I'm really worried about Tom, mom. He went up there Saturday and didn't come back. He left his bag up there."

"I know you're worried, honey, but don't be. I'm sure Chris will turn up. Lord knows, I had to quit worrying about you boys long ago – if a mother ever really quits worrying about her kids. But he'll show up. He's disappeared before, you know, and he'll come back again. You can't spend all your time worrying yourself."

Chris figured maybe she was reassuring him to reassure herself. "Maybe you're right mother, I hope so."

He didn't really believe so, but she wasn't going to believe otherwise now, and Chris felt it best, or easiest, to let her con-tinue her illusion. 'Children shouldn't die before their parents, its unnatural' she had said when Tom had disappeared before. Let her not worry now, again, what good could it do anyway?

"I'm sure he'll be okay. Come on, let me microwave some frozen green beans for you, and fry up that steak."

The freeway miles seemed shorter on the way back to the Bay Area from Sacramento. The highway glittered like a river of lights, red and white, streaming both ways across the countryside, full speed ahead, millions of joules of energy flowing along man-made channels, day and night. Within seemingly no time Chris was across the long causeway above the Yolo bypass – the flood channel of the Sacramento River – past Davis, past Dixon, past Vacaville and Fairfield, and climbing the last range of hills that separated the Sacramento Valley from San Francisco Bay.

He thought of many things as the miles rolled by. He thought about his father, and about the times and culture that would make him ashamed to have an Indian in his lineage. He thought about his mother, and why she had never told them any of this, even after their father had died. Did she still harbor some of the same sentiments of his father's generation? He thought of the tragic paradox that Tom may have been killed because he was seen as a white man seeking answers in an Indian world.

He passed the last rest stop on the long interstate, and crested the final hill that separated the central valley from the bay.

Below him spread the lights of Vallejo, and beyond, the whole San Francisco Bay area – one megacity, hundreds of cultures and local jurisdictions, large and small. Surrounded by that glistening was the vast void of lights, the bay itself. This sight never failed to thrill Chris, no matter how many times he had seen it. The gravity of the city was sucking him back now, sucking him into the swirling pools of stress and energy and creativity that made up daily life here.

Traffic became dense, but every car moved at least ten or twenty above the posted speed limit, bumper-to-bumper at seventy or eighty miles an hour, no room for driver error. Where was everybody coming from? Where were they going? Was it all really necessary?

Chris could sense his level of tension rising. Stress. One slip up here could ruin your whole day, or worse.

He was glad to pull off the frantic freeway at the Albany race track and follow the frontage road toward the marina, where he lived alone on his small sailboat.

This was better. Now, he was by the water, the pace was slower, the night was clear, and the city of San Francisco sparkled on the far side of the bay like a magic crystal palace. He was home. It felt like he had been gone for ages.

17

Back to work

Chris dragged himself up with the first light, and stopped by the French Hotel Cafe for his morning dose of strong coffee. He was in his office before the owl shift in the adjoining shop had left.

The red light on his phone blinked persistently. New voicemail. How many calls would it be – twenty? Thirty? Each one would be someone's special problem, a minute or two to listen to, save or delete, then more minutes or hours to deal with.

Chris worked at fixing other people's problems – computer problems. He knew computer problems were often people-problems as well.

He logged into his desktop computer, and found thirty-two E-mails awaiting his attention. He started listening to the voicemail ('Mailbox full. You have 27 new and 3 saved messages') as his eyes simultaneously scanned and filtered the e-mail.

Most calls were from people wanting special favors, expedited processing, people calling to say their system's broken, then calling back later saying never mind, sorry, its not broken. He wrote things down only to scratch them out when he processed later calls.

He took notes in a simple spiral notepad, jotting down and prioritizing electronic messages as he parallel-processed them in his mind. He was getting back into his groove – he'd been doing this work for nearly twenty years.

He was immersed in a pool of other people's problems when he got Robin Marquez's voice message. This jolted him back to his own problem. He jotted down the telephone number she'd left. He would call her back when he had processed all the backlog of messages.

It was late morning when he finally got to call back Robin's number. It was her office phone on campus, and he caught her just as she was about to leave.

"Robin? This is Chris Livingstone calling you back."

"Chris, I'm glad you finally called. I've been trying for days to get hold of Professor Coyote. Do you have any idea where he is?"

"I wish! He went up to a big-time at Pitch-off Mountain over the weekend and just disappeared between a couple handgames. He didn't come back. I just got back from there, trying to figure out what happened."

"I was afraid something might have happened to him when he didn't show up," Robin said, "but then I thought maybe he just wanted to get out of Berkeley or something. I'd invited him over to my place Monday night, for dinner and to talk about my thesis. What happened?"

"I don't really know, I wasn't there when it happened. I got a call Monday, and took a couple days' leave to check out things up there. I talked with people who were there, and we looked all over. But there was no sign of him, except all the gear he left in his friend's truck. I can't help but think somebody might have finally got him."

"What do you mean someone finally got him? Why would anyone want to hurt Professor Livingstone?"

Chris paused before answering. "I don't know. He's been threatened more than a few times over the years. There's a few people up there that have a lot of anger in them. They resent him, especially because he's white – or they think he's white."

Chris's group's secretary popped her head through the open doorway as she walked by. "Don't forget the meeting in the conference room in ten minutes, Chris."

Robin's voice continued on the phone. "Maybe Professor Coyote wanted to get lost," she mused. "If someone was after me I'd probably want to disappear too, unless I wanted to be got."

A technician stood patiently waiting next to Chris's open office door, holding a small disk drive in his hand. Chris held up his finger to the technician, to say 'just one minute'.

"Maybe. Look, there're a lot of things going on here right now. Maybe we could talk about all this later."

"I've got to talk to you about some things," Robin persisted. "Do you have time to get together for lunch?"

Chris groaned. He wished he could take off for lunch to meet this woman, but he didn't have time, there was too much to do.

"I really don't today. I'm swamped here until at least four, and who knows what'll be happening by then. But how about after work. I'm going to try to get out of here by five-thirty."

"Why don't we meet at six, then, down at the Berkeley Espresso Cafe?"

"Okay, why don't we make it more toward five-thirty?" It was a beautiful spring day. Chris quietly hoped to get out of the office early enough to spend the evening sailing his boat on the bay. Maybe this woman Robin would like to come with him.

"Great," said Robin. "I'll see you at five-thirty at the cafe. By the way – what do you look like?"

How could he describe himself? "Pretty much like my brother, I guess, just younger and better looking," he joked. "And I'm wearing dirty gray jeans with a blue sweatshirt."

"I'll recognize you," she laughed. "And I'm dark-haired and brown-eyed, about five-five."

"All right. We'll talk then." Chris hung up the phone. He had a date at five-thirty.

The technician stepped into the office.

"Sorry to keep you waiting, John, what's the next problem?"

18

Chris meets Robin

It was nearly five-thirty when Chris finally made it out of the office. He would have been stuck there longer if he hadn't headed toward the restroom and slipped out the back door. Some people always seemed to have problems at five or six o'clock in the evening, and they always walked in expecting Chris to fix them immediately or sooner, or at least to hold their hand in reassurance that something was being done. Tonight the swing-shift could handle whatever came up. Chris had been here long enough, he had to get away.

· He got to the cafe at five-thirty-five. A cute short-haired brunette with high cheek bones, a pert nose and slender hips came up to him when he walked through the open door.

"You're right, you do look like your brother," she said greeting him with a smile. "But I don't know if you're better looking. The professor looks a little more distinguished."

Chris had long ago learned to distinguish himself from his scholarly older brother by being deliberately more sloppy in his appearance. Jeans splattered with boat paint and epoxy were his customary working attire.

"You just mean he just has more gray hair," Chris joked. It had been a while since Chris had met a new woman, and he liked this one immediately. He wanted to make a good impression.

"Find us a table, and I'll order. What's your preference?" he asked.

"I'm already working on a caffe latte over by the window here. Why don't you order what you want and join me there?"

Chris walked up to the counter and ordered a double cappucino. It took a few minutes to prepare, and he stood looking around the cafe and the people in it.

This was one of the many newer coffee shops in Berkeley, and he had never been here before. The place was light and pleasant, and seemed to be doing a healthy business. The simple decor was spiced by the colorful and diverse people who populated the place.

A woman in an electric wheelchair motored through the open doorway and drove up behind Chris. She was a big woman, almost too big for the wheelchair.

"Good thing you had that door open now, Carlos. I hate to have to bang on it to get in here," she hailed the espresso-man behind the counter.

"We keep it open just for you, Marcia. From early in the morning 'til late at night, just for you," the espresso-man hailed back.

"You're such a sweetie, Carlos." The disabled woman looked up at Chris. "He really is my boyfriend, you know. Aren't you Carlos? You're my boyfriend."

"Como no, Marcia. What'll it be today? The regular?"

"No, I think I'll have an iced double espresso. What do you think?"

"Whatever you want, Marcia, you just name it. One iced doppio coming up. You're hitting the hard stuff today."

"Well, all my other medicines don't seem to be working, I think maybe that's what I need to kick-start me. What do you think?"

"That'll do it!"

A group a Japanese girls congregated in front of the pastry display speaking excitedly in their own language, while two more older women spoke quietly in German at a nearby table. And by the windows, behind Robin's table, a well-dressed, elderly black gentleman-scholar sat immersed in a thick book and a tall latte. Classical music played almost unnoticed in the background. Chris liked the feel of this place, with all kinds of diverse people coming together peacefully in one place,

He paid for his coffee, and was pleasantly surprised to find it was twenty five cents cheaper here than he usually paid at the French Hotel. He put the extra quarter in the tip jar, sprinkled chocolate liberally on the foamy milk head and joined Robin at her table.

"Why would Professor Coyote go up there if he knew people were after him?" Robin asked as he sat down.

"I don't think people were really after him," Chris replied. "We have a lot of friends up there. There might be somebody that resented him, but that happens everywhere. Look at the University. There's a lot of political back-stabbing going on there."

"Right, but he got out of the University when he felt it was getting bad," Robin persisted. "What was he looking for on Pitch-off Mountain?"

"He went there for the handgames."

"Just for the handgames?" Robin asked. "He went up there to gamble?"

"You sound like the cop I spoke with in Ophir City." Chris didn't mean to speak the thought, but it came out.

"It's not gambling in the sense people gamble in casinos," Chris continued. "It's a performance. It's a religion. It's a way of seeking power. He plays for the power, not for the money. If he's lucky he might win twenty dollars after playing all night. That doesn't even pay for the gas to get there. He doesn't want to win their money, he wants to play the game. The Maidu aren't a rich tribe."

"Seeking power through gambling?" Robin still sounded a little sarcastic.

"No, more like training your senses by letting yourself see with your intuition, through singing, and through team work," Chris responded. "It's great. Have you ever played the game in the course of your scholarly research into the Indians?" Chris didn't mean to sound sarcastic. Somehow he was not getting off to a particularly good start with this woman.

"Actually, I'm more into the Martis culture, and they're not around to play handgame any more," Robin explained. "The Maidu are ancillary to my main studies, in so far as their languages seem to have diverged from a common central tongue about four-thousand years ago. But to answer your question, yes, I have played handgame once or twice, and I've seen it played a lot. I don't know the songs very well, and I don't know all the rules, but I can usually sing along when I hear them. But I can't remember any of them right now, not even the simple ones."

"Yeah, some of the songs are like that," Chris agreed, warming up again. "Sometimes I can't remember a catchy gambling song five minutes after I've heard it and sung it, but weeks or months later it will just pop into my brain out of nowhere. You've been to some big-times then?"

"Oh yeah, I've been to a couple Bear Dances at various places, and I've been to the big-times over at Chaw-Se State Park. And I was invited up to Grindstone once, for the Big Head Dance."

"You know the Sierra's pretty well, then?" Chris led her.

"I've been to a lot of places, more than most people I guess."

"You know Indian Valley? There's a big-time up near there the weekend after this. I'm going up there to meet with some friends, to see if anybody's heard any rumors about Tom or learned anything more. You're welcome to come if you want."

It had been more than a year since Chris had broken up with his last girl friend, and he needed to start relating to womankind again – what better way was there than to go camping at an Indian big-time?

"There'll be Indian dancers from all over northern California," Chris encouraged, "and probably handgames too, from what I'm told. Maybe we can get into a handgame, and you can see first-hand why people drive hundreds of miles just to camp outside in the dirt all weekend and play the game."

"Are there any lakes up there?" Robin asked.

It was a strange question. Did she like to swim?

"Oh, there's lots of lakes in the area," Chris replied. "Lake Almanor's not far away. It's a beautiful place, but it's a reservoir, not a natural lake. It flooded all of Big Meadows where a lot of the Old People used to live, and lots of special places were lost. But that was way before my time when it was built. There's lots of other lakes in the area. It's up in the mountains."

"Can anybody go there?" Robin asked.

"To the big-time, you mean, or to the lake?"

"To the big-time, of course. I know all about Lake Almanor," Robin said petulantly.

"Oh sure. Everybody's welcome there, even though they don't advertise it except by word of mouth. Many big-times are open to anybody now, although some few still have a no-whites rule. And some of them are family affairs, sort of by invitation only. But a lot of them are held on county fairgrounds or state or federal parklands, and everybody's welcome. There's one held every third weekend in June right in Yosemite Valley behind the visitor's center. Some places might have no-camera and no-recorder rules for certain ceremonies and dances, but anybody's usually welcome if they're respectful."

"Well, draw me a map to the place and maybe I'll drive up there, I'm not sure what I'm doing that weekend," Robin said.

"Do you know about the sacred lake up in the mountains that Professor Coyote used to talk about?" Robin asked abruptly.

"What lake's that?"

"The lake where the Maidu used to dive for power. The lake in the center of the world."

"Oh, right. Root-snag lake. Have you been up there?"

"No, I need to go there. Do you know where it is?" she asked again.

"No, I've never been there. I've just heard about it from Tom, but he would never tell me where it was. He said if I knew, I would probably tell my friends, and they would tell their friends and soon the place would be full of people from Berkeley. He's right," Chris laughed. "If I knew, I would be telling you right now."

"He never told me either," Robin added solemnly. "He told me to consider it a mythological place, but I know that was just to put me off."

Chris said nothing. If Professor Coyote wouldn't tell his own brother and handgame partner the location of this lake, he wouldn't tell one of his students either. Chris looked at Robin and briefly wondered how close his brother had gotten to this woman?

"What do you know about Indian medicine?" Robin probed again. "Did your brother ever talk much about it with you?"

"A bit, but not much," Chris said. "I know their doctors used to suck on their patients to extract weird looking things from them."

"*Pains*," Robin said.

"What?"

"Pains," Robin said again. "They sucked pains from them."

"But they'd actually hide something under their tongue, pretend to suck it out, and show it to the patient before going out to bury it," Chris added, "They knew they had the power, but they had to show their power to their patients – the placebo effect."

"I think it was more than a placebo effect. They believed disease was caused by this pain shot into your body by the power of a person who had it in for you," Robin explained. "If you were powerful enough yourself, you could find that pain and get it out of your body. Otherwise you'd have to find a doctor strong enough to suck it out, to gather it up with her mind, with her song, and spit out the pain without taking any of it into herself."

"Uh huh," Chris grunted

"Do you know of any of the old doctors still around?" Robin persisted in seeking the depth of Chris' knowledge.

"No, the last one I knew was an old Pomo woman who used to come to the Susanville bear dance, but she died a few years ago. They're a dying breed. There might be a few others left, but they're not out there advertising for business. This stuff gets to the heart of their beliefs. I think that's where Tom got into trouble."

"What do you mean by that?"

"I don't know. I think he was getting close to some of their lost secrets of power."

"Okay," Robin asked, "what do you think Indian power is, anyway?"

It took a while for Chris to answer that one.

"I think power is something like the harnessing of the spirits with the will, like the power that drives a sail boat."

"I think they mean something more than wind power when they talk about power in the sense of the shamans," Robin laughed.

"Yeah, but then again, it's *magic* that pulls a sailboat against the wind," Chris smiled back.

"I thought it was physics," Robin retorted.

"Whatever."

After another sip Robin said, "You told me there might be someone who wanted to get Tom. Was there another woman who might have gotten him?"

"No, it's not that," Chris laughed. 'Not this time,' he thought.

"After his first treatise on the Maidu was published," he explained, "Tom brought up a couple cases of his book to the Bear Dance to give to the older people. There were several respected Indian leaders there, some from different areas. He had photos of many of them in the book, along with some of the stories he had spliced together from fragments he'd learned from each of them. They were all really proud. They respected Tom, like he was an elder in their family. Although some of them could not or would not read, they were giving books to all their relatives, and selling more to help offset the cost of the big-time."

"So someone was jealous of him up there?"

"More than just that," he said. "To make a long story short, Tom ended up wearing the special bear hide in the Sunday Bear Dance that year."

"A white man wearing the bear hide. That caused some controversy, I bet," interjected Robin.

"Right. Nobody could tell who was wearing the hide, but word got out. Tom later said that wearing the bear hide was like becoming a dancing bear – his feet were light, like he had no weight, because he was so strong, like a bear. He said that as he looked at all the people through the eye-sockets of the bear hide, he could see like a bear too, and think like a bear – kinda mean. Though people could not see his face behind the hide, he made a bear-like face and showed his teeth."

· Chris took a sip of his coffee. "They say the bear hide works on you," he continued. "If you wear it too often your arms get hairy and your teeth get pointy," he laughed.

"That sounds a little weird. He only did that one time?" asked Robin.

"Yeah, right," Chris said. "There were several people that didn't think he should have worn the hide. He never danced with the hide again. Maybe he stepped on somebody's toes. But that's all right, by the next year a great young dancer was groomed, ready and eager to be the Bear."

Chris took a couple sips and contemplated this woman, Robin, trying not to be too conspicuous. She was older and more mature than your typical graduate student, yet still seemed much younger than himself, more interesting-looking than stunning, but perky and cute, radiating an inner beauty and strength.. He wondered how old she was. Thirty? Forty? It's not something you can easily ask a woman, especially if you're off by a decade.

Chris took another sip from the tall cappucino, studying Robin again, as she turned to look at some art hanging on the wall. "It sounds like you know a lot about these things," she said, turning back to catch Chris' eyes.

"No, not really, just a few things I've picked up over the years. I lived up in that area, years ago. And I know these people are animists. They believe that rocks have souls, and animals can talk, and people can become an animal."

"And you think Professor Coyote was done in by one or more of these animists?" Robin's wide eyes probed Chris'.

"I don't know. There've been some unsolved deaths and disappearances up there, over the last few years. And I've heard plenty of stories about how the old people used to hunt deer by driving them off the cliff, and about old-time killers up there that would push their enemies off a cliff, or poison them – any way to get them. Supposedly that all ended in the 1920's, but who knows?"

"Do you think something like that really happened to Professor Coyote?" Robin asked.

"I don't know," was all Chris could say. "I'm worried, but what can I do?"

"What was that about driving deer off a cliff?" Robin continued. "That sounds like a funny story."

"Well, that's it. That's how they say the Old People used to hunt, according to the stories. They also have some kind of dance that commemorates it, I think."

"That's a Maidu story? A Maidu dance?" Robin asked.

"Right, from the Tai people."

"Tai – that's a word Professor Coyote used to use," Robin said. "He's the only one I've ever heard use that term before. But that's a funny story. I mean, the Maidu or the Tai or whatever we call them had the bow and arrow, that's one of the things that distinguishes them from the older culture. Why would they drive deer off the cliff if they could just shoot them with the bow and arrow on top?"

"The story probably comes from long before they had the bow and arrow," Chris speculated.

"Then it's not a Maidu story," Robin countered. "The Maidu pretty much by definition had the bow and arrow."

"By whose definition? I mean, the story is in the Maidu oral tradition, so what is it?" Chris argued.

"Well, it's a mystery," Robin said. "I'd like to hear the whole story from the source someday. I mean, there's a long gap between the old culture and the coming of the Maidu, maybe five hundred years, and probably brought about by two long periods of drought which made the region uninhabitable. I'd be most interested to hear this old story, especially if anybody knows it in a Maiduan language."

"I'm not sure you'll be lucky enough for that," Chris said. "There're not many people left really fluent in the old languages, as you probably well know. But I can certainly get Leonard to tell it to you in English, and he might know some relative who knows more parts to the story."

"I'd be most interested in that, if you could," Robin said again. "You see, this sounds more like a Martis story than a Maidu story, what little we know about the Martis. But we have no evidence of the Martis after they disappeared, no indication that they had any linkage to those who later populated the area. This story seems like a linkage."

"So come up to the Indian Valley big-time," Chris prodded. "Leonard will be up there and I'm sure he'd be delighted to meet you."

"I'll do that, then."

"All right!" Chris cheered. "Weekend after this at Indian Valley. I can draw you a map or you can ride up with me."

"Draw me a map, I'm not sure when I'll be free."

"Do you know where the Feather River Canyon is?" Chris asked.

"Sure."

"Okay, I'll draw the map from there."

He drew a map on a paper napkin and gave it to Robin.

Chris's cup was now empty, as was Robin's tall glass.

"I was planning on taking my boat out for a sunset sail. Would you like to come along?" Chris ventured.

"Oh, so you're a sailor. I should have guessed from your description of power," she smiled.

"The spirits in the wind. It's fantastic," Chris exuberated. "Do you want to see?"

"I always get seasick on a boat," Robin backed off. "Besides, I have way too much to do tonight."

Chris was mildly disappointed, but didn't let it show.

"But here, let me give you my home phone number," Robin said. "In case you hear anything about the professor."

'All right', Chris cheered to himself. 'At least I got her home number.'

19

The Bingo King

It had been a rocky early morning on the boat. The wind started blowing sometime in the middle of the night. It howled through the marina, causing halyards to slap incessantly against their aluminum and wooden masts, like a percussion orchestra playing atonal music throughout the pre-dawn hours.

By the time he awoke Chris felt like he hadn't slept at all. He crawled from the V-berth and stepped into the shower for a wake-up rinse off, then dressed, closed off the boat and headed up the dock and out the gate. He had a lot to do today.

The water was high now, the ramp from the floating docks to the parking lot was nearly level, not the steep incline of a low tide. The water smelled like seaweed. He was off for another day of work.

This was another of those days he wished he didn't have a job. He had too much to think about, too many things to do, too many things on his mind, to deal with the things he had to do at work.

He'd have to contact people about Tom. But whom? Maybe he would contact the newspaper to put in some kind of article or notice. But what? What do you say about someone who disappeared and maybe died? Especially someone who disappears every ten years or so – the last time only to be heard from three months later when he emerged from southern Panama painted in blue stripes, and with some rare recordings and ethno-botanical specimens from the Darien area.

Maybe he should contact some people at the university, some of Tom's old colleagues, ask their advice. Maybe they could help him.

It was still early, and he was not yet ready for the semi-ordered chaos that he knew awaited him. Heading up to work. he stopped off at the coffee bar in the French Hotel. He normally took a cappucino to-go, but this morning he needed something stronger, and time to adjust his head. He bought a newspaper from the vending machine and sat down outside with a doppio espresso to continue waking up.

He never really had been a morning person. Morning was fine if you had seen the night all the way through, if you had been up all night working on a problem, or playing handgames at a big-time, or serving watch duty on a boat making a long sea passage. Then he would welcome morning for what it was – the coming of light, a new beginning, a new day. But if he had slept at all during the night, he would crawl unwillingly from his dreams and wouldn't be fully functioning until after a couple cups of strong coffee.

He took a sip of his doppio, opened up the newspaper, and awoke immediately.

In the center of the front page was a picture of Big Bob, with a caption in huge black letters

THE BINGO KING

and the article below it began:

"Bob Mathews, spokesman for the Goose Farm Rancheria near Ophir City, California announced Thursday that his group of Concow Maidu Indians would build a ten-million dollar gambling casino at their Indian rancheria ninety miles northeast of Sacramento.

"We have everything in place now, and plan to begin construction immediately" Mathews said. "The construction of this facility will provide a tremendous uplift for the local economy, which has been hard-hit by the declining timber industry. And when we're in full operation, we'll provide over one hundred permanent local jobs. We will be open for Bingo operations by the end of the year, but plan to provide a full service gaming casino by early next year."

The article went on to explain the federal Indian gaming act, the California self-reliance initiative, and the gray area of the laws concerning which Indian groups could provide what games. It concluded by speculating on the enormous potential revenues the operation could generate, the trend it could set among other Indian rancherias, and the impact this might have on Nevada gambling establishments, especially those in Reno, if a full service casino were built.

The Goose Farm Rancheria! That was below Soapstone Hill, the place where the Tai used to collect the soft stone used to carve out their chillums, on the old road the soldiers made the Maidu people build back in the gold rush days. All the Indians the soldiers could catch were put to work on that road. The soldiers tied a white scarf around their captives' arms to identify them as 'good Injuns' – the ones not to be shot! These were the ones they forced to work on the highway.

The Goose Farm rancheria was pretty accessible. It'd be a good place for a casino, Chris thought, without thinking about it much.

He was a little hurt that Big Bob hadn't mentioned any of this when he'd just seen him Tuesday. But big money must be involved, and influential people too, to get this on the front page of the Chronicle. He re-read the article as he finished his doppio, trying to figure out what it all meant. It was too much to think about right now. He had to get on with the day.

20

Coyote in the world above

Coyote's group had many adventures on their rescue mission in the land above the sky, but eventually they got to a place where they could see Big Bird's roundhouse in the distance. They sneaked up to where they could get a good view, and saw the two young girls sunning themselves on the roof of the roundhouse. It was the same two girls, their parents recognized them

Coyote whispered 'You guys stay here while I go check this out.' He sneaked up to the roundhouse where the girls were sunning.

BAM! BANG! BANG! Somebody was chopping something inside the roundhouse. Coyote came up to the girls. 'Shh, I've come with your parents to rescue you. Where's Big Bird? What can you tell me about this place?'

One of the girls whispered 'Big Bird's not here right now. He usually goes to the world up above to bring back a human. Sometimes he goes to the world below to get them. His wife's inside now, pounding up human bones.'

'What does he do when he gets back?' Coyote asked.

'Oh, he lands right here on the roundhouse roof and tosses the human down through the smoke-hole to his woman. Then he goes in and takes off his flying clothes and hangs them up on the roundhouse wall. Then he goes out to the spring over there, and takes a long drink and lies on that rock. After awhile he looks around with his mouth open, then he takes another long drink and goes back to the roundhouse, and he and his wife eat human-bone soup.'

Coyote got good information like that from the girls.

'Look,' he told them, 'we'll do something, we'll get you out of here. Your parents are here waiting.'

Then he sneaked off and made his way back to the waiting group. He told them everything he had learned, and they all wondered what to do.

Coyote pushed out the gopher head that he always carried with him, to ask its advice.

'Oh, you're a dead man now, Coyote, there's nothing you can do. Big Bird will get you for sure, and that old woman will pound up your fore-legs and pound up your hind-legs and throw you into the pile of dead meat!'

'Oh, you always give me bad advice,' Coyote said as he tossed the gopher head aside. Then he pushed out his favorite wire grass, to ask its advice.

'Here's what you do, Coyote: you turn yourself into a fog and go drift into that Big Bird's roundhouse where his woman is pounding bones. Find a big rock and roll it toward her. When she kicks it away, roll it back at her again. Keep doing that 'til she's good and mad. Then take that rock and hit her over the head. Lay her down next to the fire and cover her with a blanket, then drift out and go down to that spring and wait for Big Bird to come take his drink. When he opens his mouth to look all around, take these pieces of flint and drop them down his throat. That will kill him fast.'

'That's good, you always give me good advice,' Coyote said, stuffing his wire grass back in its place. He found the gopher head he had tossed aside, and put it in the same place.

And so that's what he did. Coyote turned himself into fog, drifted into the roundhouse, and watched Big Bird's woman pound human bones. He saw dozens of human skins hanging on the wall. Then he found a big round rock and rolled it toward her. She kicked it back and he rolled it back toward her. She kicked it back again harder, and he rolled it toward her again. He played with her like that 'til she was good and mad, then he picked up the rock and hit her over the head and killed her. He did just what the wire grass told him.

When Big Bird came back with another human from the world above, he landed on the roof where the girls had been sunning.

'Where's my woman, why isn't she pounding?' he asked the girls.

'Oh, I think she has a headache and is lying down,' one of the girls answered.

Big Bird dropped his load of meat down through the smoke-hole of the roundhouse, then came down below himself. He saw his woman lying down by the fire covered with a blanket.

He took off his flying clothes and hung them up on the wall. He was just an ordinary person then, like anyone else. He went down to the spring to drink, and when he looked all around with his beak open, Coyote dropped the flint pieces down his throat. That killed Big Bird. Then Coyote got the young girls and they took down all the human hides hanging on the roundhouse wall and threw them into the spring.

There was another fellow still alive there that Big Bird had brought down from the world up above. 'I don't know how to get back up to my world, I'll just travel with you folks,' he said. So Coyote and the two girls and this other fellow went back to the camp where the rest of the group was waiting.

'We'll have to find another way to get back home. If we go back the way we came we'll die of old age,' Coyote said.

The next morning all those human skins they had thrown into the spring turned back into people, and, together with Coyote and his group, these people all went off to find a way back down to the world below. That fellow from the world above decided to come with them. 'I can't get back to my world, so I'll visit your world.'

Now, Coyote knew that somewhere up here lived Spider Man, who could lower people down to the world below using his cord. Eventually they found Old Man Spider, and he agreed to help them return to their world. 'I can lower you one at a time, but you have to keep your eyes closed until you're back on your own ground. If you open your eyes when I'm lowering you, the cord will break and you will fall through the sky to your death.'

So Spider lowered the people one by one back to this world, but he kept Coyote back 'til last. He knew Coyote. He tied a blindfold around Coyote's eyes and began to lower him, but just a little ways. He kept Coyote dangling on his cord.

'I must be getting close now, just about tree-top level, I can feel it now. Just a little bit lower and I'll be there,' thought Coyote. 'This must be close enough, I can jump from here now,' Coyote thought as he took off the blindfold to look around. BAM! The cord broke and Coyote went blazing down through the sky. When he finally smashed into the ground all the hair was burned off his hide, and he was a dead coyote again. Years later somebody found his broken pile of bones and tossed them into some water. Next day he emerged, a new coyote again.

21

The next week

Days passed. Robin tried to ignore the headache-that-wouldn't-go-away. She worked on her thesis to focus her mind on something, but she kept thinking of Professor Coyote, and what his brother might know of the professor's power spots.

Robin was fascinated by the story Chris had mentioned of the hunters driving deer off the cliff at Pitch-off Mountain. This story seemed too old to come from the era of the bow-and-arrow, it must have roots in the old pre-bow culture. But who? The Martis? Or the earlier California cultures, of which almost nothing is known? And how did it pass into the Maidu tradition? How did the Maidu pick up a Martis, or older, story? Did this indicate that the lost Martis language stemmed from the same Penutian family as the Maiduan languages?

She decided to incorporate this idea as a part of her thesis. 'Either I'll be laughed out of the department or they'll think I'm brilliant and give me my degree.' She plodded along.

Chris was soon immersed in the daily pressures and semi-ordered chaos that made up his normal life at work. He had little time to think of anything but the current problems – the relentless computer hackers, the trouble-logs, keeping customers happy, keeping technicians happy, keeping managers happy, handling accounts, ordering spare parts, dealing with memos and counter memos, and going to endless meetings. Every day was different, but somehow still the same.

He was on a salary, there was no such thing as paid overtime or compensatory time off. His work days began too early and ended too late. There weren't enough people to handle the increasing workload. There wasn't any money budgeted for them. His department currently had two positions open, but there was no money to pay for them.

Early one afternoon Chris came back to his office with a sandwich in one hand and a cup of coffee in the other, just as his office phone started to ring. He put the sandwich on a pile of papers on his desk, keeping the coffee. He picked up the phone on the third ring.

"Chris Livingstone," he answered.

"Mr. Livingstone, this is Micky Whittaker at the Butte County sheriff's office...."

Hearing from the police was probably not good news.

"We have part of a nearly skeletonized male body here that Fish and Game found near Pitch-off Mountain. I've read the forensics report, and I'll tell you now, I don't think it's part of your brother's body. It seems too far gone for that to me. It's been mutilated pretty badly, probably by a bear or other large animal. It's hard to tell who it was."

"You think it's too far gone to be my brother?" Chris asked hopefully.

"Yeah. They couldn't find any insects on the remains, but found some empty blow-fly pupae and beetle droppings, which they sent to the lab, so we should be able to get a date on it pretty soon. Anyway, I'm wondering if you've had any luck locating some dental or medical records we could use for identification."

"No, Tom hadn't been to a dentist for years as far as I know. He took care of his own teeth. Once he chipped one of his teeth and glued the piece back on with super glue. It held too, I don't think he ever did get it fixed."

"What condition were the Professor's teeth in?"

"Oh, they were in pretty good shape, I guess. I think he still had all of them. All his wisdom teeth too. He used to kind of brag about that."

"Uh huh, what tooth was it he chipped? The one he glued back on?"

"It was one on the upper right, from his point of view. What do you call it, the canine? Not one of the front teeth or the molars. The eye tooth."

"Uh huh." It sounded like Whittaker was making notes as he talked.

Chris continued. "I don't think he had any regular doctor. He didn't believe in them. He thought doctors and hospitals were maybe okay at fixing bones but no good at keeping people healthy. He was more interested in Indian medicine."

"Did he ever break his leg?"

"I don't think so, but unless it was broken in two pieces, he was the kind of guy who might just wrap it up with an ace bandage and hobble around until it was healed."

"He didn't like his medical plan, eh?"

"No, he just didn't like going to doctors and hospitals and dentists. He knew more than one old timer who was hauled into a hospital with a broken bone only to end up being hauled out dead of some infection three days later. He didn't have much contact with white man's medicine, as he called it. He said it was bad luck to spend time in hospitals. He was interested in herbs."

"Uh huh. Well, we're gonna have trouble making any kind of identification unless we can get as many medical records as possible – dental x-rays and chest x-rays and leg x-rays and whatever. You gotta understand, we don't get a whole body to identify when they come in, we sometimes just get a few pieces here and there. Now we've got these male remains. As I said, we don't think it has anything to do with your brother. We have another open missing that we think we can probably link this to."

"What about DNA? Couldn't you just run some DNA tests?"

Officer Whittaker laughed. "Well, if we had the big bucks that you people down there have, we could. This county's under-funded and over-budget already, and we haven't even finished the fiscal year yet. We'll take some samples and save them, but we don't do DNA here. Maybe next year though. Most of the things I've dealt with here have involved drunks, domestic disputes, car wrecks, and one bank robbery. Your missing brother's an interesting fellow. I found two of his books in the library here, and read one of them. It was pretty interesting."

"You said you had a missing person you thought might match the remains. Who was it?" Chris asked.

"Well, we think we know who it was, but we can't release any name. We're having some difficulty locating the next of kin."

"It wasn't Marty Steven was it?"

"How – did you know Martin Steven?"

He'd never heard Marty called by that name. Mart or Marty, but never Martin. It must be who it was.

"I met him two or three times. I didn't really know him that well but I met him a few times. I heard he was missing since last fall."

"Yeah, he probably fell while fishing up the Middle Fork."

Chris knew that wasn't right. "Marty hated fish. He was a red meat man. I can't picture him ever going fishing."

"I thought you said you didn't know him that well."

"I didn't, but I knew him well enough to know that. He'd really complain if the venison had run out by the time he showed up, and there was only fried salmon left in the kitchen. He let you know he didn't like fish. A lot of people will be able to tell you that much. Red meat and beer, that was his food."

"Well, that's interesting," officer Whittaker said slowly. "Maybe he was hunting or sniping up there then. I hear there's a lot of gold still in the Middle Fork."

"Yeah, it gets worked when the water's low. Where was Marty's truck?" Chris asked.

"Now, that's the funny thing. His truck's apparently been parked at his trailer since he's been missing.... Anyway, I just wanted to touch base with you. If you can locate any of those records, get them up to me."

"Okay. And I might stop by up there and see you if I pass through Ophir City, just to keep in touch."

"Well, I'm in and out of the office," Whittaker said. "The university down there must have something on him, there must be at least a chest x-ray somewhere. Mail me any records, or get someone to fax them to me. See what you can get me, okay?"

"Okay, I'll see what I can do."

Chris hung up the phone, and took the first bite of his sandwich. The message-light blinked on his telephone.

The secretary popped her head into his doorway as she walked by. "Remember the one o'clock meeting, Chris."

The phone rang again. Back to life at work.

22

Fire on the mountain

Chris still couldn't quite believe what he had done. He sat at the bar in the Triple Rock Brewery and ordered another pint of amber ale. An overhead television set droned in the background toward the street side of the bar. It was not yet five o'clock, and the brew pub was relatively empty. In another hour it would be packed with students and noisy revelers. Now it was quiet, like the eye of a storm, or a transient lull on the bay. He felt, somehow, satisfied.

He hadn't planned on quitting. But when the new Division Director announced a departmental reorganization and reduction-in-force, and told him he'd have to eliminate four technician positions from his group, Chris went ballistic. This was the same director who'd spent hundreds of thousands of dollars remodeling his own administrative offices when he'd first come in, and now the budget was hundreds of thousands of dollars short! Surprise!

Chris needed more technicians, not fewer. When the director responded that more of the load could be shifted to manufacturers' warranty service providers since people were buying new computers every few years anyway, Chris laughed and asked what they planned to do when their megabuck-projects were hung up waiting 24-hours for an outside tech to come in to fix a fifty-dollar problem. The director said they hoped for something better than a twenty-four hour response time. Chris mentioned he already had twenty-three trouble calls logged today alone, not counting the calls still open from yesterday and the ones that would be waiting for him after he got out of this meeting, and wondered how the manufacturers' service reps would be able to handle that load in a timely manner.

The director clearly wasn't pleased, but neither was Chris. At the end of the meeting Chris announced they'd only need to lay-off three technicians, since he was volunteering himself for the severance package, effective immediately.

Chris took another sip from his beer. He was happy to be out of the stress and chaos of the office. He thought about his father's grandfather, and the world he must have come from. 'The white-man's highway to the future dead-ends at the graveyard,' he thought. He would take an older trail now, and follow the handgame highway. He was tired of the white man's world. He felt, somehow, lucky.

Something in the background drone of the bar television snapped him out of his thoughts.

"...raging out of control near Ophir City has already injured two firefighters and claimed more than four-hundred acres, and there's no containment in sight. The news at five is next...."

Chris ordered another beer and watched the television. He must have watched five minutes of commercials before the newscast finally started.

"The wildfire season got off to a roaring early start this afternoon when the tinder-dry brush southeast of Ophir City erupted in a blaze that so far has consumed hundreds of acres and is still raging out of control with no containment in sight. Two firefighters have been injured, and several structures have been destroyed. George Roth is on the scene and he has this report...."

The map shown on the television showed the fire was closer to Forbestown than Ophir City, on the southern edge of the south fork of the Feather River watershed, burning in national forest land. It was probably fifteen or more miles from Pitchoff Mountain, so his friends should be okay.

But Chris couldn't take his eyes away from the images on the television. The fire raged and was whipped by hot dry winds. It was frightening to watch, he could only imagine what it must be like to be around.

He thought about how the Indians of the Sierras used to regularly set grass fires to burn the land, so raging infernos like this wouldn't have the fuel to sustain themselves.

They kept the oak forests of the foothills like park lands, free of the tangled brush and undergrowth that chokes the foothills today. They burned the land with small fires every year or so, to keep it clean and clear, to keep the young underbrush from taking hold and threatening the big trees that gave them *uti* - their acorn, their bread and soup, and their pine nuts.

Burning the land wherever they went made it easier to get around, easier to hunt and gather acorns. And easier to see any enemies waiting in ambush.

After the white man put a stop to the burnings, the land grew choked with manzanita and poison oak and star thistle and scotch broom and all kinds of brush. The springs dried up. The food and medicine plants disappeared. Now, a small fire might grow to burn up the whole forest.

As Pancho always said, ' They should give the land back to us Indians. We would take better care of it.'

After the fourth or fifth pint, Chris slowly eased himself off the bar stool and found his way back to the pay telephone by the rest rooms. He called Robin's office telephone expecting to leave a message on her voice-mail. She answered on the second ring. Chris was caught off guard. He didn't really know why he was calling.

"Robin," was all he could manage to say.

"Who is this? Chris?"

"Right."

"What's up?" she asked.

"I don't know."

"Where are you?"

"Down at the pub."

"Oh, that explains it."

"Explains what?"

"Explains... why you called." She didn't want to seem too critical of Chris's apparent inebriation.

"Actually... I don't know why I called."

"You took the afternoon off and spent it in the pub?" she asked.

"Right. Oh, that's why I called you. I quit."

"You quit? You quit your job?"

"Right."

"Why?"

"Because I wanted to. It's a long story. I thought I should tell you, in case you try to get hold of me."

"What do you plan to do?" she asked.

"I plan to go to some handgames," he said nonchalantly.

"That sounds like a good plan."

"Speaking of plans, I wanted to know if you still planned to go up to the Indian Valley big-time this weekend."

"Sure I am! I'm not going to be able to get out of here until some time Saturday, but then I'm done."

"Saturday?"

"Right. Hopefully, I can leave here Saturday morning," Robin said.

"I was thinking of leaving tomorrow."

"That's fine, you can go up tomorrow and I can meet you up there Saturday afternoon, I have the map you drew."

"Right." Chris was a little disappointed. He thought somehow she would be riding up with him.

Robin was a little concerned about Chris from the sound of his voice.

"Look, why don't you stay where you are and I'll meet you in twenty minutes," she said.

"No, that's okay." Chris didn't need any sympathy.

"No, stay where you are," Robin insisted. "I'll meet you in twenty minutes. We need to talk."

"Right."

23

The way to Indian Valley

Chris stopped by the Ophir City sheriff's office on the way up to Indian Valley. He wanted to touch bases with officer Whittaker, to let him know that he couldn't be reached at his work phone any longer. Also, he was curious about the fire over near Forbestown.

He learned that Whittaker was out for lunch, and with little probing found out that he would undoubtedly be at the Cornucopia Cafe out by the Feather River highway.

Chris saw a patrol car in the restaurant's parking lot, and found Micky Whittaker at the counter inside lingering over a pie a-la-mode and a cup of coffee. An attractive young woman, fair-haired and probably just a few years out of high school, worked behind the counter. Chris mused that this woman might be the primary reason Micky Whittaker took his lunches here. He took a seat at the counter next to Whittaker.

"They told me at the sheriff's office I could probably find you here," Chris said. "I was just passing through town. Mind if I join you?"

"Livingstone! I was just thinking about your brother!"

"Well, you think of the devil and his brother shows up." Chris meant it as a joke.

"What, your brother's the devil?"

"No, I was just kidding," Chris explained. "'Devil' is like 'coyote' among many of the christianized Maidu. But 'devil' is a little strong, I think. I mean, in the old stories Coyote's often just trying to help out in his own way, he just often screws things up and gets himself killed."

Some unintelligible police talk squawked from a radio on Whittaker's belt.

Officer Whittaker nodded, then looked at Chris. "You heard about the big wildfire that started up here yesterday?"

"Right. How bad is it?"

"It was bad. They got a lucky wind-shift last night. It blew back on itself, and it's pretty much contained now. But it was bad yesterday. It started some time in the afternoon around three o'clock. Two firefighters got trapped early on and had to take cover under their survival blankets, and one fellow ate it in his cabin when the fire swept over it – a big Indian gambler from around here, one of your buddies maybe. You know a Robert Mathews?"

"Bob Mathews? Big Bob?" The news hit Chris like a hammer.

"Yeah, Bob Mathews, the 'bingo king'. They got an ID this morning. It's funny, isn't it? King one day and dead the next."

"It's more than funny, it's suspicious," Chris said.

"It seems like that to me. But the FBI came in and took over this morning. It happened on National Forest land, and they just want us out of there now."

"How did the fire start? Do you know?" Chris ventured.

"Oh, they have all their own investigators up there now checking into that. We're not on the case. It'll be some time before they make up their report, and I'm sure we'll both read about it in the newspapers."

Officer Whittaker was apparently a little ticked-off, but he continued. "But from what I heard from the fire crew at the scene before the Feds shut us out, it looked like the fire originated just below Mathew's cabin, and the wind swept the fire right up the hill."

"How did Big Bob die?"

"Probably smoke inhalation. The autopsy should be complete later today, but they won't have a full toxicology report for several weeks."

"Why didn't he get out of the cabin?" Chris asked.

"A good question. He was just found in the cabin. Maybe he was sleeping," suggested officer Whittaker.

"And why would he be sleeping inside his cabin at three o'clock on a hot afternoon?"

"Another good question. Maybe he was up all night. Maybe he was sleeping off a drunk. We've been assured the FBI will ask all the right questions and they'll come up with all the right answers."

"Well, I can tell you one thing," Chris said. "Big Bob wasn't drunk. He quit drinking years ago. He was diabetic."

Whittaker looked at Chris and slowly spooned out the last of his pie.

"You know," he said, "we're out of the Mathews case, not that we were ever really into it. But we're still on your brother's disappearance, and if they're related that gives us an in. In my gut, I feel there's some connection between your brother's disappearance and this.Mathews death, and I'd like to pursue this thing."

"Well, there was something concerning Tom and Big Bob I think I never mentioned to you."

"What's that?"

The pretty counter-waitress came over to take Chris's order. He hadn't yet looked at the menu, so he just ordered fish and chips and a coffee.

Chris told Whittaker about the old Martis artifacts found at the Goose Farm rancheria before Tom disappeared, the ones found deep in the ground when they were excavating the barbecue pit.

"I don't know what that all has to do with anything," Chris finally concluded.

"I don't either," Whittaker said, "but it's very interesting. It says to me this casino thing should have had an archaeological report. That could hold up the project for years. And if your brother was out there at the rancheria when they found those things, and if he soon after disappeared, then we have a perfect right to look closely at what happened at that rancheria, including this big casino plan."

"And Big Bob's involvement."

"And that's where it's gonna get sticky," Whittaker said. "If those damned Feds could just work with us instead of against us, everybody would be better off. They act like they're a bunch of officers and we're just all... dog faces."

"I think everybody feels that way," Chris laughed, "not just you."

"The FBI knows about the casino thing, don't they?" Chris continued.

"I assume they do," Whittaker answered, "but they won't tell us diddly squat. They're running their own investigation. I assume they'll be looking into the whole casino thing."

"How does this relate to my brother's disappearance," Chris asked.

"That's just what I was wondering when you came in. I don't know. As far as I can tell the FBI's just interested in this Mathews' death, because it occurred on federal land. They're not interested in any other local cases."

"And what do you think?" Chris asked.

"I think it's at least a coincidence."

"Maybe," said Chris thoughtfully. "And what about the other guy – Marty?"

"This Martin Steven disappeared about eight months ago. His body was torn up by animals. He seems to have been a different kind of person, too, from what I hear, a mean alcoholic, a loner. I just can't quite put all three of these cases together."

"I don't know," Chris responded, "what about that other guy they found last year, half-eaten by a bear? Maybe we're talking four cases here."

"Oh, you heard about that camper, eh? Well, there are some similarities there, to the Steven thing," Whittaker said, "but they're all separate, probably unrelated cases. Everybody dies someday."

The waitress arrived with Chris's order. This wasn't Chez Panisse, but Chris was hungry and the food looked good.

"So how long are you in town?" Whittaker asked. "Are you heading up to Pitch-off Mountain again?"

"No, I'm just passing through. I'm headed up to a big-time in Indian Valley this weekend."

"Going up to do some more gambling, eh?" Micky asked.

Chris didn't like the way Whittaker seemed to equate Indian handgame with the casino style of gambling.

"Yeah, going up to watch some handgames and learn some new songs, I hope," Chris answered.

He was starting to like this cop, somehow. He seemed to be straightforward and honest. A little education in Indian ways would be helpful for him, Chris thought.

"It's a Spring *weda* up there, a big celebration," Chris said. "I'm told there'll be a lot of native California dance groups coming. You should try to make it up there this weekend. Things should be happening off-and-on all day and night 'til Sunday afternoon. And if you watch these handgames carefully, I guarantee it will be an eye-opener for you."

"I can't make it, I'm on duty all weekend," Micky said. "But I'd like to check out one of those things sometime."

"Well," Chris said, "you've got another chance, there's another one the following weekend up near Susanville. The Bear Dance. It's like a New Year's celebration for the Sierra Indians."

"I'll keep it in mind. Where's it held?"

"Anybody up there can give you directions. If you get lost, anybody in the Lassen county sheriff's office will know where it is – they cruise by there several times a day during that weekend."

"Well, I might make it up there if I have both days off next weekend," Whittaker said. "Any good fishing up there?"

"Eagle Lake isn't far from there, and it's one of the best fishing secrets known to man."

"Well now, that might be some incentive," said Whittaker. "I'm not much of a gambler, but I am a fisherman."

"Come up there if you can, and dress, uh, casually," encouraged Chris. "You'll see a world of difference between a bunch of friends and family singing their power songs and playing handgame out in the woods, and compulsive gamblers hanging around a smoky casino full of slot machines."

"I'll try to check it out. It sounds like these things are going on all the time around here."

"Indian culture's getting revived more and more, it's having a big comeback. Big-times are in full swing from April through October throughout the West. There's another one in a few weeks in Yosemite Park, behind the Visitors' Center."

Chris took a swig of water, then continued.

"Handgame has a lot of variations, but it's still pretty much the same, from here to the Rockies, and north to Alaska."

Some more gibberish and code numbers squawked from the radio on Whittaker's belt.

"Well, that one's for me, lunch time's over," Whittaker said as he got up to go. He left a pile of dollar bills on the counter.

"Bye, Tommie, see you tomorrow?" he hailed to the waitress.

"Thanks, Micky, see you tomorrow," Tommie responded with a sweet smile.

He turned to Chris. "Nice talking with you, Chris, it's been interesting. We'll keep in touch."

"Right. Oh, that's one thing I meant to tell you – you can't reach me any more at that phone number I gave you, so I'm hard to get hold of."

"Well, you know how to get hold of me."

"Right, right here, whenever Tommie's working," Chris joked, nodding toward the waitress.

"You got it!" Whittaker said with a smile as he left.

24

The man-killers of Chuchuya

Chris left the Cornucopia Cafe and headed up the Feather River highway, passing the old road that led down toward Pancho's place. He said a silent prayer for Pancho, but didn't stop this time. He was in cruising gear, thinking about Big Bob, thinking about Tom, and singing handgame songs to himself as he drove up the canyon.

> *yu ku tai yoweni*
> *yu ku tai yoweni*
> *kau wau wau yoweni*
> *kau wau wau yoweni*
> *yu ku dai!*

This is the northernmost route across the Sierras. The North Fork of the Feather has been claimed and shaped by gold miners, engineers and earth movers for well over a hundred years. Everywhere he looked Chris could see the signs of modern man – highway and railroad tunnels bored through solid granite, and a wild river tamed by a series of power dams, its many tributaries channeled into huge steel pipes and turbines.

On the far side of the river, the railroad followed its own grade carved along the canyon wall, across its own bridges and through its own tunnels. Whenever the highway crossed the river to run along the opposite side of the canyon, the railroad would soon also cross to climb along the other side.

Still, in spite of all these works of man, the canyon retained its own beauty and power. Chris always felt good when he drove it.

At the Quincy Y he turned north and followed the dredged river up toward Greenville. Soon he passed the terraces along the creek at Chuchuya, where a mineralized, healing hot spring once flowed, before the ground was disturbed by modern quarrying for travertine

Chris thought about the old Maidu story of the Chuchuya women. Chuchuya was one of those places Worldmaker fixed up when he was on his long walk through the new world, getting things ready for the human people he was about to make.

Man-killers they were, those Chuchuya women.

When Worldmaker came along the trail, one of them tried to wash him into the creek with a powerful geyser of hot urine. Worldmaker made it across the washout by stretching his walking stick all the way down to the creek bed, maybe two- or three-hundred feet below. But he was mad. Those man-killer women would have to go!

He came to the place at the next spot up the creek where two boys lived, Mink and Fisher. Those boys were running around helping to make the new world, running all over, making ravines and canyons and springs, and naming everything.

Worldmaker waited for Mink and Fisher at their place, and when they came home he fed them with a big bowl of acorn soup from the magic pack he carried.

The boys told Worldmaker about a huge snake that was causing problems. They couldn't catch it because it was so big it broke all their traps. They asked Worldmaker's help in catching the snake. He agreed.

Next morning Worldmaker set a couple of good sticks way up in a hole in the sky. He fashioned some kind of string big enough to catch the snake. When the snake got caught, the string would pull it up into the world above, and there would be no more big snake in this country – at least, not *that* big snake.

Worldmaker told the boys, "When you boys trap this animal, cut off a bit of the tail. Take that tail fat down the creek to the Chuchuya women's roundhouse. They tried to kill me, those women. Get rid of them! When they dance there at night around the fire in their roundhouse, take that fat and drop it through the smoke-hole into the fire, and sit on the smoke-hole. The smell of that snake will kill those women for sure. Let them die, and then smash down the whole roundhouse."

The boys agreed to do that, and the Worldmaker moved on.

A big sinkhole above the river marks the spot where the roundhouse used to be. The salty water there makes good medicine.

Thinking about the Chuchuya women dying in their smoke-filled house brought Chris back to Big Bob dying in his smoky cabin. He drove on, singing Big Bob's handgame songs.

yu ku tai, yoweni yu ku tai, yoweni
kau-wau-wau yo-weni
kau-wau-wau yo-weni
yu-u ku-u tai!

25

Big-time at Indian Valley

There were several cars already parked in the camping area, but Chris was able to find a good site on the far edge of the grounds near the creek. He parked his truck and unloaded some of his gear to claim the spot, then walked around to see who was already here.

He found Vinnie sitting at a picnic table, talking with his aunt at their family's camp site.

"Hey, Chris, you made it up early," Vinnie hailed.

"Well I quit my job yesterday so I finally have enough time for myself. Officially I'm on vacation before I terminate, but I'm already starting to feel like a free man."

He nodded a greeting to Vinnie's aunt, while he searched his memory in vain for her name.

"What are you going to do?" Vinnie asked.

"Play some handgame and do some sailing I guess." Chris decided this would be his stock response to that inevitable question.

He sat down on a stump next to the picnic table and dropped the bombshell news.

"I just stopped by the sheriff's office in Ophir City, and found out Big Bob died yesterday. He was killed in the fire."

"What? You're kidding!" Vinnie gasped.

"No, the fire swept through his cabin. He was found inside."

"Wow!"

"Bob Mathews, the gambler?" asked Vinnie's aunt.

"That's what I was told," said Chris.

"Wow!" Vinnie exclaimed again. "I can't believe it!" He shook his head back and forth. "I was just starting to wonder where he was coming from, and now he's dead."

"That's too bad," interjected Vinnie's aunt. "He was a nice man."

"They're not sure how he died," Chris added. "But the fire started somewhere around his cabin."

"Just when he becomes top dog of the mega-casino project," Vinnie added sardonically.

"Right, like the cop in Ophir City told me," Chris said, "one day you're king and the next day you're dead."

"Do the cops think he was murdered?" Vinnie asked.

"The FBI's handling the case since it was on National Forest land," Chris explained. "But the local cop thinks it's definitely suspicious."

"Just when I'd been thinking of Big Bob being responsible for Tom's... disappearance, and now this," Vinnie added.

"What do you mean by that?" Chris asked.

"Well, remember how Big Bob didn't want us to go down into the canyon that day?" Vinnie asked.

"Yeah, he did sort of discourage us."

"Right," Vinnie continued. "And remember that dance ground we found up top there, over on Pitch-off Mountain?"

"Right."

"And remember how Big Bob kept saying 'It wasn't a dance circle, there was no deer dance there.'" Vinnie added.

"Right, something like that."

"Well, I talked to Craig Jackson this morning – Kenny Jackson's brother, the dancer. He said they did a private bear ceremony there that Saturday night, but he wouldn't tell me much more. Why would BB want to hide that?"

"I don't know. He just said they didn't have a Deer Dance there, he didn't say anything about a bear ceremony," Chris said. "What happened at the bear ceremony?"

"I don't know," Vinnie said. "I tried to find out more about it. Craig said Big Bob went sort of berserk when he put on the bear hide, but he wouldn't tell me anything more, like it was a ritual of some secret society or something."

"Secret society? I didn't think the Tai had secret societies, at least not any more," Chris said.

"Well, there used to be the *kuksu* cult. It extended through the valley to the foothills. I don't think it made it into the mountains.

Vinnie continued after a moment.

"Craig's brother Kenny was one of those guys hassling Tom over at Pitch-off Mountain that Saturday, wasn't he? And didn't Leonard say it was Big Bob who told Kenny about those tapes at the university? To me it all points to BB somehow being involved in something and covering up."

"And now Big Bob's dead, so what does it all mean?" Chris asked.

"That's a good question. What does it all mean?" Vinnie pondered. "Maybe the hudessi was killing people, so somebody killed the hudessi," Vinnie said curiously.

"Do you really think Big Bob was a hudessi?"

"I don't know," Vinnie said. "He really looks like a bear-person, doesn't he? And I just keep wondering what he was trying to hide."

Chris and Vinnie talked for some time. Vinnie's aunt sat quietly listening to all they were saying. Eventually the conversation came around to the handgame.

"Are you going to be playing any handgame up here?" Chris asked Vinnie.

"I'd like to get into one. But we're supposed to dance sometime tonight and again tomorrow. My dad's bringing up all our regalia, but he's not here yet. Once we start dancing I can't stay around to play. Are there any other players around yet?"

"I just got here," Chris said. "You're the first one I've found. Is Marvin around?"

"I haven't seen him yet. He should be up here sometime this evening, though. He's usually in charge of the barbecue pit. But Beatrice here was saying she wanted to get a women's team playing against the men."

Vinnie's aunt Beatrice finally spoke up. "We did that last year at the Bear Dance, and we whipped 'em good too, beat 'em twice. We want to do that again here."

They talked a while longer, then Chris walked around to see if he could find anybody else he knew.

He saw Leonard sitting at a picnic table in his camp with an old woman.

Chris walked up to them.

"Hi Leonard."

"Good to see you up here, Chris."

Leonard introduced Chris to the beautiful old woman seated next to him.

"This is the professor's brother Chris, Eleanor. And this is my aunt Eleanor."

Chris smiled at the old woman.

"Glad to meet you, Eleanor."

She was small, and alert, with long white hair tied back with a colorful, glass-beaded hair-band. Silver-haired Leonard seemed young compared to her. 'She must be at least a hundred years old,' Chris thought. 'She must know a lot about the old ways.'

The wrinkles and valleys of her textured face reflected the terrain of the Sierra foothills, and spoke of a long life lived close to the sun-baked earth.

She nodded at Chris.

"You look like the professor," she said smiling. "I just saw him the other day."

"You saw him? Where?"

"At home. Leonard brought him by," she said, nodding toward her nephew.

"I took Tom over to Eleanor's place, the morning of the handgames on Pitch-off Mountain," Leonard explained. "He wanted to know more about *pumi,* so I brought him over to talk to Eleanor. I figured she'd know what he was looking for, if anybody did."

"What's pumi?" Chris asked.

"Pumi – gambling luck," Leonard explained. "Old timers used to use it in the handgame. They thought it made them see the bones better."

"I've heard about that plant," Chris said. "It's supposed to be dangerous, isn't it? Do you think Tom could have poisoned himself with it?"

"No, *chululu's* not that bad root," Eleanor interjected. "It 's different. But it's supposed to work good unless the other side has something stronger. I told him where my grandfather found it," the old woman said after a pause. "Maybe I shouldn't have."

"Why's that?" Chris asked.

"Maybe we shouldn't talk about these things," the old woman said.

Chris wanted to talk about these things, but knew not to push too hard. He'd ease in.

"You hear about Big Bob?" Chris asked Leonard.

"Yeah, I heard about that on the radio on the way up. His road was a short one."

"It's a shame," said Eleanor.

Chris sat down at their table and let out a loud groan.

"We never know how long our road is, or how long we'll last," he sighed. "My knees sure aren't what they used to be, that's for sure."

"Yup, the knees and joints start squeakin' first, and pretty soon you're all rusted up," Leonard observed.

Chris put down the small pack he carried around at big-times.

"You look like a real Injun gambler, with that *pulla* you carry with you," Leonard smiled, pointing to the woven rattan pack Chris carried.

"Yeah, this holds all my gambling stuff, and different kinds of medicine, too." Chris pulled out a small bottle of Old Crow from the pack. "Including this. This stuff helps the old joints loosen up. Care to join me for a little medicine?" Chris offered, coyote-like.

"Maybe just little," Leonard smiled, sliding over three coffee cups.

Chris poured some Old Crow into each of the three cups.

After a small sip, Leonard started talking about handgame luck again.

"There're different kinds of pumi, you know," Leonard said. "Not all pumi are plants."

After a nip or two of the Old Crow, Eleanor opened up a bit more too.

"That's right," she agreed. "What's lucky for one person might not work for another."

She talked about some of her old relatives, and how they used pumi in the old days.

"My uncle Fred used dried hummingbird skins for his pumi," she said, "but old Bean Creek Jack used this carrot plant. He said it worked for him. He said he could see the white bone just about every time. Everybody's got to find their own kind of pumi. If something works, use it. If it doesn't work, throw it away and try something else."

"How do you find pumi?" Chris asked.

"They grow where the Creator sowed them," Eleanor said. "But those old timers looked for luck in all kinds of things – albinos, freaks, deformed things. Things like that are supposed to work the best. They'd keep trying different things."

The old woman took another small sip from the cup, and smiled curiously. "But if you look too hard for pumi, it will hide from you."

Chris asked, "Do you think Tom was using one of those things up at Pitch-off Mountain?"

Leonard chuckled. "He just might have been, by golly. He sure was having a good run of luck in those games."

After a moment Eleanor looked at Chris and lectured. "Every plant has a spirit behind it. If the spirit likes you, it will help you. If it doesn't like you, you'd better not monkey around with that plant!"

She and Leonard talked of how the gamblers used pumi in the old days.

"Those things are supposed to help you see the white bone in the handgame," Eleanor said. "They'd see the white bone, but they'd call for the dark bone, *sulu*. That's how tricky those old timers were, they thought it was bad luck to call for the white bone too often.

"But you have to be careful," she cautioned, "if the other side's luck is stronger than yours, your pumi will turn against you. You have to protect yourself against the power of the other side's luck, as well as your own."

"How do you protect yourself?" Chris asked.

"With medicine," Eleanor said. "With your angelica or your rattlesnake medicine. Clean up the bones with your medicine before you touch them. Maybe blow through them to blow out any pumi the other side might have put in the bones."

She started talking about different poisons used in the old days in a form of low-scale warfare.

"Sometimes those old-timers would put a poison on the gambling bones," she said, "to make the other side sleepy or careless when they handled the bones, or maybe to get somebody they might have a grudge against. They'd all rub their own hands beforehand with angelica. If the wrong people handled those bones, why, that was their bad luck day.

"But it was more than just the potion," old Eleanor added, "a doctor would have to sing to it real good to make the poison work."

The old woman shrugged her small shoulders and took another small sip. "That's how our wars started sometimes, what wars we had in the old days. Someone would kill somebody from another outfit, maybe because of some past grudge or insult. So then the other outfit feels they're owed somebody or something, so they get their revenge, maybe by poisoning someone at a big-time, or maybe by going out and burning down the other outfit's dance-house. So then the other outfit's owed something. Back and forth like that, back and forth.

"There was a lot of poisoning going on in the old days," she continued. "But those days are long gone now. Still, some handgame players blow through the bones when they get them back from the other side, just to say 'I remember the old ways'. But there haven't been any poisoners around since Bald Rock Jim's time, back when I was a young woman. And that was a longggg time ago," she chuckled.

They talked and sipped around the table much of the afternoon. Chris eventually excused himself and walked around to see if anybody else he knew had arrived. He saw several familiar faces, but nobody whose name he knew or could remember.

Then he saw the bearded old man sitting on a big log bench near the handgame playing area. He was one of the oldest men around, and his big gray beard made him conspicuous. Most Indian men have little facial hair, and often pluck or shave what few hairs grow. This old-timer had a full crop.

He looked familiar, like someone Chris had met at another big-time. Surely Tom would have known him. Chris thought perhaps he might learn something from this old-timer.

A tall blond man holding a long walking stick sat talking with the old man. The blond man got up to walk away as Chris approached.

"I'll meet you back here, Jim, when I find out what's going on." The blond man spoke loudly but gently, with a slight European accent, and studied Chris as he walked up. Chris saw clear blue eyes, set in an honest face, probing him. The white man then nodded at Chris and walked away.

Chris remembered the old-timer now. He was Grindstone Jim, from across the Sacramento River on the west side of the valley. He had descended from those survivors of the long brutal march to the confines of Round Valley Indian Reservation.

But old Jim was a full-blown American patriot as well, an army veteran of foreign wars, who still proudly carried tatoos and scars from the time he spent in the European theatre of the Second World War.

"Hi Jim, I'm Chris Livingstone, Professor Coyote's brother. I don't know if you remember me."

Chris sat on the right side of the old man on the bench. "I've met you before but I can't quite remember where it was," Chris continued when the old man didn't respond.

"There's supposed to be some handgames around here," the old man finally replied in a barely audible voice. "My chauffeur's looking around to see if there's any gamblers here."

"What's your chauffeur's name?" Chris casually asked.

"Too bad the children don't play handgame here," Grindstone Jim continued softly. The old man spoke so quietly Chris had a hard time understanding him.

"When I was a boy the big kids would teach the little kids how to play," the old man said. "But us kids couldn't play with the adults. We could stand around and watch them and even sing, but they wouldn't let us play. How are the children going to learn, I say, if they don't play the game?"

Chris paused. He was having a hard time hearing the old man's words. "Do you know who I am? Do you remember me?" Chris asked loudly.

"Right," the old man said. He apparently had trouble hearing Chris too.

"You look like your brother, but you have more hair on your face, and more meat on your bones," the old man chuckled unexpectedly.

"Well, I still have a ways to catch up with you!" Chris laughed, rubbing his beard.

"What'd you say? You know, this here ear doesn't work too good. I can hear you better through my other ear," Grindstone Jim turned the left side of his face toward Chris and smiled, as if apologizing for his infirmity.

"Well, maybe it'd be better if I sat on your other side," Chris volunteered in a louder voice.

"Okay," the old man nodded his head, and Chris moved to sit next to his left side.

"When I was a kid we used to go up on the hillside and play our own handgames with the other kids," the old man continued. Chris could hear him clearly now. It was strange – now that the old man could hear Chris better, Chris could understand the old man better as well.

"They wouldn't let us play with the adults," the old man said.

"Right," Chris agreed, "I think the children should play the game. How else can they learn all about the game if they don't play it and copy their elders?"

"Right, how else can they learn?"

"Are you going to play some handgames up here?" Chris ventured. He was always eager to hear handgame teams singing and playing against each other – the more the better, even if he couldn't play himself.

"My chauffeur went to see if he could find some gamblers around. We'll play if there's some gamblers here." Grindstone Jim looked Chris in the eyes and nodded. "Me and your brother used to play some handgames together – used to do pretty good, too."

This was the opening Chris had been awaiting. "You hear anything of my brother? What happened to him?"

The old man clammed up. "I don't hear much. I don't ask any questions." After a moment he continued. "We don't talk too much, you know, that's the way we were taught," he said simply. "You ask a lot of questions."

"Well, my brother's been missing since a big-time over at Pitch-off Mountain. I'd like to find out what happened."

"Missing? He's coyote, Henom, just like me."

"What does that mean?" Chris asked.

"I don't know. Henom. Old Man Coyote. Sometimes you can't see him, but he's here."

"You hear anything about Tom? Anybody say anything?" Chris persisted.

"I don't know," the old man shrugged. "I don't hear much."

They sat in silence for a few moments watching all the people moving and talking around them. Chris saw the tall blond man across in the distance by the dance ground.

"What's your chauffeur's name?" Chris asked again, nodding toward the dance ground.

"I don't know," the old man answered quietly.

"You don't know your chauffeur's name?"

"No," he replied simply, with an emphatic smile. "I never asked him his name. I don't ask too many questions. He takes me where I want to go."

"Are you going to stay here tonight?" Chris wondered if old Grindstone Jim would be around for the whole weekend like most people at the big-time.

"I don't know. I go where my chauffeur goes. I don't ask any·questions."

"Well, I just asked because I thought maybe we could get some handgame going later."

"My chauffeur went to look for the gamblers. Grandma might be up here, along with some other Paiute singers. Maybe some other folks from Grindstone. There should be some good handgame players up here."

The tall man with the walking stick came back from the dance ground and stood next to Chris. Chris was about to introduce himself when the blond man held out his hand.

"Gunther," he said.

"Chris Livingstone," Chris replied, and then added "How do you know Grindstone Jim?"

"He's my teacher," Gunther replied softly. "He is the wisest man here. He teaches me."

Gunther turned to Grindstone Jim and spoke in a louder voice. "Grandma and her team from Susanville are talking about playing the Greenville team. Do you want to get in on it?"

"I'll just watch for awhile," Grindstone Jim answered.

Chris excused himself for the while, and went back to set up camp.

Sometime in the evening Chris heard clapper sticks and singing in the distance. At first he thought it was a handgame going on. Then he heard the shrill sounds of bird-bone whistles, and realized it must be the traditional dancers warming up the dance ground. He found his way over to the dance ground to watch.

A bonfire burned in the middle of the dance circle. Toward the front, four male singers, dressed in ordinary clothes but each with an ornamental belt draped diagonally from shoulder to waist, kept a sharp steady rhythm with split elder clapsticks while they sang their dance song. Dancers in their regalia pranced on the dirt as they circled around.

It was a deer dance. One man, naked but for a loin cloth and draped with a deer skin, wore an impressive set of antlers tied to his head, and danced at the far side of the circle near the opening. Four other male dancers in feathered costumes and carrying small bows moved slowly around the dance ground in a counter-clockwise direction, pounding their bare feet into the earth in perfect time to the clapsticks, while occasionally blowing small bird-bone whistles, each with its own piercing tone.

Lined up facing each other on opposing sides of the dance ground several women of all ages, wearing fancy deerskin clothes and colorful beadwork, danced in place as they held scarfs between their outstretched hands and slowly waved their arms from side to side.

As each hunter-dancer approached the deer-man, the two would seem to lock eyes, although the hunter wore a band of yellow-hammer feathers across his eyes. The deer-man's eyes would widen with fright.

Each hunter would draw his bow string as he approached, and make a step toward the deer-man as deer-man backed away as if in fear. As the hunter danced away, the deer-man danced forward again toward the fire. The other male dancers turned their heads from side to side every few seconds as they slowly circled.

After a while the lead singer quivered his clapstick momentarily to call the circling hunter-dancers back to a line in front of the singers. The deer-man stayed where he was. One by one the hunters slowly danced back to line up in front of the singers, and the lead singer brought the song and dance to an emphatic stop.

"Ho!" several people from the observing crowd called out in applause.

The singers talked quietly to each other for a few seconds, then started the same song again. The dancers circled away again in the same counter-clockwise direction, and continued the same dance.

They repeated the same dance four times, as a blessing sent in four directions. Then the chanters began another song, which began another dance, again danced for each of the four directions.

They did several dances. After the last movement of the final dance the lead singer quivered his clapstick continuously as the male dancers circled the dance ground and followed each other out, followed by the women dancers, followed by the singers.

As the dancers left the dance ground, several in the observing crowd shouted out long ho's and hoo's of appreciation and applause. Chris joined them, it had been a beautiful dance, and seeing it in the flickering firelight had made it extra special.

He went back to his campsite to think about the deer dances, the hudessi, Big Bob, and his brother....

He started up his own campfire. As he watched it burn he thought about that old man, Sumkano, who lives in the fire. Sometimes in the distance he could hear the sound of more Indian music, more drums beating through the night.

The next morning Chris wandered through the area looking for other friends who might have arrived.

Marvin had come in late last night, as had Rod Beckman, a white man who sometimes played handgame. They were both standing around the large barbecue pit on the far side of the outdoor kitchen area. Huge logs and rounds of wood burned in the pit, and the men had to stand back several feet to get away from the intense radiated heat.

"Hi Marvin, when did you get in?"

"I didn't come in 'til late last night. I couldn't get out of the shop until almost seven last night."

"You hear about Big Bob?" Chris asked.

"Yeah, right, Vinnie told me all about it," Marv said. "Man, that's a real shocker, huh?"

"Really! I don't know what to think about it. Bingo King one day and dead man the next. I mean, if he was killed, if it really wasn't accidental, it opens up a lot of questions."

"Right. I'd give it a snowball's chance in hell of being accidental," Marv opined. "When that kind of money is involved? We were just talking about it. When's the services?"

"I don't know. He died Thursday, and I guess they autopsied him yesterday."

"His people are probably holding a wake for him right now," Marv said. "I'll stop by his aunt's on the way down."

"Was he a Christian?" Chris didn't know why he asked the question, but he knew a lot of traditional people who had also been christianized by various missionaries, and had somehow integrated the dichotomous religions into their lives with varying degrees of success.

"Well, some of his family were Mormons," Marv replied, "but I don't think he ever joined the church. I'll bet there's a Mormon preacher at his funeral, though."

They all stared for a while at the big logs burning in the fire pit.

Finally, Chris asked "Well, what's on the menu for tomorrow? You planning on roasting a big deer in there?"

"Right," Marv said. "We got a *sumi* we're going to put in late tonight. And we've also got a few hundred pounds of *wolem sumi*."

"Wolem sumi?" Chris asked.

"Right," Marv explained. "White man's deer. Beef. And somebody brought up a few hundred pounds of salmon from down at the hatchery, so there'll be plenty to eat all weekend. They're frying up the fish in the kitchen now."

"Maybe I'll go check it out," Chris said. "Maybe they have some coffee over there too."

"They do – go for it!" Marv said.

"When will the handgames start? When's the dancing?" Beckman asked.

"Who knows?" Marvin said. "We're on Indian time here."

Grindstone Jim had been watching the handgames all day. Old Grandma and her family were playing against the

Greenville Maidu, and had won the first two games in fairly short order, drumming out a new song every time they had the bones to hide, never singing the same song twice, no matter how lucky it seemed to be.

The Maidu team played with grass, fancy style, using big wads of grass called *bodau's* to hide the bones, which they tossed into the air like expert jugglers in rhythm to their gambling song. The Paiute women played more sedately, without grass, using a large colorful shawl to cover the hiders' hands while they rolled the bones.

Grandma, a tough-looking Paiute from Honey Lake – at least eighty years old and probably more – pounded her big round deerskin drum while others on her team hit sticks on a log in a rhythm that moved slightly in and out of unison.

The Paiute team sang on and on in their haunting voices. The sound of Grandma's drum echoed from nearby hills, and came back in a kind of counter-point that could sometimes be heard in the moments between the regular drum beats.

Then, suddenly, the game was over. One last missed guess, and now there were no more counting sticks to lose – or win, depending on where your sentiments lay.

The crowd dispersed when the game ended. Some went over to Grandma's side to collect their winnings, others wandered off to look for some food or to stretch their legs. Grindstone Jim approached Chris.

"Too bad your brother ain't here," Grindstone Jim said as he came over. "We could take Grandma now, I know we could. She thinks she's on a roll now. It's a good time to go after her. She'll probably double her bets, she thinks she's so hot."

Grindstone Jim looked Chris up and down, sizing him up. "Let's you and me be partners in this next game," he finally said. "We'll get up a pot and challenge Grandma's team. She's all stoked up now, she's won twice already, so she thinks she can't be stopped, but we can get her now. Your brother and me did pretty good on occasion," he winked.

"Sure, why not? You, me and who else?" asked Chris.

"Well, I've got some people who want to bet on a game, and you can help come up with enough to match her stake. We can get 'er! Check these out."

Old Jim pulled a leather pouch out of his pocket and shook out two sets of gambling bones. They gleamed like old ivory.

"I made the white ones out of bear." He handed Chris a polished hollow bone.

"Mountain lion is best, 'cause they don't check if you accidentally shake 'em into the fire," Jim continued. "And these with the black stripe I made out of deer. I hid some gambling luck inside 'em, and plugged the ends with madrone. The luck calls to me when I guess for black."

"But there's two things to learn about this next game," Jim said sternly. "First, there's one Captain and I'm the Captain. When it's our turn to hide, I'll handle the bones first, and I'll decide which one of us will hide 'em for the next go-around. If you don't feel like hiding 'em when I pass 'em to you, you pass 'em back to me and I'll choose someone else. And if Grandma's side makes a call and they miss you, pass the bones back to me anyway. This goes for all your people too. Even if you think you're on a roll, you pass 'em back to me. I'll decide who's going to hide 'em next. If you're on a roll I'll probably give 'em back to you to hide again. But maybe not. I'm the Captain!

"And second, and most important for this next game with Grandma," Grindstone Jim cautioned, "if you're hiding the bones, you sneak a look over at me when she calls you. Before you show her your bones, you look at me. You look for a sign from me that its okay to show yourself. Otherwise you just keep singing and keep hiding."

"That's fine with me, I'd feel better having you be the Captain while I'm around here anyway," Chris grinned.

"Good, but you remember, don't show 'er your bones 'til I give you the nod."

After some while Grindstone Jim finally found enough backers to make a reasonably challenging bet. With Chris's twenty and Gunther's ten, and a little help from bystanders and friends, they'd amassed a fair amount of money. It was enough. Grandma's team was on a roll, and they quickly came up with enough to match the challenge.

When the pot was duly collected, and the money matched bill for bill and tied in a scarf placed to one side between the two teams, Grandma threw five counting sticks over to Grindstone Jim, keeping five sticks and both pairs of her own bones herself.

"Let's start. We hide 'em. You call us," Grandma said curtly.

"No way, we hide 'em first, and we use my bones. You won the last two games!" argued Grindstone Jim.

"You're a clown, Jim, but you're right about just one thing: we won the last games. And we'll win the next. Let's go! This is new teams. You guess us," and Grandma's teamed jumped into their song.

> o yoko no   o yoko ne
> a honi nameya nameya ne wa
> honi nameya nameya ne wa
> o yoko no   o yoko ne

Grandma's partners began to pick up on the song, and Grandma pulled her hands out from beneath a scarf at the same time her daughter Star showed her hands.

"Ho! *Tep*" cried Grindstone Jim instantly, pointing out with his right hand.

Grandma looked at her daughter, who looked back at her.

"Pass 'em over, I called both black bones to the right, in your left hands. I got ya both, I know I did."

"That's cheating, we weren't ready yet," Grandma feebly protested.

"Don't matter, Grandma. Like I said, we hide 'em, we start 'em," joked back Grindstone Jim. He seemed to be hearing just fine now. Grandma and Star tossed over the bones, and Grindstone Jim began to fire up a song.

> *heni no we, heni no weni we,*
> *heni no we, heni no weni we.*

One by one Grindstone Jim and his pick-up team started finding their rhythm and their individual songs that blended together into one.

> *weni no we heni no wendem we*
> *weni no we, heni no weni we*

Chris heard the words as similar English sounds,

> *winny no way, hinny no winny way*

Everybody sang slightly different syllables to the same melodic rhythm.

The song wove on and on, endlessly repetitious patterns and variations, creating a fabric of melody and rhythm, simple but powerful, subconsciously enticing someone on the opposing side to guess wrong. From time to time Grindstone Jim would holler out a taunt of *nawol, nawol,* as if to say 'Come on, guess us, we're tired of singing.'

Finally Grandma grunted. "Ho, *tep!*" She pointed to her left. Chris stole a glance toward Grindstone Jim, who nodded with his eyes, and Chris showed his hands. She'd guessed Chris correctly! But Grindstone Jim showed the bones he was hiding, and she'd missed him. Chris tossed the bones that had been guessed to Grindstone Jim, who tossed them across to Grandma. Grandma reluctantly tossed over a counting stick, mad at herself for missing Grindstone Jim."

"Catch me if you can, Grandma!" Grindstone Jim laughed as he boldly held out his hands."

"Ha, gotcha! *tep-yos*" cried Grandma as she held up the white bone in her left hand.

"Arrgh" grunted Grindstone Jim as he tossed the bones he held over to Grandma's side. "That didn't work too good. I'll teach myself not to try that again," he grunted.

Now Grandma's side started singing.

wai yo-
namea wai-yo-o, namea wai yo, namea wai yo
—wai-yo!
yoko wai o-o
namea wai yo

Others on her side started helping out the song:
wai yo, hamea wai-yo-o, hamea wai yo, hamea wai yo
Each person seemed to sing it a little bit differently, but still it was the same song with the haunting beautiful melody.
wai yo, amea wai-yo-o, amea wai yo, amea wai yo
They started swaying their bodies and hitting sticks on the long log in front of them to keep up the now-building rhythm of the song.

wai yo-,
nameya wai-yo-o, nameya wai yo, nameya wai yo
—wai-yo!
yoko wai o-o nameya wai o

After some time Grandma gave one set of bones to her daughter, and kept a set for herself to hide. She held her bones in one hand while she waved around a bright silk scarf in the other hand, moving her body around, back and forth, weaving her song like Spider Woman weaving a web, singing to trap you, weaving, singing, waving....

wai yo—
namea wai-yo-o, namea wai yo, namea wai yo
—-wai-yo!
yoko wai o-o namea wai yo

Eventually she brought her hands together under the scarf, then quickly pulled them apart. Just as quickly Grindstone Jim shouted out his guess:

"Ho! *We!* – you better have both black bones over there where I'm pointing, or you owe me those bones," Grindstone Jim grinned, with a twinkle in his eye.

Grandma looked at her daughter, Star, who looked back at her. They both threw their bones into the dirt toward Grindstone Jim.

"You cheated again," Grandma sulked jokingly. "We weren't ready yet."

"It don't matter, you'd no winny anyway, ready or not," laughed back Grindstone Jim as he quickly started singing.

>*no weni no weni no weni no wen*
>*no weni no weni no weni no wen*

He picked up a few counting sticks and hit them into the palm of his hand to keep the fast rhythm.

>*no weni no weni no weni no wen*

The song began to pick up some steam. Chris started singing English syllables again

>*no winny, no winny, no winny, no win*
>*no winny, no winny, no winny, no win*

Grindstone Jim passed one set of bones to Chris. After some time playing with the bones behind his back, feeling them until he himself didn't know which hand held which bone, Chris brought his closed hands out front, then crossed his arms as he sang.

>*no winny, no winny, no winny, no win*

Grindstone Jim soon held his closed fists in front of him also, and waved his arms as he sang.

>*no weni no weni no weni no wen*

After some time of this, Grandma brought her pointing stick in front of her and began waving it around, as if dowsing or testing different calls with her spirit.

"*We, este*, she finally hollered as she made her call.

We was a common call that the white bone was held on the side toward which she·was pointing. Grandma used the old-fashioned call '*este*' which meant 'down the river', or 'away from the *kumi* door'.

They played outdoors here, and there was no roundhouse door, but Grindstone Jim knew what she'd called. Sierran rivers flow generally westward, downriver. The Tai used to play the gambling game in a roundhouse, where the door faced east, upriver. The pot was placed between the players, away from the door, where it could be watched, with a fire between it and the door to make it hard for someone to grab the pot and run out the door. Grindstone Jim instinctively knew 'downriver' meant toward the side the pot was placed.

Still, he didn't show the bones in his hands. He kept on singing. Chris looked for a sign but saw none, so he and the whole team kept on singing too.

no weni, no weni, no weni, no wen

"Come on, show 'em. You heard the call," Grandma pointed now. "*We!*" Still Grindstone Jim did not show.

"Come on, toss 'em over," she shouted as she started to take out her drum and begin her side's gambling song, in anticipation. Slowly Grindstone Jim started exposing the bone hidden in his left hand, showing more and more of the white bone, until... the black band in the center clearly marked it as the dark bone. She had missed Grindstone Jim.

But Chris still had his bones hidden, as Grindstone Jim had not yet nodded his okay. Chris and Grindstone Jim sang stronger now as their team helped pound out the rhythm by clapping sticks together

no weni no weni no weni no we

"Come on, wannabe! Show your bones too!" Grandma demanded. "Shake 'em out!"

Chris was about to, but looked at Grindstone Jim. Grindstone Jim looked straight ahead, still singing the song

no winny no winny no winny no way

"Come on, wannabe! Don't look at him. I'm calling you!"

Chris sang on. He could see peripherally that Grindstone Jim was still staring straight ahead, as if to say "not yet, hold on a little longer...."

no winny no winny no winny no way

"I called you, wannabe son-bitch!"

Grandma was getting agitated now. "Show me your bones!" Grandma stood up into the center area between the two teams, waving her pointing stick.

Chris shouted back in self defense, laughing "I'm no wannabe, Grandma, I'm a half-breed Pawnee gambler." Grindstone Jim laughed and kept on singing, and Chris kept singing too, while the rest of their team pounded out the rhythm.

no weni no weni no weni no we

Grandma waved her arms wildly and began hitting Chris's head with her pointing stick. "Show me your bones, you wannabe Pawnee horse thief!"

Grindstone Jim quietly nodded to Chris, who shook the bones out of his hands onto the ground, showing... the black bone where she had called for the white. She had missed Chris also.

Grandma staggered back to her seat, defeated, sulking.

"Two sticks, Grandma, two sticks!" Rod Beckman shouted out. "Toss 'em over!"

Star called across to Chris, "Hey, Pawnee wannabe, now you know what it's like to be an Indian."

Grandma didn't make more calls. She seemed to become deflated. Her teammates carried on, missing more calls than they made. Before long the game was over. Grindstone Jim's team had won.

While they divvied up their winnings, Grindstone Jim chuckled to Chris, "That's an old Injun trick. When you wouldn't shake out the bones, she got mad. And when you get mad, you lose some of your power."

Marv came over to them with a big grin on his face.

"Where have you been, Marv? We were looking for you before the game," Chris hailed.

"I think I'd better take this boy down to the woodshed," Marvin said to everyone around, putting one strong arm around

Chris's waist and more-or-less marching him out of the handgame area, across the bridge over the creek and down toward the old barn. He didn't say a word as they walked. When they came to the barn door he held it open for Chris, then followed him in, shutting the door behind him.

Marv walked over to a shelf on the wall and pulled a bottle out of a brown paper bag.

"Ten years old, it says," he said, handing the bottle to Chris, "and I guarantee you it's at least a year or two older than that. We don't drink here except on special occasions – like this."

Chris took a swig from the bottle, wondering what was going to come next.

"Don't mess with Grandma! She's one tough lady!" Marv warned.

"She really lost it there, didn't she," Chris chuckled.

"Yeah," Marv smiled. "She really lost it at the end there." He laughed to himself, shaking his head as he pictured the scene again, then he got serious. "But don't mess with her. She's one tough lady. She's probably packing." He took a small sip from the bottle, to let what he had said sink in.

"What do you mean she's packing?"

"Packing. Packing a gun. She probably has her little revolver in that purse she carries around."

Grandma? Eighty or ninety – or whatever – year old Grandma, carrying a gun around in her purse?

Marv pulled out a Pall Mall cigarette and lit it before he continued. "She shot a guy at a handgame once. Over at the Lassen rancheria. Actually a couple different guys at different times, I think. She thought someone on the other team was messing with her so she pulled out her little pistol and shot him."

"What happened?"

"The fellow was hurt pretty bad. They took him to a doctor. I think he survived," Marv said nonchalantly.

"What happened to Grandma?"

"She was drunk. Her people talked to her and let her know what she did was wrong."

"Didn't the cops get involved?"

"Oh no, nobody called the cops. These people like to handle things themselves, you know. That was a long time ago. That guy never pressed charges, and he never messed with her again, that's for sure. She still drinks too much, and I'll bet she's still packing. That's why I'm telling you now, don't mess around with Grandma... unless you really know what you're doing. Just a friendly warning. Did old Grindstone Jim put you up to that?"

"Yeah, sort of," Chris admitted. "He said he knew we could get Grandma if I never showed until he nodded. I guess he knew what he was doing."

"Yeah, but did you know what you were doing?" Marv warned. "You don't want to rile up anybody here. Most folks are real friendly toward you now, especially after this thing with your brother disappearing and what not. But watch out for who your friends are, and what enemies you make, that's all. A little friendly advice."

He offered the bottle to Chris, and then took another swig himself.

"And now back to our regularly scheduled duties," Marv said, capping the bottle, putting it back into the brown bag next to the assorted turpentines and motor oils on the shelf in the old barn.

"Hey, wannabe." One from a group a tough looking young Indians called out to Chris as he walked back up the hill from the barn to the handgame area. "Come over here!"

'Careful,' Chris thought. 'No clear way to avoid them without obviously changing course.' He didn't want to be hassled but:...

"What's up?"

"Hey wannabe, come on over here." Several shirtless young men stood around an old Chevy with its doors open and rock'n roll music blasting out of a tape player. "Where'd you learn how to play handgame, anyway?" the one with a tattoo of a mountain lion on his biceps asked.

"Here and there. I've been playing for awhile," Chris carefully answered.

"Well," the young tough said, "we're gonna put our money on your side next time. But you better win, 'cause you know what? If you don't win, we're gonna get even!" They all laughed.

Chris laughed with them. "My luck's gonna run out sooner or later," he said.

"Well, you better be lucky next time, or we're gonna get even!" They all laughed again.

Chris headed back to his camp site by the creek. He found Robin unpacking her car next to his truck.

"Hi, Robin, I didn't see you drive up," he greeted her.

"I saw you playing the handgame over there, but when I parked my car and came back, the game was over and you were gone," she said.

"Yeah, Marv took me down to the barn to show me some things," Chris said.

"You know that Big Bob guy I was telling you about, the one that's starting up the casino near Ophir City?" Chris asked her.

"Yeah, what about him?"

"Well, he's dead. He was killed Thursday in the fire down near Ophir City," Chris said.

"You're kidding! What happened?"

Chris told her all he knew about the fire and how they found Big Bob in his cabin. She was as surprised as everybody, and suspicious. They talked more. Then he walked with her to the kitchen area to introduce her to the fried salmon, acorn soup, and camp coffee.

26

Winning and losing

The big guy wearing a black baseball cap backwards on his head approached Chris. Chris assumed he was Paiute because he wore a big T-shirt blazing the block-letter words

PYRAMID LAKE PAIUTE
AND PROUD OF IT!

"I'm Nevada Big Waters from over in Nixon. I saw you guys playing Grandma's team. You want to play some more? We'll challenge you. Where are you guys from?"

"We're from all over," Chris answered. "I'm Chris Livingstone, from the Bay Area for now at least," he said, rising and extending his hand. Big Waters had a huge hand and a hearty handshake. He looked young, at least a lot younger than Chris – maybe twenty-five or thirty. But Chris knew age was a hard thing to guess with some people.

"Jim's from over at Grindstone," Chris continued, nodding toward the old man on the bench. And I think Gunther's from over in Germany."

"I'm from right here," old Grindstone Jim corrected.

"This here is my wife Sally," Big Waters said proudly, introducing the small, pretty woman with a raptor feather in her hair, standing next to him.

"Why don't you get your people together," Big Waters said to Jim, "and we'll get another handgame going. How much money can you get up?"

"How much you need?" Grindstone Jim smiled. "We've got Grandma's money to finance us now."

"Don't worry, we plan to take that money of Grandma's back to Nevada with us, where it belongs," Big Waters responded with an earnest laugh. "We'll get up what we can then, and challenge you."

"Okay, I'll try to round up the rest of our team so we can get our donations together," Chris said. "We'll meet over in the handgame area."

Chris found Gunther and Rod Beckman. They were both up for another handgame. Marvin was busy preparing the salmon, and Vinnie was with the dancers. But with Robin and himself and the three others, they'd have a good team. But where was Robin? She was nowhere to be found.

The two teams lined up across from each other, with a small fire burning between them. Those who wanted to play hunkered or sat in the front row, and other bettors and supporters stood behind the players, to watch and help them sing. The pot was placed between the players, to one side, where all could watch it.

Big Waters won the.initial call of the bones, so they played with his big wooden Paiute bones, calling for the white bone, Nevada style.

Big Waters team included two of his cousins, both big Paiute men wearing baseball caps and sun glasses. Big Waters and Sally wore sunglasses too. Some gamblers feel it helps you hide the bones if the other team can't see your eyes.

Big Waters and Sally began singing their simple, beautifully haunting gambling song.

o wi o wi he yo
o wi o wi he-e yo
o wi o o-wi-he-yo

There were no words, just the sound of their two voices harmonizing their lucky syllables, somehow evoking memories of the beautiful desert mountains and springs around Pyramid Lake. Chris wanted them to keep singing this song forever – he didn't know whether to laugh or cry. He was entranced.

o wi o wi he yo
o wi o wi he-e yo
o wi o o-wi-he-yo

Big Waters and Sally sang on. Big Waters passed the bones to the two big gamblers squatting beside him, and they began to roll the bones, shifting them between their hands, keeping them hidden while rotating their fists about each other.

o wi o wi he yo
o wi o wi he-e yo
o wi o o-wi-he-yo

The hiders waited for the song to build its magic.

o wi o wi he yo
o wi o wi he-e yo
o wi o o-wi-he-yo
o,
o wi o wi he yo–

Both hiders were finally ready. They brought their fists out in front to be guessed.

Grindstone Jim still captained the Maidu team, and he made the first guess.

"Ho, *tep!*" he cried, pointing to the left, calling for the bones with the black stripe around the center.

"*Tep* you called?" asked Big Waters.

"Yup! Tep, over here. Toss 'em over."

The Nevada gamblers showed their white bones where Grindstone Jim had called for the dark.

"*We*! Should've just called for the white bone, like we do," joked Big Waters while he sang. "Then you would've won both of 'em. You owe us two sticks."

Grindstone Jim tossed over two counting sticks. The Nevada gamblers sang away, small, pretty dark haired Sally harmonizing with the three big Paiute men in baseball caps and shades.

o wi o wi he yo
o wi o wi he-e yo

The same two hiders hid the bones again, and brought their hands out.

Grindstone Jim studied the holders, looking for some clue. Finally he swooped his left hand to the left, this time calling "*we*!"

He was calling for both the hiders to be holding the white bones the same way as last time. He missed them both again. They had both switched!

"Two sticks!" Big Waters hollered.

Grindstone Jim tossed over two more counting sticks.

Grindstone Jim whispered to Chris. "You see any better than I do?" he asked.

"I've had the guy on the right both times," Chris answered, "but I've missed the guy on the left."

"Well, one set of bones is better than none," Grindstone Jim said. "Here, try to get 'em both." He handed Chris the pointing stick. "Go for the guy you know, and hope you get 'em both," old Jim advised.

Chris studied the hiders, but he didn't know what kind of clue he was seeking. He had a hunch to guess *right*, but he switched the hunch for the guy on the left, the one he'd been missing.

"Ho! Outside!" Chris shouted, holding the pointing stick horizontally. The hider on the right immediately threw over to

Chris the bones he was hiding, while the hider on the left flashed the dark bone in his right hand where Chris had hoped for the white bone. Chris should have followed Grindstone Jim's advice.

Big Waters and Sally kept singing.

o wi o wi he yo
o wi o wi he-e yo

Grindstone Jim tossed over another counting stick to pay for Chris's missed guess.

"*Demi*," old Jim said, pointing to the pile of un-won sticks in front of Big Waters. They'd lost five sticks already, the game was half over.

The counting sticks, or *demi*, must be won before they belong to either side. At the beginning of a game the sticks are usually separated into two equal piles of 'raw' counting sticks, one pile for each team, Some teams prefer to begin the game with one large pile of unwon sticks. It doesn't matter, because all losses are initially paid from the collection of unwon sticks. When won, the sticks become 'cooked', because in the old days they were tossed over the fire to the other side when won. The cooked sticks are kept separate from the uncooked sticks. If the raw sticks were initially divided, and one side runs out of uncooked sticks to pay for missed guesses, the other side tosses over whatever uncooked sticks remain.

Big Waters tossed the five demis over to Grindstone Jim, so Jim could pay for any more missed calls.

Big Waters and Sally kept singing their simple haunting tune.

o wi o wi he yo
o wi o wi he-e yo

"Ho!" Grindstone Jim threw the bones he held onto the ground in front of him in a dramatic call, trying to match the other side.

"Arrgh!" the hider on the opposing side groaned in defeat, throwing his bones across to Grindstone Jim.

"All right! Let's go!" cried Chris, trying to energize the team.

Grindstone Jim started singing an old Maidu gambling song.

> *a tun na weo wene*
> *a tun na weo wen ne*
> *he yana hana weo wen ne*
> *he yana hana weo we ne*

It was an old song that everyone on the team seemed to know, more or less, and they all sang it loudly, if not in tune.

> *a tsun na we yo wene*
> *a tsun na we yo wen ne*
> *he yana hana we yo wene*
> *he yana hana we yo wene*

Big Waters pointed to the five uncooked sticks now sitting in front of Grindstone Jim.

"*Demi*," he said, and Grindstone Jim tossed the uncooked counting sticks back over to Big Waters.

Grindstone Jim handed one pair of bones to his chauffeur Gunther, and kept a pair himself. When he brought his hands back out with the hidden bones, he waved his arms freely from side to side and swayed his body with the music, dancing in place.

When Gunther finally brought out his hands, Big Waters made his call immediately.

"*Tep*! *Bewi*!" Big Waters shouted, clapping his hands and holding them.

"What does that mean? Make your call with your stick!" Grindstone Jim hollered out as he kept singing and hiding.

"*Tep*" Big Waters repeated, pointing his stick downward.

"I thought you Nevada boys were going to call for the white bones!" old Jim protested, throwing his bones over to Big Waters.

"That's unless I call for the black bones, like I did now. I held my hands to show *inside*," Big Waters explained.

"Well, use your stick to point when you call, so we know what you mean. We don't speak Paiute over here," Grindstone Jim growled.

Big Waters had caught Grindstone Jim, but he'd missed Gunther. Big Waters tossed one of the uncooked sticks over to Grindstone Jim.

a tun na we yo wene
a tun na we yo wen ne
he yana hana we yo wene
he yana hana we yo wene

Gunther brought his hands out, and Big Waters immediately made his call.

Ho! *We,* " he said holding the white bone in his right hand. "You'd better put a black bone in this hand, or your song's over!" He caught Gunther this time.

The game went on that way. Big Waters' team won two or three sticks for every one that Chris's team won.

o wi o wi he-e yo
o wi o, o wi he- yo

Jim was soon down to his last stick, while Big Waters team held both sets of bones.

"We'll take that stick, game's over, we won," said Big Waters.

"No, let's play out the last stick," pleaded Jim.

"No way! If you guess both wrong again, you have no way to pay us all that you owe," Big Waters countered.

He was right. Those were the 'house rules' here. The game was over.

Chris got up to stretch his legs while Big Waters' team and their backers gathered around their Captain to collect their winnings.

'Well, you can't win them all. I'll have to avoid those toughs, if I can,' Chris sighed as he reached into his pocket to pull out the last cigarette from his pack. He didn't really smoke much, except at big-times, when he'd bring along a few packs to have something when people tried to bum from him. It was a thing he had learned from his brother as a way of meeting people at a big-time. But now he felt like a smoke.

A big sack of herbs plopped down on the earth at Chris's feet.

"Here, this is better for you!"

Chris looked up to see Marvin.

"This is special Indian tobacco," Marvin continued. "The only place it grows is up by Tree Lake. I try to get up there every year to pick a bunch. The Old People used to pick it regularly, but the patch is getting smaller every year now. You've got to pick it to make it grow. But sometimes I get stuck in town and can't get up there."

"Where's Tree Lake?" Chris casually thought he might like to go there himself some time, to gather a little tobacco, to help the patch spread again.

"It's northeast of here a ways, over by Clear Creek. The patch is on the southeast side of the lake. Not much left of it now. It used to be spread out more." Marvin was quiet for a moment, then continued.

"It's a special holy place for the Old People, up there. But now logging roads cut through the area, and fishermen and weekend warriors go up there, and sometimes trash-out the place."

A holy lake of the Mountain Maidu! Could this be the place where people used to dive for power? The place whose location Tom never revealed to him, nor to Robin?

"Is that the lake with the old dead tree in the center?" Chris tried to conceal his excitement.

"Right, that's the one. Root-snag Lake, some people call it. You've been there then?"

"No, not yet," Chris said, "but I've heard a lot about it from the stories.... Maybe we could post some 'No Fishing' signs around the lake to keep it from getting trashed."

"Nah, that wouldn't work. Forest Service would raise a stink, and most people would ignore the signs anyway. Wouldn't keep out the hunters either, but I don't think they're the problem. But roll up some of this *pani*, or stick it in your pipe. I think you'll like it. Maybe it'll help you in the next handgame – looks like you need it!" Marv chided. "I've gotta go check the barbecue pit now."

"Thanks Marvin," Chris said. "Thanks a lot!"

Chris couldn't wait to tell Robin what he had learned from Marv. He found her coming up the hill as he headed back to camp.

"You missed the handgame. Ever find your power lake?" he asked her, like a kid brother holding out on what he already knew. He knew she had probably been up here asking all the older people about the lake.

"I was talking to Leonard," she said, "asking him about the lake. He said he didn't know anything about it. But he'd heard about a similar place, but got a little vague about it."

"I found your lake," Chris said with a smile.

"What?"

"I found your lake. Tree Lake. This tobacco comes from there." Chris showed her the tobacco in the paper bag.

"Where did you get this?"

"Marvin gave it to me. He just dropped it in my lap," Chris replied. "He said he goes up there every year."

"Marvin! I haven't talked with him yet. We've got to go there," Robin said.

"Monday, after the handgames."

"Tomorrow. You've already played your handgames," Robin argued.

"There's still more handgames! And you've missed them all so far," Chris countered.

"There're always more handgames!"

27

The world below this world

Once they knew its name, Tree Lake was easy to locate on a Forest Service map of the area, What wasn't so easy was to find the right road to it. The map indicated a maze of back roads and logging trails leading up to the lake from both the north and the south. It looked like a decent road to the lake went up along Clear Creek from the west. Marv had mentioned Clear Creek. That must be the right approach.

What the map didn't show was the terrain – high mountainous country, crossed with many streams and large creeks, each with its own canyons, small and large. What looks like only a few miles on a map might turn into several hours or a full day, when the realities of the terrain become apparent.

Still, if weekend warriors could reach the lake as Marvin had said, it couldn't be too difficult a road. Chris and Robin agreed the best approach from here seemed to be from the southwest.

They planned to build a primitive sweat, and to camp at the lake a day or two. Robin intended to swim to the hole in the lake to dive for power as the Old People used to do. She said if nobody could find the pain she felt within her head, she'd have to find the power to get it out herself.

Chris wanted to camp in the woods, to sweat, swim and fast, to try to figure things out before getting more deeply involved in anything. If he found a little power here too, all the better.

After several wrong turns onto logging roads not marked on the map, Chris and Robin finally followed the rutted road through the pines, made a final sharp turn, and pulled onto a big meadow filled with a light blue haze of new lupine blossoms that surrounded the sparkling bluer waters of a sub-alpine mountain lake. At its center, what appeared to be a twisted leaf-less tree came out of the water. From the shore Chris couldn't tell if this was part of some old dead tree growing on an island in the lake, or part of a root coming out of the water.

But this was definitely the right place. Chris found the tobacco gathering ground on the southeast side of the lake just where Marvin said it was – a small patch, covering probably less than a quarter acre. Although he didn't need any more tobacco, since he still had plenty in the bag Marvin had given him, he picked the leaves of a couple plants in a symbolic gesture. "They need to be picked for the patch to grow," Marvin had said.

Chris talked silently to the spirits of the place, and buried a small quartz crystal he carried with him for luck – a gift for the spirits behind this place.

Chris and Robin walked around the lake's shore, looking for the right spot to build the sweathouse. Chris found a big level spot by the west side of the lake.

He had helped build a sweat lodge before, in preparation for a Bear Dance. Although he'd never built one by himself, he basically knew what to do. He needed some willow branches, young enough to bend without breaking, old enough to be long and strong. He began hiking around the water's edge looking for willow. Robin wandered around gathering firewood.

He found a good-sized patch where a small stream emptied into the lake, and started hacking away at a long tough branch with his Swiss army knife. The branch was too old, too tough and it didn't want to yield easily.

He was fighting the willow for a few minutes, and accidentally jabbed his hand with the knife before he realized... this was all wrong. He hadn't asked the willow, or the spirit behind the willow, for its branches. He was like any other white man, just coming in, cutting things down and taking whatever he wanted. Especially here, by this special lake, by this stream, he should act differently. The tiny bits of Pawnee within him still lived. He would behave better now, he resolved. He could have been struck down by a rattlesnake. He apologized to the willow for hurting it, and explained what he wanted, and why.

"We would like to use your branches to build a sweat lodge," he said. "We would like to cleanse ourselves, and to learn more of the ways of this place." He reached into his pocket to find some kind of gift to leave. Finding no more crystals there, nor cigarettes, he pulled out the colorful bandanna he had used for hiding bones in the handgame, and he tucked that into the earth next to the willow.

Whether the willow branches cut more easily after he'd made his offering, or whether he had just refined his technique for cutting with his small knife, Chris soon had eight thin poles – enough to build the new lodge.

"We're going to need eight holes dug, each about a foot or more deep, and spaced equally around in a circle," he told Robin. "I don't have a lot of blankets with me for covering it, so we'll have to keep it small, no more than six or eight feet in diameter."

Chris kicked out a circle of approximate size, then sat down in it. "This is pretty good, but we can make it even a little smaller. We've gotta make sure we'll have enough covers to seal it up real good.

"And we're gonna want to have the opening facing east or southeast, toward the rising sun." Chris glanced at the sky and toward the east, trying to figure where that point would be. He took one of the willow poles, stood in the rough center of the circular area, and, using the pole like a huge pencil and rotating his body in place, marked a more precise circle in the earth.

"We'll want our opening about here,' he said, "so we'll put the first pole here next to it." He marked the spot with a rock. Then he took another rock, went across to the opposite side of the circle, sighted a line through the center of the circle to the first rock, and put another stone down at the spot opposite the first.

"We'll put the next pole here." Then he sighted a point on the circle between the first two, and marked another spot. He continued until he'd marked all the spots along the circle.

"We need to dig these down deep enough so the poles won't come out when we bend them over."

"What do you mean *we*, white man?" Robin smiled.

Chris continued unfazed. "And let's be sure to talk to the Earth before we puncture her skin. We don't want to hurt you, Mother, we just want to build a nice sweat lodge for this place, like the people of old used to do." Chris talked like that to Robin and himself, and to whatever might be listening out there.

They built the stick frame in this manner – talking to trees, talking to dirt, talking to the lake. If they were in the city behaving this way, people would think they were crazy, and the psycho-police would lock them up, put them on Thorazine and place them in front of a TV. But the city itself was the crazy place – in this place talking to inanimate objects was the right and proper behavior.

"I don't think the Old People built their sweat lodges this way, not around here anyway," Robin critiqued as she eyed the structure. "They sweated in their roundhouses, not tents."

"That's probably true, but I saw a traveling Pawnee build one like this at a bear dance a couple years back. It worked great. Of course it was bigger than this thing's going to be." Chris eyed the small circle on the ground skeptically. Why had he built it so small?

"They had sweats going down by the creek, all day and night, all that weekend," Chris continued. "They do it every year now. The first year anyone who wanted could take a sweat, as long as they stayed in for the whole ceremonial round. But last year's bear dance, some traditional men wouldn't go near the place, because women had also sweated in there the year before."

"They were freaked out by men and women sweating together?"

"More than that the men and women sweated together," Chris said, "but that the women sweated in that same place at all! It wouldn't matter if the women sweated separately, this guy considered it bad luck just to have women sweat in the same house that men used. Even though the house was more of a tent, and the frame had been open and exposed to the weather all year, he wouldn't go near it, he was afraid he would get sick."

"Yeah, right, like women carry some kind a disease."

"Right, they can certainly get to you some times," Chris joked, as he thought 'This Robin is no traditional Maidu woman.'

"Well, I'm not sure I'd want to use any sweathouse after a man used it. Men can be so... you know...."

Chris didn't know how to respond to that one, but she was still smiling so he said nothing.

"And in view of that fact, it's only right that I should get to sweat first," Robin continued, "Because men can be so messy.

And because you apparently don't have any qualms about sweating in a woman's sauna."

"Wait a minute. This isn't a woman's sauna. It's not even built yet and I've already lost control of it," Chris moaned.

When the poles were vertically in place and tamped down in their holes, it was merely a matter of bending opposing poles to the center and tying them together, forming a dome-like structure.

Chris spread blankets across the willow ribs to complete the structure.

"It looks a little small," mused Robin.

"Yeah, well you do the best you can with the materials at hand," replied Chris.

"No, I mean it's fine, it's just right, for me anyway. There's no way we're both going to fit in there at the same time, especially if you put a bunch of hot rocks in there."

"Well, we'll see how many rocks it takes to heat it up. I think it'll be okay."

It was now late afternoon, and the sun was below the near-by hills in the west. Chris and Robin wandered along the shore of Tree Lake looking for stones to use to heat the little sweat lodge.

It's important to use the right kind of rock in a sweat. River rock or other stones with pockets of water vapor in them can explode like a little bomb when heated for a long time in a hot fire. They picked out volcanic rocks a little bigger than large grapefruit. These were perfect for their intended use.

Two by two, Chris and Robin carted the rocks over to the site of their sauna.

After several trips they had enough stones collected. They piled the rocks into the center of the fire pit, and built up a good fire around them.

Through the hours Chris fed wood to the crackling fire as he and Robin talked about life, and traded stories and songs.

Finally, when the stones began to glow slightly, Chris used his shovel to carry the rocks one-by-one into the small sweat lodge.

With four hot rocks in the sweathouse, it was obvious there would be room for only one person at a time.

"You're right, with the hot stones in there there's only enough room for one person," Chris told Robin. "So go for it. I'll take care of the stones for you, at least for the first round."

"Okay," she said. "I'll tend the stones for you next."

Robin took off her clothes as if she were just slipping off her jacket, and crawled into the small sweathouse. Chris pulled a blanket down over the entry.

"More heat!" she demanded.

Chris took a small coffee pot from his truck and filled it with lake water. He got on his knees and poked his head into the sweathouse.

"Here, try some water on the rocks," he said as he splashed some water onto the rock by the door.

"Whoa!" Robin cried out.

A cloud of hot steam filled the small tent-like structure. Chris backed out instinctively..

"All right! Close that door!" Robin commanded.

"You all right?" Chris asked.

"I'm fine, it's perfect now."

Robin started chanting slowly to herself.

> *yong gong goi yong gong goi*
> *yong gong goi yong-gong-go!*

Chris tended the fire. He listened to Robin singing her song. He thought of his brother, and about Robin.

He had never heard this strange song Robin sang. He took a stick and began hitting it onto a rock to beat out a rhythm to accompany her.

> *yong gong goi yong gong goi*
> *yong gong goi yong-gong-go!*

"More heat!" Robin finally hollered. 'Bring in another stone."

Chris dug out another hot rock from the fire and carried it on his shovel to the entrance.

He pulled open the blanket door. "Where do you want this?" Chris asked.

"Put it over here," Robin pointed.

All Chris could see was her bare arm pointing next to the doorway. Chris carefully placed the hot rock on the dirt floor.

He sprinkled a small amount of water on the new hot stone, then backed out and sealed the blanket door as the steam enveloped the tiny structure."

"Whoa!" Robin cried out again, "No more heat! That's enough!"

After a while Robin started singing again. She sang several rounds and variations of the same song.

After maybe half an hour she suddenly opened the blanket door and ran naked into the lake, disappearing under the water for several seconds.

At first Chris thought she was swimming for the center of the lake, and he got up to run in after her. Then she reappeared and swam back toward shore.

She swam like a fish, or more like a dolphin, using her body like a fin, with minimal arm strokes. She waded the last few feet to the shore and stepped out of the water.

"This feels great!" she cried out as she stretched along the shore line.

Chris studied her form through the flickering glow of the fire. Clouds of steam poured off her skin.

"It's great that we're not, like, involved with each other, that we can just be friends like this, no hassles," she finally said.

Chris didn't know quite how to take that.

"Well," he justified, "we're both on some kind of power journey now. I don't quite know what I'm looking for and I'm not sure you do either. For me, it has to do with the handgame.

"And when you're on a power search," he continued, "you abstain from sex, or you'll get distracted and weakened. That's one thing the old-timers always agreed upon."

He appraised Robin's form. "But I can still appreciate beauty when I see it! I mean, your swimming form, that is. You swim like a dolphin."

"I love the water," she said simply. "But now it's your turn. You need to sweat yourself."

Chris carried the old stones out of the sweathouse on his shovel, and carried in a batch of new hot ones. He filled the pot with fresh lake water, sprinkled some on the rocks, and crawled into the small tent. Robin sealed the blanket door behind him.

Inside, the little sweat lodge was totally dark except for the faint glow of the stones. Chris poured more water on the hot rocks, and steam quickly saturated the air.

Sweat soon covered Chris. At first the heat burned his lungs, and he got down low to periodically breathe some cooler air. Soon it had cooled enough, or he had acclimated enough, that he thought he could sit upright and breathe normally.

"Whoa!" he hollered, as he bent down low to breathe the cooler air again.

When he could sit up and breathe again, he remembered the song he learned in Pitch-off Mountain Canyon and began singing.

Wo-nomi mo-mi, Wo-nomi mom
Wo-nomi mo-mi, Wo-nomi mom

He sang several rounds and variations of this song, which soon turned into a handgame song he'd heard somewhere.

windum no we, heni no windem we
heni no we, heni no windem we

"What are you doing singing a gambling song in there?" Robin hollered at him.

"What do you think I'm doing? I'm a handgame player. These songs just pop into my head."

After sometime Chris could take no more heat, and he too dashed naked from the sweat and jumped into the lake.

The icy water instantly felt invigorating. He quickly pulled himself to the shore and got out. The night was cool, but Chris felt flush with warmth.

Chris and Robin alternated sweats and swims throughout the night. Robin sang her medicine songs and Chris sang his gambling songs.

When the sky was light, but before the sun rose above the eastern ridgeline, Robin ran out of the sweat lodge.

"Let's go!" she shouted, diving into the lake and swimming out toward the center.

The old-timers always swam in pairs when they sought power at the lake. One of the swimmers might find the power and become a doctor. The other, who helped the one whom the lake gave the power, would at least have good luck throughout his life.

Chris jumped into the lake and swam after her.

The lake felt frigid. Chris hadn't had the luxury of being the last one to sweat.

Once in the water and away from shore, the island in the center seemed even farther away than ever. Chris doggedly swam on, trying to keep pace with Robin.

Finally, he made it out to the root-snag tree, following Robin. Chris treaded water while he caught his breath. He hadn't swum this far in a long time without the aid of fins.

Robin looked at him as if to say "Well?" then rolled forward and swam straight down in the water.

Not quite ready, Chris took a lungful of air and dove after her.

He swam downward, through clear bluish water. The tree now looked like an ancient serpent reaching toward infinity in the darkness beneath. He saw beams of light dancing through the water. He couldn't see Robin. The pressure on his ears became intensely painful, and he needed to breathe. He turned around and headed back to the surface, where he rested, hanging onto the old tree snag.

He waited for some time for Robin to reappear. He waited for what seemed like minutes, when she popped to the surface wearing just her smile.

"Robin!"

She tilted her head first to one side, then the other, and kept smiling.

They swam in silence back to the beach by the little sweat lodge. Robin flew out of the water like a penguin. Chris barely made it back. He struggled out onto the little rocky beach on all fours, like an old dog, panting.

She said nothing, she just kept smiling.

Finally she said, "I think my headache's gone."

"Tell me what you saw."

"Amazing," Robin said. "I swam down and down, and came to a cave in the water down there, like a big lava tube. In the tube I could see a patch of dim light. I didn't feel at all like I was out of air. So I swam way back into the tube toward the light. Luminous, frog-like beings swam with me. At the light spot I popped out into a little pond. The light was like a full moon shining through a layer of clouds. Pebbles of a hundred different colors, like the inside of abalone shells, lined the shore of the pond. Something told me to take a pebble and leave. It seemed easy to get in there, but hard to get back, like something pulling at me. There's another world down there," Robin added.

She opened her palm to show Chris a small, flat, dark rock. "It was rainbow-hued down there. Now it's just a little black stone."

"You can give it to me if you don't want it," Chris volunteered.

"No way!"

Chris remembered an old story.

"One old man used to fly to hidden places in his dreams. He spoke of a place in the desert east of here, where there used to be a huge lake, far larger than Pyramid Lake is today. Ancient beach lines around all the mountains there mark its shorelines. He traveled beneath that ancient lake, deep within the earth, to a world under this world. He found water-washed stones the hue of ten rainbows there – like the pebble you brought back. Hold on to that pebble. It's your luck."

"We must make an offering to thank the spirits of this place," Robin said.

The sun, who watches everything, sped across the sky. Morning turned to late afternoon, and soon long fingers of shadow began to reach toward the lake. From the cracks and crannies high above the lake, some spirits, *kukini*, watched these strange neo-Indians cavorting about. They watched them hang feather offerings, *yakoli*, on the bushes around the shore-line. The kukini listened to their unintelligible prayers.

'What kind of tribe are these? What are they doing here?' they wondered.

The kukini heard the two pray under a reddening sky. A sweet smell reached the high cliff face – tobacco, *pani*, from Chris' pipe. Attracted to the pani, the spirits flew down from the cliff and fluttered around, unseen by the two humans. Wind rustled the leaves of nearby trees.

Robin said, "We've had a long day. I've got to get some sleep."

"Me too," said Chris. He spread out their sleeping bags.

Soon Chris snored away. But strange dreams came to Robin – she heard music, Indian songs, all night long.

weni heni we hu we hu!,
weni heni we

Chris awoke as sunlight touched the trees around the lake. He sat up and looked around. Robin's sleeping bag was empty.

He walked along the shoreline, enjoying the morning air. Part of a handgame melody, probably a piece of some song he once heard but had since forgotten, popped into his head, and rolled round and round.

tai we, tai we

tai-we tai we

tai we

Near the creek a small plant with a bright green top like a young carrot waved in a slight breeze. The song rolling through his brain took on new words.

lucky root–

lucky root–

lucky root, lucky root

lucky root–

He got down on his knees to look at the plant. He sang to it in his mind.

lucky root–

lucky root–

lucky root, lucky root

lucky root–

"Pull me up," the little plant said to Chris. "I want to come with you. I can help you win the handgame."

The song kept rolling through Chris's mind as he dug the dirt out around the root. He knew it would mean bad luck if he broke the root. He gave a slight tug on the wild carrot top, and the root slipped easily out of the ground. It was thin and white, smaller than a little finger, and smelled something like celery root.

"I want to take you with me," Chris said, this time aloud. "I want to use you in the handgame like the old-timers did."

"Take me," the plant said, aloud also. The voice startled Chris. "Wrap me up. Keep me warm. I can help you."

Chris talked to the spirit of the mountain. He was starting to think like an Indian.

"Help me," he said. "I want to take some of your grass to keep my lucky root warm. You can be my lucky grass too."

He left a gift of some tobacco from the bunch Marv had given him.

Chris gathered a few handfuls of long grass while the gambling song circled in his mind. He wrapped the grass carefully around the lucky root, brought his pumi back to camp, and put it in a small pouch in the pack that held the rest of his gambling gear.

Robin was nowhere to be seen. He started to look for her when he heard her shriek. He looked toward the source of the shriek, and saw her way up in a fir tree, laughing and crying, naked.

"Robin," he hollered, "come down,"

She began to howl like a coyote, then screamed like an eagle. When Chris approached she made chirping noises. Something was seriously wrong with Robin – she had become possessed by spirits, *kukini*, and couldn't control them.

Chris ran to the tree. "Please, Robin, come down."

Robin shrieked at him again. Chris climbed the tree and finally managed to get her down. She was all scratched up and crying.

'Now she's really lost it,' Chris thought, 'and I've gotten into water way over my head.'

"Chill!" Chris ordered.

Robin began laughing hysterically as Chris tried to dress her and comb her hair.

"Take control. You've got to get control of that spirit inside you!" he commanded. "Sing if you can."

Robin began singing over and over a dance song about the gray squirrel, sowali. she'd heard at the big-time.

> *so wa wa lemi*
> *so-o wa wa loli*
> *so wa wa lemi*
> *so wa wa lo*

This seemed to calm her.

Chris managed to clean up the camp site while they both sang. Finally he said good bye to the lake, and got Robin out of there. Hopefully she would snap out of it soon. He still had to get her and her car back to the city.

28

A week on the hard

What a let-down to come back to the city! Chris should have stayed in the mountains, but he was used to working, and didn't know what to do with his free time. While Robin tried to get control of her spirit, Chris decided to haul out his boat for annual maintenance and a new coat of bottom paint. The local boat yard wasn't busy, and he was able to get the boat out of the water and 'on the hard' the same day.

Having the boat to work on, and the time to do it, kept Chris mindlessly busy all week from early morning until after sunset. He washed and wet-sanded the hull, and put two coats of anti-fouling paint on the bottom. His boat had only a little exterior woodwork, but each handrail and companionway-slat and other piece of trim had to be scraped and sanded and coated with several layers of varnish. Each layer took a day to dry.

Chris wanted to take off with Robin Friday morning to head up to the Bear Dance. But when he got the boat back in the water Thursday afternoon, he noticed a minor problem.

It was late Friday afternoon by the time he and Robin finally got out of town, and that put them right in the middle of rush hour. But Chris was happy to be getting out of the city, going up to the Bear Dance and camping out in the woods again.

Robin seemed to be in full control of her spirits, and was again herself. But she was now possessed, and strove to learn all she could of power spots and spirit helpers.

It had been a long week, and now it was a long drive. Chris felt worn down from dealing with Robin, and worn out and sore from all the physical labor he had been doing. His legs felt cramped from the long ride in his old truck.

It was nearly dark when they passed Ophir City, and almost ten o'clock when they reached the upper part of the Feather River canyon near the Quincy Y.

He remembered a nearby hot spring, and slowed down to look for the exact spot to pull off the highway.

Chris recognized the spot at the last minute and pulled over.

He and Robin scrambled down the short dark trail to the small concrete hot pools alongside the Feather River.

They both slipped off their clothes and eased into the hot water.

"Oh, this feels great!" Chris sighed loudly. "This is exactly what I need!"

It was only then he noticed someone else soaking in the adjacent cooler pool right next to them, near the river.

"Oh, sorry," Chris said, apologizing for intruding on this stranger's peace and quiet.

· "Right. But that's okay, might as well meet here as stumble over each other later trying to set up camp in the dark at the Bear Dance." The voice sounded familiar. It was Marvin!

"Marv! What are you doing here?" Chris greeted.

"I'm soaking in a hot bath, what does it look like I'm doing? It's been a tough week."

"Well, it's funny to bump into you here," Chris said.

"Right," Marv drawled. "But not half as funny as the last time I came up here, last winter. I stopped in at Woody's bar up top there to have a few beers, then came down here to soak up and clear my head up a little, if you know what I mean."

"Right!"

"I came down here just like you two now, except I came down the easy trail from the bar. I got out of my clothes and into that tub you're in now before I noticed this other big fellow soaking in this tub I'm in now."

"Just like we stumbled into you."

"Right," Marv continued. "It took me a while to realize something was funny with this other fellow, then suddenly he steps up and I see this big buck getting out of the tub, big antlers like this on his head," Marv said stretching his arms. "He got up and just glared at me for awhile, like I had interrupted his private bath. Then he high-tailed it up the bank toward the road, the way you just came down."

"Your kidding," Chris said, "You interrupted a deer taking a soak in the hot spring?"

"Right," Marv said. "If it was red bats, I'd know it was the beer. But it was a deer, a big buck!"

They talked deer stories and hot-spring stories, and Marvin told jokes, as they all relaxed in the hot water by the cold rushing river. They left the hot spring late. Well after midnight they finally rolled down the little road that led to the Bear Dance grounds.

Chris and Robin drove up the hill to find a place to camp away from the majority of other campers and their noise. Marvin followed in his own pickup.

They could hear the drums and singing of a handgame chant coming from the old roundhouse.

Chris wanted to get down there to the handgames, but Robin was tired from the long drive and the soak in the hot spring. She spread her sleeping bag next to the truck to sleep under the stars.

Chris and Marv wandered down the hill toward the sound of the drums and singing. Another big-time was beginning, another Bear Dance, another new year.

29

At the Bear Dance

Saturday morning Big Waters' two cousins challenged Chris to a handgame.

"You guys got any players here?" they asked.

"You guys got any of Grandma's money left?" Chris countered.

Would-be players slowly gathered around a ramada next to the dance ground. Chris was the de-facto captain of the team this game, and the responsibility left him with a bit of nervousness. Hundreds of dollars were in this pot, this was a serious duel with worthy opponents.

These big Paiutes looked tough, like they were made of stone. They all wore blue jeans, baseball caps and – a sure sign of serious Indian gamblers – sunglasses!

Everyone here was on an unspoken search for power. A win would yield a boost in prestige, respect, and personal power.

Robin wasn't with Chris. Where was she this time? He had Marvin and Vinnie and Rod Beckman and a few other players on his team, but he wanted to get Robin into a game.

The game was not long underway when Chris heard a small voice in his left ear.

"Let me call. I can *see*," said the voice. The voice belonged to a small black-haired Paiute boy about twelve years old.

"You don't have a bet out, you're not in the game," Chris said. This was a heavy game, and Chris didn't need to be distracted by a kid! Who was this kid anyway, and whose side he was he on? After all, it was probably this kid's relatives Chris was playing against now.

"Let me call them, I can see," the kid insisted. Chris didn't answer him, but kept him in his mind. 'Is this some kind of Paiute trick? Who is this little guy?' Chris wondered.

The first time Chris called the bones, he called his own hunch and missed both ways. Two sticks lost, just like that!

"Let me call them. I can see them," the kid said again.

"OK, where are they now?" Chris asked.

"*Mowi* – on the inside," the kid replied.

Immediately, Chris moved to guess *mowi* to test this form of hunch, but before he could, both hiders on the other side put their hands behind themselves and switched the bones. Maybe the kid was on to something!

"OK, where are they now? – but whisper to me, don't talk out loud," Chris quietly commanded.

"Guess outside now," the kid whispered. "They both switched them."

"Huh! Outside!" – Chris grunted out before the other team had a chance to switch them again, gesturing by holding out his fist with the thumb and little finger pointing outward. The big

Paiute holders on the other side shook their heads in surprise and disgust, and tossed the bones over to Chris. This time Chris had caught both of them!

Chris quietly tested this young helper's hunches throughout the game. Whenever he or one of his partners guessed, they were usually wrong. Whenever Chris followed the young boy's hunches, he won.

He eventually let the boy tell him where to guess each time, and his team walked away winners.

'Thank you little pumi,' Chris thought.

After the game, Chris joined Marv at the barbecue pit. It was now loaded with green wood – dozens of oak and pine logs – but wasn't yet burning. They talked awhile, then headed over to the outdoor kitchen to get some coffee.

Where is Robin? Chris wondered.

Nevada Big Waters challenged Chris's team to another handgame, and the betting list was soon closed. Marvin got down on his haunches to make up the pot, matching one's and five's and ten's and twenty's with Big Waters' wife Sally. Robin was nowhere in sight.

"We'll use our bones," Big Waters said.

Big Waters, like most Paiutes, played with big wooden bones that couldn't be completely concealed in a small fist.

"No, let's use our bones, yours are too big," Chris argued. "We like to call for the black bone here, too," Chris added.

"We like to call for the white bone. We like to play with our bones. Let me look at your bones."

Chris tossed over his set of lucky bones. They were made from deer leg, about the size of a woman's thumb. The two dark bones were marked by a single piece of electrical tape around the center.

Big Waters examined Chris's bones and tossed them back to him.

"Okay, let's match for the bones and the start, then," Big Waters volunteered. "Whoever wins the match, we play their way with their bones."

"Okay, I'll match you," Chris said.

"All right, call 'em," Big Waters said as held out his closed hands.

"This way," Chris said instinctively, holding up the black-banded bone in his right hand and the white bone in his left. He called them right.

"All right!" Marvin cried out approvingly. "We use our bones!"

Chris noticed an ancient-looking beetle clinging to his shirt cuff. He had seen this strange bug before, at Pancho's place. This time somehow Chris knew he was going to win.

Someone on Chris's team immediately started up a song before Chris could start the one he had been hearing in his mind.

yu ku tai yo-weni, yu ku tai yo-weni

"All right!" Marvin cried out, and he too started singing the song. Chris rolled the bones in his hands and soon joined in.

yu ku tai yo-weni, yu ku tai yo-weni
kau-wau-wau yoweni kau-wau-wau yo-weni
yu ku-u tai!

Chris took one set of bones himself and passed the other pair to Marvin to hide. Chris tried to empty his mind as he rolled the bones around in his hands.

yu ku tai yo-weni, yu ku tai yo-weni
kau-wau-wau yoweni kau-wau-wau yo-weni
yu ku-u tai!

Chris felt the bones hidden in his hands. With one thumb he could feel the hollow smooth white bone, while his other thumb felt the banded black bone. At some point when the team began to find the song, Chris brought his hands out to be guessed. Marvin did the same.

Big Waters made his call instantly.

"*Tep*," he called, with his index finger pointing downward, to call a 'heart shot' – both black bones on the inside, between the two holders.

Chris looked hopefully over to Marvin while still singing the song. Marvin looked back and shrugged his shoulders. Big Waters had guessed them both. Chris and Marvin tossed the bones over to Big Waters' side.

Big Waters hit his big round deerskin drum and began singing his gambling song.

BOOM!

o- o-ho   *BOOM*   *o i o-ho*

BOOM

o o-ho!

BOOM!

o i he ha he ha!

o o-ho o i he ha! he ha!

o o-ho o i he ha! he ha!

o o-ho o i he ha! he ha!

o o-ho o i he ha! he ha!

Big Waters passed one pair of bones to his cousin Roy and hid one pair himself. As soon as they brought their hands out Chris called them immediately.

"HO! Outside!" he called, clenching his pointing stick in the center and holding it out horizontally. He didn't know why, but it seemed the right call. Big Waters and his cousin looked at each other, and their song abruptly stopped. Chris had guessed them both too.

Big Waters tossed both sets of bones over to Chris, who started up a new song.

(spiritedly)

he - yo he yo

he - yo he yo

he yo he-e yo

he - yo he yo

"All right!" crowed Marvin. This was an old Tai song he knew well.

Chris passed one set of bones to Vinnie and the other set to Marv, then picked up his clapper stick and joined in the rhythm.

They sang and sang, and when Vinnie and Marvin had finally both brought their hands out to be called, Big Waters hollered out his call.

"*Tep!*," he cried, holding his guessing stick horizontally, calling 'black-bone outside' also.

Marv and Vinnie looked at each other and stopped singing.

"Gee," cried Marvin, "we were just getting warmed up."

He and Vinnie tossed their bones over to Big Waters, who had already started singing his same old song.

BOOM!
o– o-ho   o--o-ho
BOOM!
o- o-ho!
o i he ha! he ha!
(faster)
o- o-ho o i he ha he ha
o- o-ho o i he ha he ha
o- o-ho o i he ha he ha
o- o-ho o i he ha he ha

Big Waters handed one set of bones to Sally and kept the other to hide himself. When Sally brought her hands out from under her shawl Chris saw a shadow cross one of her hands, and figured he knew how to guess her. When Big Waters brought his hands out, the left one facing Chris looked darker also.

"Ho! Tep," Chris shouted out, holding his pointing stick in his left hand and sweeping it leftward. Sally stopped singing and looked helplessly at Big Waters. Big Waters shook his head and tossed the bones over. Sally handed the other bones to Big Waters, who then tossed them over to Chris too.

"Good call, Chris," praised Marvin. "Just the way I would've guessed 'em," he laughed.

Big Waters shook his head back and forth.

Marvin started prancing on his haunches, singing his song.

a wanda no, a hai wa lo
a hai wa li a so-mi ko
a hai wa li, a so-mi ko

The team started picking up the song, and occasionally Marvin threw in some variations,

I sold my cow to play handgame
a hai wa li a so-mi ko
a hai wa li a so-mi ko
I lost my cow, I bet my wife
a hai wa li a so-mi ko
a hai wa li a so-mi ko

Chris passed one pair of bones to Marv and held one pair himself. He and Marvin used to have some good luck with this song. Chris waved his arms with the rhythm as he rolled the bones in his hands.

a wanda no, a hai wa lo
a hai wa li a so-mi ko
a hai wa li, a so-mi ko

When he noticed Marv was about to come out, Chris rolled a bone into each hand and brought out his clenched fists simultaneously with Marv.

Big Waters guessed them immediately.

"Ho-o *Tep!*" he hollered, pointing his stick rightward. He got both Marv and Chris again, and they each tossed their bones over.

Big Waters started up his same old song again, and passed the bones to Sally and Roy. But Chris guessed the bones correctly again as soon as Sally and Roy brought their hands out.

Something was happening – Chris was hot, but Big Waters was hot too, and again guessed both Chris and Marvin. What was going on here? What kind of gambling luck was Big Waters using?

The double-calls went back and forth four more times like this, with each captain making perfect guesses each time. Big Waters and Chris kept looking at each other and shaking their heads in disbelief each time another perfect call was made.

Then Robin came up behind Chris just as he made another perfect call. She looked stunning. She was dressed like an Indian dancer, wearing a buckskin dress and moccasins, with a rabbit-bone necklace. Three magpie feathers dangled from her hair.

"Robin! You're here! Quick, make a side bet," Chris commanded.

"How do I do that?" she asked.

"Just take some money out and put it between the teams, under a small rock or something. Ask if anybody wants to make a side bet. Somebody might match it."

Robin smiled at Big Waters with her beaming eyes, and put a dollar bill down in the dirt.

"Side bet anybody?" she asked.

Big Waters beamed a smile back at her as he quickly took out a dollar bill and stepped forward to match Robin's side bet. He was captivated by her. Chris hoped Big Waters' wife Sally didn't notice.

"All right, Robin, you're in now," Chris told her. "Here, hide these bones and don't let them catch you."

He handed her a pair of the bones and passed the other pair over to Marvin.

Chris finally remembered the gambling song he'd heard with Marvin and Vinnie down in Pitch-off Mountain Canyon, and started singing.

> *Wo-nomi mom-i, Wo nomi mom*
> *Wo-nomi mom-i, Wo nomi mom*

"All right!" Marvin pitched in and started singing along.

> *Wo-nomi mom-i, Wo nomi mom*
> *Wo-nomi mom-i, Wo nomi mom*

Chris picked up his clapstick and beat out a steady rhythm of about three beats a second.

Wo-nomi mom-i, Wo nomi mom
Wo-nomi mom-i, Wo nomi mom

Marvin rolled the bones all around between his hands, waving his arms in an elaborate manner. Finally he brought his hands out to be guessed. Robin brought her hands out as well, with a broad smile and big shining eyes.

Big Waters watched intently, and used his pointing stick as if to test different calls. He pointed to the left, then to the right, then back to the left again, then swung it like a pendulum down the center. Finally, he hollered out "*mowi*," and pointed downward to indicate the bones lay down the center. Marvin groaned loudly and looked over at Robin, who kept singing through her smile. ·

Marv had been caught, and he threw the bones he held over to Big Waters. But Robin showed hers as she kept singing. Big Waters had missed.

"All right!" Marv cried out his approval. "Let the women do the hard work for us," he joked. "She won us one stick, let's make it a home run!"

Big Waters tossed one of the five counting sticks in front of him over to Chris, who caught it and stored it behind another pile of five counting sticks. One stick had been won now, had been 'cooked'. Nine more to go.

They kept singing the song and beating out the steady rhythm.

Wo-nomi mom-i, Wo nomi mom
Wo-nomi mom-i, Wo nomi mom

Big Waters looked at Robin and shook his head. She held out her hands, ready again.

Big Waters called her again, using the pair of bones Marv had tossed over to him, guessing that she had switched. She had held.

The singers sang louder when they saw Big Waters had missed again. Their song became more powerful. Big Waters shook his head again and tossed another stick over. Chris caught it and stored it with the other cooked stick. Two down, eight to go. The hiders sang on.

Wo-nomi mom-i, Wo nomi mom
Wo-nomi mom-i, Wo nomi mom

Robin rolled the bones around and was soon ready again. Big Waters kept shaking his head smiling, then passed the bones he held over to his cousin Roy. Maybe Roy would have better luck guessing her.

Roy studied Robin intently for several minutes, waiting for the singers to tire, waiting for the song to stumble a moment or lose its intensity. Finally he called out his guess. "Hup!" he shouted, showing his bones, guessing Robin had switched. She had held.

Roy shook his head and passed the bones back to Big Waters. Big Waters reluctantly tossed another counting stick over to Chris's side. Chris stored it with the other cooked sticks. Three down, seven to go. The singers sang on.

Wo-nomi mom-i, Wo nomi mom
Wo-nomi mom-i, Wo nomi mom

Robin brought her hands out again. She had hidden the bones the same way three times in a row, she wouldn't try to get away with it four times in a row! Big Waters made his call.

"Hup!" he cried, holding his white bone in his left hand, black in his right, guessing she had switched. She had held them again.

Big Waters kept smiling at Robin and laughing to himself, shaking his head from side to side, wondering 'who is this woman?' He tossed another stick over to Chris, who placed it next to the other cooked sticks. Four down, six to go. Chris's side sang louder now, and faster.

Wo-nomi mom-i, Wo nomi mom
Wo-nomi mom-i, Wo nomi mom

Big Waters handed the one pair of bones they had won to his wife Sally. Maybe she would have better luck guessing Robin.

Chris had a sudden feeling that Sally would guess Robin. 'Change hiders' a little voice urged. He nudged Robin, and she passed the bones back to him. Sally would be guessing Chris this time.

Chris decided to hold the bones the same way Robin had been hiding them.

Wo-nomi mom-i, Wo nomi mom
Wo-nomi mom-i, Wo nomi mom

The change of hiders surprised Sally. She had been expecting to call Robin, now instead she had to guess Chris. Perhaps she should have handed the guessing bones back to Big Waters, who apparently wasn't having any trouble seeing Chris, but she didn't. If she had, Chris would have passed the hiding bones back over for Robin to hide again.

Wo-nomi mom-i, Wo nomi mom
Wo-nomi mom-i, Wo nomi mom

Sally finally let out a quiet Ho! and held up the black bone in her right hand and the white bone in her left. Chris showed his bones and kept on singing, she had missed him too.

Big Waters reluctantly tossed over another counting stick. Chris caught the stick and put it next to the other cooked sticks. Five down, five to go. They were on a roll. Sally handed the calling bones over to Big Waters. Chris handed the bones back to Robin for hiding.

"*Demi*" Big Waters said, pointing to the pile of five unwon sticks in front of Chris. Big Waters was out of sticks to 'pay' for missed guesses. Chris tossed the five 'uncooked' sticks over to Big Waters.

The hiders kept singing their song:

Wo-nomi mom-i, Wo nomi mom
Wo-nomi mom-i, Wo nomi mom

Chris's voice was becoming a little hoarse. The Paiutes waited for the song to weaken before making another call. Chris softened the song, sang more quietly but with the same driving rhythm. The rest of the team followed, singing softly but with a quiet intensity.

Big Waters made his call.

"Hup!" He showed the white bone in his right hand. Robin quickly showed the black-banded bone, opposite facing him, in her left hand. Robin had switched. The song surged a little louder.

Wo-nomi mom-i, Wo nomi mom
Wo-nomi mom-i, Wo nomi mom

Big Waters shook his head looking at Robin, still laughing to himself. Robin kept smiling and singing and brought her hands out again for another call.

Wo-nomi mom-i, Wo nomi mom
Wo-nomi mom-i, Wo nomi mom

Big Waters passed the bones to his cousin Roy, but Roy shook his head and passed them on to another heavy-set gambler in dark glasses standing behind them. Big Waters tossed another counting stick over to Chris. Six down, four to go.

The big gambler in the dark glasses, and wearing a Caterpillar baseball cap, rolled the bones and snapped them into his hands in a fancy gesture.

"Ho!" he cried, holding the white bone in his right hand, the same call Big Waters had just made, guessing Robin had switched. She had held. He shook his head too, and handed the bones over to Big Waters. Big Waters tossed another stick over to Chris.

Seven down, three to go.

"All right!" Marvin crowed. "Home run, Robin!"

Wo-nomi mom-i, Wo nomi mom
Wo-nomi mom-i, Wo nomi mom

Big Waters kept shaking his head, looking at Robin and smiling. He handed the bones to Sally, but she shook her head. He looked over to Roy, who took the bones, rolled them into his hands for a few seconds, then shouted out "Ho!" and threw the bones onto the ground. The white bone landed off to the left and the marked bone off to the right, guessing she had held. Robin shook out her bones. She had switched.

"Wow!" someone shouted.

"All right!" sang out Marvin.

"Way to go, Robin!" cried Chris.

Big Waters shook his head and muttered something. He reluctantly tossed over another stick, which landed in the center area between the teams. Chris had to get up to retrieve the counting stick, which he put with the other cooked sticks. He looked at the pile to see how they were doing. Eight down, two to go.

The excited players' singing surged louder again. Robin was on a phenomenal run.

Wo-nomi mom-i, Wo nomi mom
Wo-nomi mom-i, Wo nomi mom

Robin brought her hands out again quickly, singing softly through her smile. Big Waters looked over to Roy, who shook his head 'not me'. He looked to the gambler in the sunglasses and Caterpillar hat, who took the bones, and looked intently at Robin. He wasn't smiling, but Robin was, right at him.

Wo-nomi mom-i, Wo nomi mom
Wo-nomi mom-i, Wo nomi mom

Finally he called.

"Ho, *Tep!*" He shook the black bone in his left hand, then showed the white bone in his right, guessing she had held. She held up the white bone in her right hand, showing she had switched. Then she showed the black-banded bone in her left hand, just to show Big Waters team that she wasn't playing any tricks on them.

"All right!" Marvin crowed.

"Home run Robin! Home run!" someone shouted out.

Big Waters looked down at the two sticks in front of him, shook his head again and tossed one of the counting sticks over to Chris, who stashed it with the others he had. Nine down, one to go. The song surged louder.

Wo-nomi mom-i, Wo nomi mom
Wo-nomi mom-i, Wo nomi mom

Robin brought her hands together and separated them quickly. She was ready again, and now she was singing louder too.

Big Waters looked over to Sally, who nodded 'no thanks'. He glanced at Roy, then at the big man in back. They all seemed to say 'No, this is on you, Big Waters'.

Big Waters shouted out "Hup!", simultaneously throwing the black bone off to his left and the white bone off to his right, guessing Robin had switched.

Robin looked Big Waters in the eyes and kept singing as she threw out the white bone from her own right hand, and the black bone from her left. She had held. They had won.

Chris's team started clapping their sticks and hollering in celebration. Chris sat where he was, nodding his head in disbelief and smiling back at Big Waters, who sat there shaking his head in disgust.

Robin smiled at Chris with glistening eyes. "I see what you mean about the handgame now," she said.

It was then that Chris noticed Officer Whittaker in the crowd of onlookers. He nodded to him and Whittaker nodded back.

Big Waters got up and came over to shake Chris's hand. Sally followed.

"Good game," he said. "In fact, I'll never forget this game!"

"It was awesome. How do you explain something like that?" Chris asked.

"That streak at the beginning where we both kept making the right calls back and forth, how many times? Eight or ten times?" Big Waters remembered.

"And then Robin's home run, what a streak of luck!" said Chris, introducing Robin who was standing next to him.

"And where did she come from?" Big Waters laughed. "We never should have let her play," he said, looking into Robin's shining eyes and taking both her hands in his. "I'm Nevada Big Waters, from Pyramid Lake. I want you on my team."

"I'm Robin Marquez."

"I never should have matched your bet," Big Waters laughed. "As soon as you came in and started winning I knew we were done for. If I hadn't matched your bet you'd never be in the game."

"And we'd both be hoarse from singing and nobody would have won any sticks yet, the way those calls were going," interjected Chris.

"That was good calling," praised Big Waters.

"That was a good game," added Chris.

"Better for you guys, with Robin on your team," Big Waters said, shaking his head again. "Every time I looked at Robin I'd get confused and not know which way to guess. I felt this funny itch in the wrong place, and knew whatever I guessed would be wrong."

Chris thought about the ancient-looking beetle that had been on his shirt. Where was it now?

Big Waters and Sally walked around to shake hands with the rest of Chris's team. Big Waters' cousin and the other gambler from Nevada still sat on the far side, not smiling.

Marvin picked up the scarf full of money lying between the two teams and began distributing the winnings, reading a list of names from a small scrap of paper.

"Captain Chris, twenty bucks in, forty bucks out," Marv said happily, handing Chris two twenties.

Micky Whittaker walked up to Chris.

"Looks like you guys did pretty well," Whittaker commented as Chris tucked the forty dollars into his jeans.

"Micky! Ummm... glad you could make it up. So what did you think of the handgame?"

"It's pretty interesting, all that singing's really neat. I think I understand the game too. You're guessing for where the marked bone is."

"Right, that's pretty much it," Chris said, oversimplifying it.

"So it's pretty much a fifty-fifty game," Whittaker continued.

"What?" asked Chris incredulously.

"A fifty-fifty game. You're guessing for where the bones are, and you're either right or wrong," Whittaker explained. "It's a fifty-fifty game in the long run."

Chris shook his head. "Were we watching the same game?" he asked. "First of all," he continued, "each team starts out with two people hiding two sets of bones. So the caller has a one in four chance of getting it right. And how many times did it go back and forth at the beginning of this last game. Eight times? More? So what's the odds of a one-in-four call being right eight times in a row?"

"Each call is an independent one-in-four chance then," Whittaker argued.

"And then when they couldn't guess Robin – what's the chance of their losing ten straight calls, if it's really a fifty-fifty game?"

"Well, again, when you're guessing just one person you've got a fifty-fifty chance each time," Whittaker reasoned.

"And ten times in a row?" Chris argued.

"Then it's a unusual streak, but still, in the long run it should be a fifty-fifty game."

"So it might seem," Chris said. "But some people have good-luck days when others are having bad-luck days. Some people can see the bones one day and not see them the next. In a handgame the team captain can feel out his players to find the ones who are having a good luck day. That way the whole team can ride the luck of a few people, and beat what you call the fifty-fifty odds."

"Maybe," Whittaker argued, "but in the long run it should still even out to a fifty-fifty game. You can have lucky streaks when you're playing the slot machines too, but in the end they're less than a fifty-fifty game."

He paused, then added "Are they going to play this game in that casino they're building?"

"No, I think it's just going to be a regular casino, but you probably know more about it than I do."

Chris hadn't thought about it before, but Whittaker's question suddenly excited him.

"But that's a great idea!" Chris said. "Why not? They could have an area of the casino where they could do handgame tournaments and have open betting. It would put the Indian into Indian-gambling, and people could hear the old songs and see some of the magic of the game. What a great idea!"

"It just seems that if the Indians are going to get into the gambling business they ought to at least do it in their traditional ways."

"Well," argued Chris, "some of them want to go where the money is. They're tired of being the poor cousins of modern society."

Chris and Micky Whittaker talked for some time. Chris told him about the overall Bear Dance and what it meant, and mentioned there would be several other dances and more handgames throughout the weekend, day and night, before the actual group bear-dance on Sunday.

Micky mentioned he was camping up at Eagle Lake with a buddy who had a boat, and he wanted to get back up there tonight so they could be out on the lake fishing before dawn.

"So this Bob Mathews was one of the bear-dancers?" Whittaker asked. "What are they going to do without him?"

"No, he never was a bear-dancer, if you mean the man who wore the hide in a Bear Dance, as far as I know," Chris answered. Then he joked, "You've got to be light on your feet, from what I've heard, when you put that skin on. Big Bob weighed a ton!"

"Well, they found one of those things in the cellar underneath his cabin," Whittaker continued, "an old bear hide, with lacing all the way up, rigged to be worn as a costume. It was about the only thing left in the place after the fire. Maybe he was just storing it there for somebody."

"Was it a grizzly hide?" Chris asked. Maybe Big Bob really had been a hudessi. Or maybe this was some relic from one of Big Bob's ancestors. "Or was it a black bear with a white spot on it?" Chris knew the people used *muda*, the black bear with the white 'sticking spot', for their ceremonial hides in the Bear Dance. That was the special bear whose hide gave the power.

"It was a big brown bear hide, Chris. It might've been a grizzly. It looked like a real antique. The mouth was rigged up to open and close."

"Why didn't the hide burn up in the fire?" Chris asked.

"It was in a trunk in the fruit cellar beneath the cabin," Whittaker answered. "It didn't even get scorched."

"Were there any herbs stored with it?" Chris asked.

"Herbs?"

"Herbs," Chris repeated. "Like wormwood or angelica."

"No, it was just in a trunk by itself down in the cellar."

Something sounded funny. The sacred hide used in the Bear Dance had to be bedded down with wormwood, with *munmumi*, and put away with prayers to sleep between ceremonies. The hide would become dangerous if it were not put away properly, and any person wearing it would become dangerous too, and be in trouble. Marvin had told several stories over the years of the ill-fate that befell those who didn't take special care of the bear hide, and didn't retire it properly when it was through being used. This was abuse of the bear hide!

Chris wondered. Maybe Big Bob had been on the path of the warrior, and gotten in over his head. He'd been evasive about the dance ground at Pitch-off Mountain. What was that all about? And why wasn't he captaining his own team during that last handgame? That sixteen-stick game lasted all night long – he could have easily slipped away for a long time unnoticed.

Maybe the curious professor had wanted to look more deeply into the Martis site on the Goose Farm rancheria. That would have held up construction for sure. Big Bob couldn't afford the long delay, he needed to get the casino in operation before the Amador Miwoks or somebody else might beat them to it. Or maybe the professor knew Big Bob was a hudessi. Maybe the Professor had to go.....

But what about Marty Steven? If Big Bob really were a modern grizzly-man, he'd probably killed others too. Could he see Big Bob getting rid of Marty Steven? Yes, for sure, Chris thought. Marty could make an enemy of anyone.

Maybe the grizzly-man had gotten rid of other people too, those supposed fishermen that occasionally washed up downstream, and that unidentified camper ripped up last year.

Big Bob always had a touch of impatience, and was used to having things his way. He was used to winning. And he even looked like a bear.

But he must have been working with other people on the casino project. Some other people must have known about the Martis artifacts at the casino site. Big Bob had been their driving force, and Big Bob took care of the problems. Now Big Bob was gone, and somebody else would surely soon be running the project. Who would it be?

Chris showed Micky the outdoor kitchen area, where there were several plastic tubs full of cold fried salmon and home-fried potatoes. The main barbecue would be tomorrow, Chris said, but there was always plenty of food available for everybody all the time, and there was a cauldron full of camp coffee and another of bean soup for those who wanted to stay up all night.

The last handgame of Saturday started after midnight in the ramada next to the dance ground. It lasted all night long and then some. Late in the pre-dawn morning a staggering drunk – it was Kenny Jackson – came by the ramada to get warm by the fire that separated the two gambling teams. He staggered in and stepped between the two logs, right on the scarf full of money that made up the pot, while one team pounded their drum and sang their hiding song.

"Hey! Get out of there!" someone shouted at Kenny.

Kenny stared down at Chris.

"Hey, wannabe," he said confusedly as he looked Chris straight in the face. "I thought you were dead."

"Hey! Get out of here! You're stepping on the pot!" somebody from the other team yelled.

Kenny looked around to see who was confronting him. He was standing between ten to fifteen serious gamblers, old to middle-aged, and some of considerable stature. Unable to possibly win any confrontation, especially in his current condition, Kenny backed away from the fire a bit, but still stood unsteadily between the two groups, keeping warm by the fire as the handgame continued, staring straight at Chris, who tried to ignore him.

The game went on and on, back and forth. Finally the early sun poked its light through the leaves and branches of trees in the eastern hills. A few old men and women gathered around the nearby dance ground. It was time for the special sunrise ceremony of the Bear Dance, the time when all people present are encouraged to let their heart speak.

The gamblers paused the unresolved handgame to let the ceremony proceed on the adjacent dance ground.

The leaders and their helpers hung the sacred, old, black-bear hide, draped with wormwood. onto a post on the side of the dance ground, next to another pole planted in the ground and draped with Indian flags, tassels of maple bark representing Rattlesnake.

One of the older people, a leader, spoke for a while to the ancestors in an old Maiduan language, in exhalted poetic intonation. Then he spoke in English.

"Welcome to our Bear Dance. On this kind of day, everyone should be friends and get along with one another.

"This place is all sacred ground – the dance ground, the kumi, the handgame area – these are all sacred places. If you have a light heart, join us as friends and share our ceremonies.

"We are born of this land. This earth, *Kodo,* is our Mother. This sun, *Wonomi,* is our Father. As long as He is in the sky, He hears everything we say, He sees all that we do. When Wonomi sets beyond the jagged mountains, He prays that we have clean hearts.

"So like the people before us, we begin this big day, this beginning of a new year, with a sun ceremony.

"We remember the people who have passed on this year," the head-man continued, "and all our people who've passed on in years before. We keep you in our hearts. We think of you who are sick and can't be here with us today, and those who died. I want to tell you the big man's casino will come, and will help all of our people. At the end of our days we will meet in the big roundhouse inside the mountain."

The head-man turned to one of the helpers next to him and asked softly, "Have I forgotten anything?"

The helper whispered back "What about Marty?"

The head-man then added, "Oh yes, and cousin Marty, we hope you find your peace now."

"He Wenai!"

"Ye Wenai," those gathered replied.

Then the headman turned to the group of those present and said "Would anyone else like to step up and say something?"

"I've shumthin' to shay." Drunken Kenny staggered out from the ramada and onto the edge of the ceremonial dance ground, where the sacred bear hide hung draped with worm-wood.

"I have... something to say." He spoke a little more clearly now. Stepping onto the dance ground was sobering him.

Everyone stood or sat still, not knowing what kind of anger or hatred to expect from this drunk. Kenny himself didn't know what words were about to come from his mouth.

"I have to... have to say..." he stammered, "we have to come together. We have to help each other now. I'm sorry for the hurt we've caused. We can't be fighting each other all the time. We're all people on this same planet. We have to help each other, love each other, respect our older people and our ancestors."

"We have to help our world. Our mother is sick, she needs our help. She is sick because of all the greed. And her people are sick too. We have to stop our greed, our anger and hatred and jealousy. We have to come together. We've come here to pay respect to brother Bear and brother Rattlesnake. They live here. But we pay respect to our mother Earth too, because we all live on her. We come here to ask brother Bear and brother Rattlesnake to help us, not to hurt us. We ask them to help us and we will help them. We are here to find peace for our families and ourselves. We are here to all learn to get along with each other. That is all I have to say."

"*Ye Wenai!*"

"Ye Wenai," everybody responded.

The land affects people in many ways, and the spirit of the land spoke straight through Kenny.

Chris stepped onto the dance ground next.

"On this day especially," he said, "I think of my brother, and of our grandfather's father." He paused, not knowing what to say. "We don't know. what happened to you, brother. Maybe we'll never know. But when one coyote dies, another shows up in its place. It's not easy to kill a coyote! We'll be looking for you, Coyote. And if we find your bones or ragged hide some-where, we'll take them to a special lake in the mountains, and throw you in, and next day you'll crawl out, new and whole again."

"Ye wenai," everybody nodded.

The handgame continued soon after, and within an hour Chris's team had pulled it off. They won again. It was a new day, a new year.

The sun rose higher over the ridge. Robin wanted to go down to the creek to do a round of sweats. The day was already getting warm, and Chris couldn't get into the idea of sweating for an hour. He would rather find a shady spot under a tree and think about gambling luck, and his last two wins. It had been some night!

First they stopped by the outdoor kitchen. Volunteers were frying up quantities of scrambled eggs and sliced potatoes, and putting them into plastic tubs for people to serve themselves.

Robin had a light bite. But Chris heaped his paper plate high with a pile of potatoes and eggs, which he washed down with a cup of black camp coffee.

After breakfast, Robin walked down to the sweat lodge by the creek, while Chris went back up to the camp to find his shady spot.

Chris had hardly finished counting his winnings when Robin stormed back to camp.

"Those sexist pigs wouldn't let me sweat!" she fumed.

"What?" Chris groaned.

"They wouldn't let me sweat. I went down to the sweat by the creek and they wouldn't let me in. They said they're doing men's sweats."

"Right."

"They can't do that. It's not right."

"Right," Chris groggily agreed. He felt like he'd been up for days.

"I want to sweat," Robin complained.

"Right," said Chris.

The crowds started showing up before noon for the big day. Most of the handgame players still wandered around, even after the long night of gambling, while the Maidu dance group and the visiting Big Head dancers alternated sets on the dance ground.

Marv and some other helpers pulled the venison and beef from the barbecue pit. A free meal of meat, fish, fry-bread, salad, acorn soup and home-made cakes was soon being served to the hundreds of visitors.

People milled around the dance ground after the big afternoon meal, and many of the older people sat on the split-log benches that defined the dance circle. Marvin walked onto the dance ground.

"All right," he hollered out, "we're going to start the Bear Dance now. We want to get everybody in on this. We're going to form several circles on the dance ground. Everybody get a piece of munmumi from the pile up here. This is our medicine for the bear. When the bear-man comes by you, gently brush his hide with this medicine, to soothe him, to calm down the bear. Don't beat him with the munmumi, just brush him gently, soothe him down.

"Let's get all the young children up here first to make the inner circle," Marv continued. "Come on! All you kids come over here, and we'll start a circle in the center."

Marvin directed the children to the center and tried his best to get them to all hold hands and form a circle. It was clear Marvin enjoyed this role immensely.

"Then we're going to want all the older people to form more circles around the kids. Come on! Everybody who's not too sore or too old, get up here," he hollered out.

People swarmed onto the dance ground, although many of the older people still sat on the benches surrounding the ground.

There were so many children this year Marv split the inner circle into two circles.

Five larger concentric circles of more than a few hundred adults formed around the two inner circles of children.

"Now we want you all to hold hands with the people next to you, and we're going to practice the dance. Each circle turns a different direction from the one within it. We're going to start the kids' circle going counter-clockwise, then the next circle going clockwise, the next one counter-clockwise, alternating like that. We'll go around like that a few times, then we'll stop, and then we'll start up again and each circle will move the other way and go around a few times. Let's practice. You guys go like this," and Marvin showed the children how to dance by lifting one foot after another and slowly navigating a circular path.

The concentric circles of people started moving around the dance ground in opposite directions.

"All right, that's good. Now everybody stop, and now start circling in the opposite direction," Marv hollered.

The circles began falling apart now, some people stepping to the right while their neighbor stepped to the left while they still held hands.

"Remember which way you're supposed to go," Marv hollered out. "Slow down. Watch the old people."

They practiced like this for some time, until Marvin announced "Okay, you've all graduated. Congratulations! Let's let the singers take over now, and we'll start the Bear Dance!"

The lead singer spoke up from the front edge of the dance ground.

"We'd like to warm this up with a welcome dance," he said, as the four men began softly hitting their clapper sticks into their palms and singing.

paudem chikeni wele ho-o
paudem chikeni wele ho-o

Marvin got the seven circles moving in their proper directions, in step to the music, about one beat a second. He had the most trouble with the innermost circle of small children, who sometimes didn't want to hold hands with their neighbor, or wanted to run off to somebody in another circle. Marvin herded them around gently and got them to dance.

The dancing crowd slowly circled the ground.

paudem chikeni wele ho-o
paudem chikeni wele ho-o

Finally the lead singer quivered his clapstick and brought the song to a close. That dance was for the East, the place of birth. Now they would dance for the South, the place of youth, of life.

He soon started the song again, and the circles of dancers started moving in the opposite direction.

paudem chikeni wele ho-o
paudem chikeni wele ho-o

The concentric circles of dancers slowly rotated in opposite directions. Finally the leader quivered his clapstick and the song stopped again. Next they would dance to the West, to the place of older age.

The singers started up, and the dancers again reversed their directions.

paudem chikeni wele ho-o
paudem chikeni wele ho-o

After the third time around, the leader ended the song again, and after several seconds again started up. This was for the North, the place of our ancestors, our wisdom, our death.

paudem chikeni wele ho-o
paudem chikeni wele ho-o

The dancers again reversed themselves. A cloud of dust rose over the dance ground but a gentle breeze soon carried it away.

After four slow circles around the dance ground the welcome-dance ended.

"You did good, real good," Marvin yelled out to the crowd. "You've all got your master's degrees now. Now just stay right here, and we'll continue with the Bear Dance in a few minutes."

The lead singer and an elder helped take the bear hide off the pole at the side of the dance ground, and placed it on – all right! Vinnie would wear the hide this year!

Marvin took the long pole with the tassels of Indian 'flags' representing Rattlesnake, and started leading the bear-dancer around the dance ground, as the singers started the bear-dance song to the same slow rhythm.

> *weda, weda, wulu nai*
> *o-o wulu, wulu nai*
> *weda, weda, wulu nai*
> *o-o wulu, wulu nai*

Seven circles of hundreds of people holding hands moved in opposite directions on the dance ground. Marvin, carrying the long rattlesnake flag, followed the bear-dancer slowly between the circles. Each person brushed the bear-man with wormwood, munmumi, whenever he was within reach. Some of the young children aggressively beat the bear with their wormwood.

"Don't beat the bear, just brush him gently," Marv hollered. "Soothe him. Nice bear."

Sometimes the bear-man would try to nose-up to a young girl or an older woman. They always either laughed or ran away.

The song went on for a full circle of the dance ground, as the bear-man danced among the circling people, who calmed that bear with wormwood.

> *weda, weda, wulu nai*
> *o-o wulu, wulu nai*
> *weda, weda, wulu nai*
> *o-o wulu, wulu nai*

Then the singers stopped.

"Okay," Marvin called out, "now start circling the other way!"

The singers started up again, and the dance circles moved in the opposite direction. This was for the South.

weda, weda, wulu nai
o-o wulu, wulu nai
weda, weda, wulu nai
o-o wulu, wulu nai

The bear-man broke through one circle and began nosing around and dancing his way past people in the next circle.

Near the end of the fourth circling, the dance for the North, Chris saw a swirl of dust in the northeast, a few hundred feet away, down the hill near the sweats. A whirlwind! A dust-devil! Within seconds, it had moved all the way up the hill from the sweat to just outside the dance circle.

It grew huge now, like a tiny tornado four or five feet in diameter. The noise overpowered the singers, and the dancers stopped as they watched this wild Whirlwind-woman.

She stayed on the east side of the dance ground for a long moment. Dust and leaves swirled everywhere. Then she shot straight up into the sky like a twisting arrow. Soon all that could be seen of her was a tiny backward S high overhead.

Everybody was stunned, awestruck. Somebody sang out a long *Ho!* and others quickly joined in.

Soon the singers continued, to finish the final dance.

weda, weda, wulu nai
o-o wulu, wulu nai
weda, weda, wulu nai
o-o wulu, wulu nai

The lead singer quivered his clapstick and the song came to an end.

Marvin addressed the crowd.

"Okay, folks, you all got your doctor's degree on that one! Look what all that dancing brought up!" he said, pointing up to Whirlwind-woman, high in the sky.

"Now we're going to follow the bear off the dance ground," Marv said, "around the *kumi* and down to the creek. We'll start with the outer circle first. When we get down to the creek, we'll wash with the munmumi to get rid of all the bad thoughts and bad things that have happened over the past year. Say a silent prayer, wash up and toss the munmumi into the water to let all the troubles flow downstream."

The singers started up again with the same song.

> *weda, weda, wulu nai*
> *o-o wulu, wulu nai*
> *weda, weda, wulu nai*
> *o-o wulu, wulu nai*

The bear-dancer circled the dance ground and slowly exited at the break in the circle on the north. Marvin broke the outside circle of dancers nearest the dancing bear, and started the line of people following the bear-man out, circling once around the *kumi*, then moving slowly down to the creek. The singers sang on as all the people slowly filed off the dance ground.

> *weda, weda, wulu nai*
> *o-o wulu, wulu nai*
> *weda, weda, wulu nai*
> *o-o wulu, wulu nai*

Marvin half-led and half-followed the bear, carrying high the long pole draped with Indian flags. When they came to the creek, the bear-man knelt by the water. Soon hundreds of people scrambled along the creek bank, washing their faces and hands with the sacred herb and cold water. Stalks of wormwood floated down the stream.

Marvin took the first 'rattlesnake' tassle – made from the paper-thin inner bark of a maple tree – off the Indian flag pole, and said a silent prayer as he hung it as high as he could reach in an oak tree. He then helped Vinnie from the bear hide. They brushed the hide with munmumi, then hung it in the same tree, draped with more bunches of munmumi.

Chris headed back toward his camp. He wanted to be alone for a little while, to talk to his lucky root, to thank it for helping him win those handgames. Robin followed him up the hill.

Chris found the scarf that held his wad of medicine grass and the lucky root. The grass was there but the lucky root was gone.

"Oh no! My lucky root's gone! It ran away!" Chris cried.

Robin looked at him sheepishly. "It didn't run away. I ate it."

"You what?!" Chris hollered.

"I ate it. I saw that scarf lying here, and when I opened it, the little root said 'Eat me.' So I did."

"You can't eat that thing. It could kill you!"

"Not that root. I feel good," Robin said, smiling.

"How could you do that? That was my *pumi*," Chris wailed.

"You wanted me to win that game, didn't you?" Robin asked, her eyes shining.

Soon the big-time ended, and most of the visitors had left. A brief rain fell over the grounds, settling the dust and dissolving the footprints of all the strangers.

30

A night in the kumi

The night in the roundhouse was always a special time, after the Bear Dance was over and the weekend visitors had left. Then many of the remaining people would get together around the fire, beneath the smoke hole, to tell stories, sing songs, and talk about the Bear Dance. Leonard and Marvin were there, along with Vinnie, Chris, Robin, Rod Beckman, Big Waters and Sally, and some of their people.

First they talked about the whirlwind.

"What do you think about that thing?" asked Chris.

"That was the spirit of some ancestor visiting," said Marvin.

"Maybe it was the Professor paying us a visit," said Vinnie.

"It was the Big Man," said somebody else.

"The Great Spirit," said Leonard, "the great spirit of this place."

They also talked about the handgame, and Robin's incredible run of luck.

"Luck comes to you when it likes you," Leonard said, looking at Robin curiously. "You have found some luck. Some people never find it. Others don't know how to handle it when they do find it. You must be careful with your luck."

After a moment he continued. "One fellow found some gambling luck up on Red Mountain. He tried to dig it up with a stick, but halfway down the root broke. He knew this meant he would lose at handgame whenever he gambled. He got mad, and yanked the root up and threw it on the ground, cursing.

"On the way back to camp he got sick. Luckily, Bald Rock Jim happened into camp and realized what had happened. He didn't think he could save the fellow, but he tried. He doctored him, sucked and sucked, and finally he sucked up this root, the size of a turnip that had already begun to sprout. Another five minutes and that fellow would have been a goner."

They talked some more about gambling and gambling luck.

"You know how a fellow knows if he's gonna win or lose at handgame?" Leonard asked Chris.

"How?"

"He finds some yellow-hammer feathers. The night before he's gonna gamble, he ties the feathers together to a little rock and puts the feathers in a gentle current in the stream, so they're standing upright, anchored to the stone. If they're still standing up in the morning, he's gonna win. If they're lying flat, he's gonna lose."

"What if they're all washed away?" Chris asked.

"Then he better go fishing!" Marv laughed.

Eventually the conversation turned to Big Bob and the grizzly men.

"Do you really think Big Bob was a modern-day grizzly-man?" Chris asked Vinnie, or anybody else around. Chris was almost convinced, but he wanted some confirmation.

"It all adds up," Vinnie said. "I keep wondering about that Pitch-off Mountain dance. Why did he say it never happened?"

Vinnie paused a moment, then continued. "They must chase the deer there, don't you think? I mean, in our deer dance we use our bows and hunt the deer as we dance around. I was thinking, they probably chase the deer around in their dance, like they used to do on Pitch-off Mountain."

Rod Beckman said, "Better watch out Vinnie, keep wearing that hide and you might turn into a bear-man yourself!" Beckman laughed, but nobody joined him.

"No," Leonard said, "the bear-dancer becomes the bear when he puts that hide on, it's the bear dancing in that circle. But maidum pano hides himself in the grizzly hide, he doesn't become a bear. He kills for his own motives, and hides behind the grizzly skin. He's still a man."

"Why else would BB have kept that bear hide?" Vinnie asked.

"What bear hide?" Leonard interjected.

"The cops found an old bear hide in a fruit cellar underneath Big Bob's cabin," Chris explained, "a bear-man outfit, rigged to be worn by a man."

"A grizzly hide?" Leonard asked.

"The cop didn't know. It was old and big and brown, though."

"Where is it now?" Leonard seemed agitated as he questioned Chris.

"The cops still have it, I imagine," Chris said.

"We've got to get that hide. We've got to calm it down, hold another bear dance and put it back to sleep, before it kills again."

A look of surprise flashed across Marv's face, then he stared long and hard at Leonard.

Vinnie speculated "Maybe in the old days the maidum pano sometimes did wear the hide at the Bear Dance, maybe the people soothed him and all the man-killers, like they soothe the spirit of the bear and the rattlesnake."

"No," Leonard disagreed, "the bear-dancer is a holy man, he is on a path. A maidum pano is a man-killer, on a different path, the path of a warrior."

"But that's what the Bear Dance is all about, isn't it? Soothing the spirit of the beast," Chris asked.

"Ye wenai!" Marvin agreed.

"So if Big Bob were on the path of the warrior, what do you think really happened to him?" Chris asked anybody.

"Well, from what you've told me," Marv said seriously, still looking at Leonard, "the bear hide got him."

Marv paused before explaining, then looked at Chris. "Remember that time there was that split over who was going to run the Yosemite Bear Dance? When Chico Pete took the bear hide out of the shed where it slept, and stuffed it into his car trunk to take it back to Sacramento? Everybody told him not to do it. Maybe that was before your time. He got killed in a car wreck before he made it home! Then his brother stored that hide in his garage. He soon lost his job and his wife left him. They wanted me to bring that thing back to the shed where it belonged. 'No way!' I said. They finally had to get a Miwok doctor to come to Sacramento, to calm down the bear and put the hide back to sleep. You're asking for trouble if you don't know how to take care of the sacred hide."

"Maybe Worldmaker killed maidum pano, to make the world a safer place for people," Vinnie volunteered.

"Worldmaker sleeps now," said old Leonard curiously. "The People have to take care of some things themselves."

Marv looked intently at Leonard, who stared straight ahead.

Somebody started singing:

> *yu ku tai yo-weni, yu ku tai yo-weni*
> *kau-wau-wau yo-weni kau-wau-wau yo-weni*
> *yu ku tai!*

but the words soon blended into English :

> *You could die, yo-weni, You could die, yo-weni*
> *Kau-wau-wau yo-weni kau-wau-wau yo-weni*
> *You could die!*

The conversation eventually turned away from man-killers and Big Bob, and everybody lightened up. Marv told many long stories and jokes, and Vinnie too felt light-hearted and in good spirits. He had worn the bear hide in the dance, but now he had turned back into one of the guys again. They all talked, and shared stories and songs around the fire in the roundhouse.

Vinnie started singing a soft haunting dance song.

> *hutuma hu tuma*
> *he ye yoyo he yoyo he ya*
> *he ye yoyo he yoyo he ya*

"Well, what are you going to do now?" Marvin finally asked Chris.

The question didn't register with Chris. He was wondering what he was going to do with Robin. "What do you mean?" Chris asked.

"With your life. What are you going to do with you life? Now that you don't have a job any more."

"Oh, I'm going to play some more handgames. And then I'm going sailing," Chris gave his stock reply.

"That sounds like a good idea. Need some company? On the handgames, that is. I've got a couple weeks off."

. "That depends on whether Robin comes with me," Chris answered half-jokingly.

"Well, I wouldn't be offering to come gamble with you if Robin weren't coming along with us," Marv laughed, patting

Robin's leg. "You don't think I want to travel just with you, do you?"

"I thought you probably had an ulterior motive there, Marv," Chris smiled.

"Let's just say I know where the Luck is now," Marv laughed again, winking at Robin.

"Seriously," Marv continued. "There's some big handgames coming up. We could do pretty well. Next week there's Yosemite, but there's also another big-time at Schurz over in Nevada – probably more gamblers over there at Schurz. Then there's action in eastern Nevada over at Duckwater, and then the big tournament over at Cedar City, Utah. There's a five-thousand dollar pot at Cedar City, I hear."

"Five thousand bucks?" Chris asked, his eyes widening.

"Right, five thousand bucks. Double-elimination tournament. Twenty-five hundred for first place, fifteen hundred for second and a grand for third. The entry fee's a hundred bucks a team. With Robin's luck it should be easy pickings."

"What do you think, Robin?" Chris asked.

"I'm ready for more!," Robin beamed. "You've got me hooked now, but I don't know how long this luck will last!"

"Okay, I'm game," Chris said. "We can hit Schurz, and then check out Spencer's Hot Spring on the way over to Duckwater and Cedar City. Let's hit the handgame highway!"

"All right!" chimed Marv.

Epilog

Back to Berkeley

Chris pulled off the freeway at the first Berkeley exit, and continued along the frontage road toward the marina, winding down from the long hot trip through Utah and Nevada.

They had done well on the handgame highway – cleaned up in the tournament at Cedar City as a matter of fact. But by the time they passed through Winnemucca, Robin was riding with Marvin, and by Lovelock, Marv and Robin were a team of two heading toward Nixon for more gambling with the Paiutes. Chris drove back to Berkeley alone.

He didn't mind, he was ready, finally – Robin was just too much for him! But he did miss his fifteen hundred dollar share of the winnings that she still carried with her. He was broke now, and he'd had to use a credit card for the gas to get him home.

He was broke, and hungry. He turned up University Avenue toward campus rather than down toward the marina, then took another left at San Pablo to head back north toward Albany and the countless good restaurants along Solano Avenue.

He'd charge up a good meal before going down to his boat and slipping off the dock lines for a long sail. But first he would stop off at his post office box. His severance check from work should be there by now, and he needed the money.

He found a parking space right across from the post office, a few blocks from the restaurant. Free parking, no meters – that's what he loved about Albany.

It felt good to get out of the truck and stretch after the long drive. He walked into the small post office.

He opened his mail box, pulled out a big pile of mail, and started casually looking through the bills and magazines for his check. When he came to the red and green-trimmed envelope with Mexican postage, he froze. He recognized the handwriting.

With a feeling somewhere between anger and ecstacy he opened the envelope, and read:

'Hi ya, Chris,

I hope you haven't been worrying about me. I haven't heard from you since I went to the handgames on Pitch-off Mountain. I found some great luck gambling there. Then after one of the games we held a private bear dance with a few insiders. Wow! Big Bob went kind of crazy when he had that bear hide on, and I had to get out of there pronto!

Julie was there too. You remember her, and how I like mature women. (She's the last remaining fluent speaker of Tai.) We fell madly in love, and went off to do a little 'anthropological research'. You know I am a firm believer in participative ethnology! It was glorious. But then I had to finish my 'Food for Peace' project in Oaxaca. Julie didn't want to come with me. I tried to reach you before I left, but you were off somewhere and your voice mail box at your work was full.

Now, I'm in the mountains of southern Mexico. I have a little problem here – nothing really. I was accused of a bizarre crime. Some *Mixe* men said I had turned into a coyote and had killed a bunch of their chickens and a young burro. So they beat me up and robbed me right in the main square of Ayutla. If my now good friend Colonel Ochoa and his men had not saved me I might have been killed. Unfortunately, during the scuffle – I don't remember much about it – I growled and I bit one of the robbers so severely he had to be taken to a hospital in Oaxaca City.

I'm still here in Ayutla, on indefinite detention. Although I'm sort of free, for I only have to sleep in the jail at night, I pretty much stay in it all day, just to be where the kids can't taunt me or the men threaten me with sticks.

Brother, I am still hurting from my beating and need medicine. I just eat tortillas with chiles, and get black beans once a week. So much for my Food for Peace project.

Hermanito mio, please help me by sending $1500 via American Express office in Oaxaca City to Colonel Alfonso Ochoa Mendoza. You know I'm good for it. And I know I can rely on you.

Your brother, Tom
PS Please get me out of here soon!'

'All right!' Chris cheered. 'That old Coyote never dies.'

Ye wenai!

Glossary

acorn bread - leached acorn meal, a staple food

Ayutla - capitol of Mixeland, a remote village in
    Mexico

bai e buna - gambling call, 'you don't want to feel
    that black bone over there or you'll lose it!'

big-time - big get together, a pow-wow

bodau - ball of grass which wraps bones in the grass
                game

bones - objects guessed in a handgame

demi - counting stick in a handgame

camputi - village, camp

cha - gambling guessers' taunt, asking hiders to 'roll
    'em again'. The request is usually ignored

clapstick - percussion instrument made of split elder
    stick

clapper - a clapstick

·este - a gambling call for the bones 'down the river',
    toward pot

gambling song - chant sung while hiding bones in a
    handgame; *hilom soli*

grass game - handgame played with wads of grass to
    help hide
handgame - gambling game, bone game, stick game,
    grass game, hand game
heno(m) - coyote
hilom - gambling
    hilom soli - gambling song
hinduku - white bone, best of mountain lion or bear
hompu - gambling call, 'upstream", away from pot,
    'toward the door'
honi - heart
    honi bodau – gambling call, 'down the center'
hudessi - man-killer; a warrior so fast he dodged all
    arrows
Ino O - site of Maiduan fertility rock
joint grass - equisetum species; looks something
    like a rattlesnake
kaiyenuk - gambling call 'changed', 'switched'
kukini (kakani) - spirit
kodo - earth
kuksu – 'secret society' among north-central California
    tribes
kumi - roundhouse, used variously as a dance house, a
    sweat house, a gambling house or for other activities
    by different groups
maidu - person; also name of a group of Californian
    Indian tribes
maidum-pano - bear-man; *hudessi*
menuk - gambling call for holding, 'same as last
    time'
mowi - gambling call for the dark bones inside, a 'heart
    shot'
Mixe - a remote tribe in Mexico
momi - maiduan word for water; momoli
munmumi - California wormwood
mude (muede) - maiduan word for black bear

nawol - gambling taunt by the singing side, asking callers to 'clap your hands and guess, we're tired of singing'.

noi - gambling call, 'inside', 'mowi'

notokoyo - mountain maidu

outside - gambling call, called bones on outside away from center

pain - intrusive disease object

pani - maiduan word for tobacco

pano - grizzly bear

power - Qi, mana, personal energy, medicine

pulla - a pouch for carrying gambling equipment

pumi - gambling luck

rattlesnake root - sanicula species

roll, rolling the bones - hiding the bones

roundhouse (round house) – used variously as a dance house, a sweat house, a gambling house or for other activities by different groups; *kumi*

sewi - river, also, gambling guess for 'outside'

sola - rattlesnake, 'singing bite'

sohoho - gambling taunt by callers, 'roll 'em again'

sulu - black-striped bone, best from deer fore-arm

sumi - deer

sweathouse - kumi, dance house of the mountain maidu

tai (tai'm) - northern foothill maidu

tai yam - Sacramento Valley

tanku - southern foothill maidu

tep - gambling guess for the dark bone

tepyos - gambling guess for the plain bone, 'tep reversed'; *we*

tsium sewi - middle fork of (Feather) river

uti - acorn

we - gambling call for the white (plain) bone

wole - white man

wolem sumi - white man's deer, cattle

Wonomi - 'the one who never dies', the sun, god

we - gambling guess for the plain (white) bone.
    (pronounced as English 'way')

yamani - mountain

    hedem yamani - these mountains, the Sierras

    hodem yamani – those (coastal) mountains

yayakit - gambling call, 'down the center'

yayalsip - gambling call, 'the door side', 'away from the pot'

yayadal - gambling call, 'away from the door', toward the pot

ye wenai! (he wenai) - an exclamation 'that is good', 'amen'

yellow-hammer - flicker, type of woodpecker

yokuslomi - gambling call, 'outside', 'sewi'

Author's notes

This is a work of fiction, set in the near future. The Pitch-off Mountain rancheria does not exist as described, nor does the Goose Farm rancheria, nor the casino that my imagination created for that place.

The physical land forms and places described are real, as are the maiduan stories and lore integrated into this work. Although many of these events were inspired by real experiences from my twenty-five years of playing handgame with various tribes of California and Nevada, the people and events described are creations of my imagination, with the exception of Bald Rock Jim, a well-known old-time Concow Maidu doctor of the Pitch-off Mountain area who died in the 1920's. I've used the name Robin in tribute to two women of nearly the same name who are wonderful handgame partners, but the character is totally fictional. I'd particularly like to thank both men who called themselves 'Coyote Man', whose work was inspirational for this book, and my good friend Dr. M. Makooi, who generously lent me his laptop computer for months at a time, which greatly facilitated the writing of this book during my travels.

A multi-media CD designed for viewing on sound-capable computers equipped with web-browsers such as Netscape or Internet Explorer is available from the publisher and included with some editions of this book. This CD includes a digital version of this book embedded with the sounds of the hand games and songs from stories, including more than sixty song clips from recordings made between 1962-1999.

Many gambling songs consist only of 'lucky syllables', and have no literal meaning, so language is no barrier to enjoying them.

In trying to represent the sounds of Indian songs in print,
I've standardized on the following approximate vowel pronunciations:

a is pronounced as in English father;
e as in English day;
i as in English see;
o as in English hope,
u as in English true

The handgame, in its diverse forms, is played throughout
much of the United States and Canada, especially in Nevada,
California, Oregon, Washington, Idaho, Montana and Utah.
The Aleuts picked up the game up from Kashaya Pomo people
when they were brought by the Russian traders to Fort Ross in
California, and the handgame then spread back to Alaska.
Many local variations exist. It's known by many names, including
Grass Game, Bone Game, Hand Game. Stick Game,
Gambling Game, Peon, Tep-Weh, Tep-Wi, Ch'enlahi and many
others.

I've attempted to accurately integrate old-time Maidu
handgame calls and songs as far as I know them. Most of these
songs can be heard on the multimedia CD which is available as
a companion to this book. Sound clips of these songs are also
freely available at the web site

www.yerbabuenapress.com

I hope my Maidu and Paiute friends and other handgame
players will forgive me for any transgressions and errors I have
made. A significant portion of the proceeds of this work will be
donated to the Yamani Maidu Bear Dance Foundation and the
Maidu Dance Group.

Bill Rathbun

For further reading

This short list is by no means complete but represents some of my favorite source books on California Indian people. Some of these books are out of print but can be found through your local library.

<u>The Northern Maidu</u> Roland B. Dixon. The classic work on the Maidu cultrure, written in the early 1900's.
<u>Maidu Myths</u> Roland B. Dixon

<u>The Maidu Indian Myths and Stories of Hanc' ibyjim</u>, edited by William Shipley, forward by Gary Snyder. A beautiful translation of ancient Maidu tales told by Hanc' ibyjim in the early 1900's.

<u>Sun Moon and Stars</u>, Coyote Man. These stories join the memories of several Maidu old-timers to recreate major pieces of the Maidu mythology. Out of print, but limited copies available on the web.
<u>The Destruction of the People</u>, Coyote Man. The history of the Maidu people from the memories of the surviving old people.

<u>Indians of the Feather River</u>, Don Jewell. Stories and memories from the author's years of working with the Maidu people.

<u>Flutes of Fire</u>, edited by Leanne Hinton. Essays on California Indian Languages.